Of Iron and Gold

Of Iron and Gold

by
Lexa Luthor

Luthor Publishing
2020

Of Iron and Gold
© 2020 By Lexa Luthor. All Rights Reserved.
Luthor Publishing
www.LexaLuthor.com

Editors:
RJ Creamer
Julia V.

Cover Artist:
May Dawney of May Dawney Designs
www.maydawney.com

ISBN-13 (ebook):
978-1-952993-00-8

ISBN-13 (paperback):
978-1-952993-01-5

First Edition – July 2020 – 01

Contents

Chapter 1

Mallory bit back a snarl after the strike to her shoulder, then ignored the sting on her skin, having grown used to the pain. She followed the others in front of her. Their iron chains dragged against cold stones, their cotton clothes stuck to their frozen skin, and their bare feet were coated in mud from the week-long walk in the rain.

Last week life had been a notch better than it was today. However, she had grown accustomed to her meaningless purpose after being sold into slavery. The moment those first shackles were anchored to her wrists, she had been confused and lost… until she attempted to fight back. Her first master had stripped her of her clothes, her freedom, and her pride. Then her name had been stripped away and replaced by one that mocked her. She lost everything including her inner Alpha.

In recent years, she made it a habit of holding onto the one thing that was still hers, and only hers. *My birth name is Aubrey*, she repeated to herself each month so she wouldn't forget. Even though her master had beaten her Alpha nature from her, some hopeful fragment of herself clung to a sliver of what had been her freedom; she held it in her birth name.

Days ago her master sold her for a few coins to a knight from Coldhelm. The temporary master, Sir Philip Anson, rode high on his pearly white horse, gazing down at the commoners milling through the streets of Coldhelm. Around him were several Beta workers, who were in charge of the slave train Mallory was chained to. The workers were nicknamed "keepers" because their sole duty was to "keep" the eleven slaves in line and obedient. Normally there was one keeper for every six slaves, depending on the slaves' breed and age.

The citizens of Coldhelm parted like a wave as Sir Philip Anson turned left onto a larger, busier street as his slaves continued the march through to the capital. Mallory peered around the other slaves' shoulders and took in the sight of the stone castle that towered over the city's small thatched homes. Whipping her head back, damp strands of hair flung from her face, and she gazed upon the eerie structure that loomed ahead of them.

The square castle sat on a hilltop, which made it nearly impossible to scale. There were four visible levels, and the highest level had a grand balcony; most likely the top floor was for the king and queen. Two gigantic towers rose up on either side of the structure, and the red metal roofs stood out against the graphite-colored stone. Long, distinctive banners hung from nearly every window. Each banner had the mountain lion crest of the House of Wymarc. As the procession neared the castle, the royal guards stepped forward to block access to the stone bridge.

Mallory couldn't make out what her master said to the guards, but they were allowed to pass, then continued onto the bridge. Once past the gate, their view opened up and the magnificent Tharnstone Castle stood before them. To the right and left there was a rift so deep that death would come to anyone who fell from the bridge. Wind and pellets of rain struck Mallory's face, but she didn't care, too fascinated by the castle.

At the next gate, another set of guards halted them before signaling for the iron gate to be raised. Once the gate was high enough to march under, their group passed the gatehouse to enter the inner ward. They were corralled to one area while their owner spoke to a well-dressed, portly man. Within seconds the keepers shouted orders for the Tharnstone soldiers to assist them.

A keeper yanked the chains Mallory and the other slaves were connected to. She rumbled a few times but followed the caravan to the right and entered through an open doorway. At first it was dark, but after a few paces there were torchlights lining the hallway. It was musty and dank, but at least they were out of the wind and rain. The keepers kept the slaves in single file while the three soldiers led them through the maze of halls.

"Line up, slaves," a keeper ordered when they reached an empty storeroom.

A soldier removed shutters from several windows around the room, allowing the murky light of day to pour into the room. The group of royal soldiers positioned themselves behind the line of slaves.

With a heavy sniff, Mallory recognized the familiar scent of grain; she'd spent her early adulthood as a farm slave. A few pieces of dried barley were wedged between the stones, but the chatter from the door opening brought her attention to the flood of people coming into the room.

Six Tharnstone soldiers entered first, followed by the same portly man, who was waving his hands about and chatting with their master. The next man was tall and burly, every bit a true Alpha. He wore refined clothes with gold accents against the dark attire. His golden crown was simple, but it signified his status all the same.

Mallory *hated* King Wilmont Wymarc.

"What did you find for me, Philip?" Wilmont asked.

Philip folded his hands in front of his body. "A variety, my king."

"I asked for good stock, not variety." Wilmont stood with Philip and the portly man at the far end of the slave line.

"Of course, my king. I brought you a variety of good stock." Philip had a charming smile that seemed to soothe Wilmont's annoyance.

"Fine. Let's get on with it."

Philip signaled two keepers; each went to the slave closest to them. The keepers pulled their daggers from their hips, then started to cut away the first slave's shirt and pants. Once the slave was nude, they moved onto the next one and continued down the line.

By the time the keepers reached Mallory, she'd clenched her hands and gritted her teeth, holding back a fighting growl. She closed her eyes and blocked out the close proximity of the keepers, who smelled as foul as she, but at least she had a reason, having been walking for a week straight. Their hands crawled over her as they pulled and yanked at her clothing, slicing it away. Once they finished, Mallory's skin prickled from the cool air. She opened her eyes and concentrated on the noblemen's conversation.

"This one is a good," Wilmont said in front of the third, then stopped in front of the next slave in the line. "This one is too old, Philip."

"He's still good stock." Philip pushed against the slave's bare chest and argued, "He is solid and healthy. According to his former owner, this one's never been sick."

Wilmont huffed and argued, "He's still old. His seed is probably all but dead by now." He went to the sixth one and growled at Philip, who was to the right of Wilmont. "I said no Betas."

"B-b-but he's well equipped." Philip grabbed the Beta slave's penis, presenting it to Wilmont. "As you can see for yourself."

"Still a Beta," Wilmont growled and continued down the line. "The finest warriors are produced by *Alphas.*"

By the time the nobles made it to the slave before Mallory, Wilmont had selected three Alpha slaves worthy of whatever he had in mind. Displeased with the tenth slave, Wilmont stood quietly in front of Mallory for a moment. Then he barked with laughter and turned to Philip, who was red in the face. Next to Philip was the portly man, and he looked between Mallory and his king.

"Is this a joke, Philip?" Wilmont clapped Philip's shoulder and said, "You have always had a sense of humor that I admire."

Philip shuffled on his boots, then said, "It's not a joke, my king." He bit his lip and studied Mallory from head to toe. "She fits exactly what you have been searching for."

Wilmont snorted and folded his thick arms. "I said *good* stock." Narrowing his eyes at Mallory, his lip curled when he said, "Not a *degen*."

Mallory inhaled Wilmont's choking scent and her growl almost broke free, but she swallowed it. Her entire body trembled with fire and heat after hearing the slur about her breed. *Better a degenerate than a fucking murdering bastard*, she seethed to herself.

"She's still an Alpha," Philip reminded. He reached between Mallory's thighs and clutched her penis, displaying it to Wilmont, who chuckled but then frowned at Philip's continued seriousness. "They say *degens* get bigger during their rut... much bigger." He released Mallory. "Sire, she is everything you're looking for." He started ticking off the list. "Young, healthy, strong, big, handsome, intelligent, and light haired."

Wilmont bared his canines at Philip and snapped, "A *degen* will not touch—"

"My king," the portly man interrupted, "perhaps we should leave this decision to the princess."

Wilmont held his gaze over Philip's head and appeared to weigh the idea.

"Acrin makes a great suggestion, my king." Philip smiled at Wilmont and said, "You want the princess to have some options."

The portly man Aerin shifted closer to Philip's side and looked over Mallory, then grabbed her face. "My king, the princess's aversion to Alphas is well known." He lowered his hand and looked at his king with a determined expression. "But *perhaps* an Alpha with soft features will be more to her liking."

After several grumbles, Wilmont huffed. "We'll keep the *degen*." He stomped off and headed to the storeroom's exit.

"What shall I do with the others, my king?" Philip asked, shadowing his ruler.

"They're useless to me." Wilmont paused in the doorway and peered over his shoulder at Philip. "Dispose of them." Then he was gone with Aerin in tow.

Mallory sucked in her breath, but a sword was already unscabbarded. The first and second slaves were gutted in swift order. With a jerk of her chains, she tried to move, unsure how she could save them. But then the slave next to Mallory took a blade through his back and out his stomach.

"N-no," Mallory rasped and grabbed the slave as he fell off the sword. She cradled his head against her chest as he bled out, breathing slower until he died in her hands.

A keeper shoved the dead slave off Mallory, then unlocked the chains from the dead slave. "Get up," he ordered her.

Mallory clenched her jaw, still holding down her snarls. She rose and followed the three remaining slaves who were escorted from the storeroom. This time the sounds of the chains were louder from the excess dragging on the floor. At the doorway Mallory gave a sidelong look at the seven murdered slaves, whose blood flowed into the crevices in the floor.

The journey through the castle's depths were endless, and when they arrived in a dungeon that reeked of piss, feces, and rotten egg, Mallory nearly lost the few contents in her stomach from this morning's meal. She placed her hand onto the cold wall and prayed her stomach would settle.

The last keeper neared her and struck her bare ass with a wooden rod. "Keep moving."

Mallory pushed off the wall and faced the keeper, who was at least a foot shorter than she. She clenched her hands when he didn't balk under her dominating presence, thanks to the beating rod and sword he carried with him. After releasing a frustrated rumble, she ducked under the doorway and followed the remaining Alpha slaves into the dungeon that was lined with cells on either side.

One by one the guards unlocked the slaves from the chain line and pushed them each into an empty cell. When it was Mallory's turn, the soldier behind her informed the keeper that the very last cell was specifically for her. The keeper grunted and neared Mallory's side.

Mallory stared down the length of the dungeon, ignoring the hoots from the prisoners who had their faces against the bars. She dug her blunt nails into the iron chains between her wrist shackles and willed her inner Alpha to stay calm.

"Pick up the chain, *degen*." The keeper pointed his wooden rod at the long length of chain that once held ten other slaves. The links were the size of Mallory's palm and every fifth link held a shackle for each slave's wrist and ankle. "Pick it all up and go to that cell." The keeper raised his rod to the cell at the end on the right. "*Now*," he growled.

Breathing harder, Mallory bent over and collected as much chain as possible, then walked down the aisle, but several shackles dragged behind her.

"I said pick it up, not drag it, *degen*!"

Mallory paused and looked at the iron tangled in her hands and arms, but saw the last of it cascaded over her arms and touched the floor. With gritted teeth, she tossed the chain over her broad shoulders, having it spill over her back. Tangling her fingers into the chains and shackles, she hefted the remainder off the floor, then continued down the aisle. Her legs and arms trembled from the weight against her weakened body, but she pushed herself forward.

Prisoners went silent, but the three Alpha slaves who had traveled with her cheered and hooted. They slammed their fists against the bars and growled when the keepers tried hitting them with their rods.

Mallory was panting and sweating when she reached the end of the hall. She turned to the empty, open cell and almost threw the chains down, but restrained her desire. The arrogant keeper would use it against her.

The keeper stomped up and folded his arms, staring at Mallory's strained features. He then leaned forward and whispered, "You think you're proving something, *degen*."

Mallory remained focused, refusing to allow the keeper's taunts to get under her skin. She paced her breathing and waited for the tiny bit of permission from the keeper who now controlled her world.

"Drop the chains," the keeper ordered.

Twisting to her left, Mallory tossed them and pulled off the lengths from her shoulders; all that remained was the end still shackled to her.

After a grunt the keeper worked the iron key into each lock and allowed the shackles to fall to the floor. He indicated toward the open cell with his beating rod, lowering it once she was inside. Next to him a soldier shut the gate and turned the key in the lock, then left with the keeper.

Mallory clutched the bars and peered between them, watching and listening to the keepers talk to the soldiers. Their voices were low, until a newcomer snapped an order at them. Sighing, Mallory went over to the bench and sat down. After such a long, damp walk this morning, it was a relief to be off her feet, and the earlier rush from the events in the storeroom were wearing off.

A chill settled over her nude body. She drew her legs up onto the bench and pulled them against her chest, seeking a measure of warmth. The cold stone wall at her back did nothing to help. As she sat there, her mind wandered back to what happened in the storeroom. It wasn't unusual for Mallory to be mocked about her breed and nature as an Alpha. People called her a degenerate or a perversion. To be called a *degen* was the most common of all the slurs. She was also used to being touched and fondled by her owners, everyone fascinated by both her penis and breasts. Usually it ended in mockery, specifically about her slimmer-sized equipment and lack of balls.

But despite her unnatural breed, King Wymarc still spared her life. The nobles had mentioned the princess, who sparked Mallory's curiosity. It seemed as if Mallory's fate, along with the remaining Alphas, was in the hands of the princess.

The loud gush of water filled the dungeon and brought everyone to the bars of their cells. A Tharnstone soldier pointed a water hose down the center of the aisle and used it to spray the floor, which kicked up the stench. He hollered over his shoulder for more power and walked down the aisle. The water pressure increased and pushed the dirt, human waste, and rotting food toward the massive drain at the end of the hall. Driving all the waste into the drain, he then hollered again; the water stopped, other than the constant drips.

Two soldiers sprinted down holding three buckets and a long brush. The soldier with the hose turned to Mallory's cell and pointed it at her.

"Pump the water!"

Mallory scrambled back when the blast of water roared past the bars and struck her. She yelled as the icy shards cut against her skin, and her heart thundered against her chest. Backing up, she went into a corner, but the water followed her before it was cut off. Slumped against the wall, she braced herself with her arms on her thighs and lifted her head when the cell's gate swung open.

One soldier rushed in and used a soapy brush to scrub Mallory down. The brush's rough bristles clawed into her already tender, frozen skin and left long red streaks. Mallory clenched her teeth, but bared them at the soldiers. Just as she took a step closer, another cold blast pushed her against the wall. The soldier with the hose laughed, then turned the water to the rest of the cell, spraying it down until all the muck went into the drain.

Mallory huddled on the floor, body curled forward, and gasped for air. Her entire frame quaked from the brutal wash down. She crawled to the bench; the only place slightly warmer than the stone floor. Balling up, she closed her eyes and blocked out the other prisoners' cries.

Silence fell over the dungeon after the soldiers finished cleaning everything and everyone. For a moment, Mallory slept lightly while her body temperature rose. But more banging startled her, and she sat up on the bench, prepared for another round.

This time the three soldiers returned to her cell with items in hand. After unlocking the door, two entered, set the things down, then left and went down the row of cells.

Mallory unfolded herself from the bench and crept over to the clothes and tray of food. Once she was sure it was safe, she held up the tunic and pulled it over her head. Slipping on the pants, she tied the string across her waist. Kneeling in front of the tray, Mallory sniffed the bowl of soup and tested it by dipping her fingertip into it, but the flavor was bland. The large hunk of bread would at least offer some weight in her gut.

Sitting on the edge of the bench, she drank the soup and sopped up the juices with the bread. She struggled against her hunger to eat slowly. She returned the tray near the cell door, then went to the bench while everyone else slurped their food.

The keepers arrived sometime later and informed the soldiers to collect the four Alphas. Without hesitation, the soldiers gathered the clothed Alphas and barked at them to follow. Again, Mallory fell in at the end of the line and ducked out of the doorway of the dungeon. Behind her, the keeper stayed close and occasionally shoved the end of his rod into her back.

They were led up to the ground floor and escorted into a different room warmed by the gigantic fire in the stone fireplace. Dreary sunlight streamed through stained-glass windows. From the tapestries and pillars, it appeared to be a great hall. Ahead of them was a dark wood, tiered dais that had three empty thrones, two of which were on an upper level. The keepers positioned the prisoners in front of the dais.

Eight soldiers flooded into the great hall from a side door and spread out around the dais. The four keepers remained behind the slaves; from the corner of her eye, Mallory watched them straighten their backs when the nobles filed through the side door as well.

King Wilmont Wymarc headed the procession, followed by Philip, Aerin, and a soldier with brilliant bronze armor. The last person to enter was a young woman, who appeared to be in her late teens. Her shoulder-length brunette hair was split into two braids. She wore a beautiful, long emerald-green dress with its short train dragging behind her. When she stood on the upper dais with Wilmont, her intense blue eyes scanned the Alphas one by one.

Philip and Aerin were on the lower level of the dais. Whereas Aerin remained at one end, Philip walked to the middle, closer to the royals. "Princess Kinsey Wymarc," he said and held out his hand at the slaves. "May I present to you the best Alphas in the kingdom."

"Yes, yes," Wilmont brushed off, then turned to the princess at his side. "The best stock that money can buy." He rubbed his dark goatee.

Philip cleared his throat and folded his hands together. "Perhaps you would like to take a closer look, my princess." He bowed his head and waited for her decision.

Kinsey pursed her red lips, then tore her attention away from the slaves to address Philip. "I would like that, Sir Philip."

Philip beamed and offered his hand to Kinsey, who took it as she descended the dais. He guided her to the first Alpha, who was at the opposite end of the line from Mallory.

The bronze-clad soldier shifted his position closer to Kinsey, shadowing her. He looked to be the princess's personal guard.

"Do they have names?" Kinsey asked.

Philip smiled and replied, "Whatever you see fit to call them, my princess."

Kinsey took small, timed steps as her eyes dragged over each slave. Her features remained neutral, until she stood in front of Mallory. Her stare lingered, and a peculiar light entered her bright blue eyes. "I thought you said they were all Alphas."

"Yes, princess." Philip smiled at Kinsey. "They are all Alphas."

Mallory fought to remain still and breathed in Kinsey's sweet scent, which raced to her head. Kinsey was an Omega, an unmated one. For a beat, Mallory's lip curled, but she strangled her Alpha's natural reaction to an Omega. She continued to stare straight ahead, fighting to not look at the princess, who stared so intently at her.

"Is she..." Kinsey struggled to find her words and looked at Philip for help.

Philip had a soft flush to his cheeks. "Yes, my princess she is equipped. Do you wish to make certain?"

Mallory tensed and gritted her teeth, prepared for her drawers to be dropped to the floor. Since being sold into slavery, she was quite accustomed to people wanting to see her genitals to prove or disprove her Alpha nature. Everyone overlooked her Omega-like qualities, forgetting she was both breeds together.

Kinsey released a soft sound, something between a rumble and growl. She shook her head and replied, "Perhaps another time."

"So what do you think?" Wilmont asked, stepping down from the dais with soft booms. "Are there any you wish to forego immediately?"

Mallory prepared to be cast out, then run through with a sword. *No Omega wants a degenerate Alpha*, she reminded herself. With her burning eyes staring upward, she waited for her final sentencing.

Kinsey neared the dais but remained on the ground floor, then turned back to face the slaves. "They all please me, Father."

Wilmont huffed and puffed up his chest. "All of them? You are certain?"

"Yes, Father." Kinsey turned to Philip and said, "You did well. Thank you, Sir Philip."

Philip bowed to Kinsey, then turned back to the soldiers and keepers. "Please escort the princess's Alphas to their rooms."

Chapter 2

Princess Kinsey Wymarc drifted out to the balcony off her bedchamber and studied the beautiful mountains beyond the castle. They were grand and daunting, stretching on forever. After the recent rain, specks of green now dotted the mountainsides. Soon spring and summer would be here.

A heavy knock from the main door disrupted her quiet moment. She returned to the bedchamber and called, "Come." A smile tugged at her lips when her younger sister bounded into the room.

Agatha rushed across the distance after shutting the heavy door. She grabbed her sister's hands and asked, "What were they like? Were they all handsome?"

Kinsey sighed, then sat down on the wooden trunk at the foot of her bed. "They were big brooding Alphas, like our father."

Agatha rolled her eyes and dropped her shoulders. "How can you hate Alphas so?" She hopped onto the foot of the bed next to her sister.

"I don't *haaate* them." Kinsey watched Agatha swing her legs and considered when her sister would be given away to an Alpha. Unlike Kinsey, Agatha's future and duty to the kingdom entailed a marriage-alliance. "I just find them very boorish and volatile."

Agatha huffed and leaned forward, cupping her chin in her hands. "I think they're all handsome."

Kinsey chuckled at her sister's romantic ideas about Alphas and the relationship between them and Omegas. From childhood, Alphas and Omegas were taught about their strict roles—until an Omega was bound to an Alpha, and only then would an Omega truly understand the value of having a mate who cared for them. Where Agatha bought into the norms, Kinsey did not. At one time, it didn't matter what Kinsey thought, because her older brother Devon was destined to take the crown. But his death changed everything, especially Kinsey's future.

As the next in line to rule, Kinsey had newfound control over her fate, and the old talks about who to wed Kinsey off to were gone. The kingdom's future rested squarely on Kinsey's shoulders as the queen-to-be. But for Agatha, nothing had changed for her and that seemed to appeal to her, at least Kinsey had assumed, until recently. There were biting remarks and mutters about unfairness each time their parents mentioned prospective husbands.

"Many Betas are handsome and far better natured than Alphas," Kinsey said.

Agatha huffed and peered over at her sister. "Father says I'll most likely be wed to a Beta prince."

Kinsey squeezed her sister's thigh and argued, "It could change. We can never be sure what will happen."

Agatha gave a soft rumble, then straightened up. "Please tell me what they were like? Will I get to see them, at least once?"

Chuckling as she stood from the trunk, Kinsey walked over to one of the sofa chairs in the sitting area. "I don't see why not." She paused and caught her sister smiling from ear to ear. "My sister should have a say in whom I choose."

Hopping off the bed, Agatha rushed over to her sister and grabbed her hands. "I wish to see them now! Mother said there're four Alphas."

"Aggie, they just went to their rooms," Kinsey argued. "They had a long journey here."

"I know, but we could just peek." Agatha pouted and tugged on her sister's arm. "Please, sister." She shifted closer and leaned into Kinsey, hugging her.

Kinsey accepted the hug, nuzzled her sister's cheek, and hummed low in a rare show of affection. As kids they had been close and often snuggled together, but into their teenage years, they only shared affection when one of them was upset. "All right. We can go see them, but we can't stay long."

Agatha squeezed her harder, nearly taking all the air out of her, then bolted across the room and yanked the door open all while urging her sister to hurry up. Kinsey rolled her eyes but left the bedchamber.

Two guards stood sentry outside her door and waited for the princesses. The soldiers had been assigned to the princesses when they first started to walk. Agatha was on her second guard; she had caught the first guard having sex with a servant. Wilmont all but beheaded the guard, then ordered Huxley as her replacement.

Kinsey had been assigned Gerald. He had sworn his blade to the House of Wymarc, and when Kinsey became a young teen, he had gone to her in private, kneeled, and pledged his life. Kinsey wanted to deny his pledge, not believing anyone's life was worth hers. But rejecting Gerald's pledge would have broken him.

When the sisters hurried down the hallway, Huxley and Gerald followed them without question. Kinsey guided her sister to the west wing where the Alphas were being held until she made her final choice. The wing had six rooms but only four of the doors were guarded. The first guard straightened his stance when the princesses arrived, then waited for his orders.

"Wait here for us," Kinsey told Gerald and Huxley. "We wish to see the Alphas," she told the guard outside one of the Alpha's room. "We'll start with this one."

The guard nodded, turned, and knocked on the door once before entering the room. He kept a hand on the hilt of his sword and ordered the Alpha to get up.

Kinsey couldn't see past the guard's body blocking the doorway. It was for their safety, as well as protecting Agatha's young eyes. Once the guard stepped aside, they were allowed to go in and meet the Alpha.

The Alpha took a few steps closer and stood in the center of the small bedchamber. Wearing nothing but loose pants that hid his lower half, his upper body left nothing to the imagination. His chest was muscular, and six pads of muscles lined his stomach. A tiny trail of dark hair traveled from his belly button and disappeared beneath his pants. The veins in his arms stood out as he hooked his hands in front of his body.

Like his eyes, his hair was black as night and very short. His dimpled chin added to his gruff appearance. On his neck a dragon tattoo crawled up the right side from his shoulder, and several old scars trailed down his left arm. She could only imagine their history in battle.

Kinsey inhaled his distinct scent. While in the great hall, she couldn't discern each of the Alphas' pheromones, especially since they'd been cleansed down just prior to the meeting; however, a few hours later, his unique scent was noticeable.

He smells like my father, she thought and frowned.

Agatha, however, was giggling, clearly showing her youth while remaining by her sister's side. "Where were you born?"

The Alpha cleared his throat and replied, "On a farm in the Cushar Kingdom."

"That's why his eyes are so dark," Agatha whispered.

"I know." Kinsey tilted her head and eyed the bulky Alpha. "How did you come to be in the Kingdom of Tharnstone?"

"War," he said with a huff.

"He was probably a soldier," Agatha whispered.

On the losing side, Kinsey concluded. She grabbed Agatha's shoulder and directed her out of the room. "Rest well," she said to the Alpha on her way out.

The next Alpha was several years older than the first one and appeared less dominant. He was still a strong presence, regardless. His features reminded Kinsey of her father, which she hadn't noticed earlier in the great hall. She hoped it was just the bad lighting in the room.

The third Alpha was in similar shape as the first Alpha and about the same age. He was slightly shorter but plenty taller than Kinsey and her sister. His shirt's seams strained against his bulging muscles. Unlike the first two Alphas, his hair was long, curly, and light brown. His eyes were a smoky gray, and when her sister cooed, Kinsey all but dragged Agatha out of the room.

Approaching the last Alpha's room, Kinsey shifted on her feet while the guard went into the bedroom first. She nibbled on her lip until the guard stepped aside to allow her and her sister to enter. Her eyes locked on the Alpha. Forcing her attention away, Kinsey smirked at Agatha's gawk.

"It's a *degen*," Agatha whispered loud enough for everyone to hear.

The guard grunted but remained silent.

"Agatha," Kinsey warned and shot her a glare for the vulgar word. She huffed at her sister, then gazed over at the Alpha, who stood beside the foot of the bed.

"Sorry," Agatha muttered and looked at the floor but only for a moment. Her attention focused back on the Alpha, and she stared just like her older sister was doing.

Kinsey studied the Alpha in the firelight's glow. In the great hall, she had thought the Alpha was strange. All her life she had associated Alphas with hulking, muscular warriors who grunted and growled about everything. Her father was the super Alpha of them all.

However, this Alpha was different. She was still very tall and large, but her features were softened by feminine lines. Her short and shaggy straight hair, coupled with freckles across the crest of her cheeks, gave her a cute air. Between broad shoulders were the perfect swell of breasts that contradicted the muscles hidden under the clothing. According to Philip, the Alpha had the appropriate tools to handle Kinsey's needs.

"Where are you from?" Agatha finally mustered the courage to ask.

The Alpha didn't meet Agatha's eyes and continued to stare into the distance. For a beat, it seemed as if she would ignore Agatha's inquiry, which didn't settle well with Kinsey. "I have forgotten."

Agatha frowned and folded her arms. "How can you forget where you are from?"

Kinsey sniffed at the air, drawing in the Alpha's spicy scent. Like the Alpha herself, it was different and also intriguing. She touched her sister's shoulder and replied, "Sometimes we forget things that are better forgotten."

Agatha pursed her lips and said, "Like that time I fell from the balcony."

Rumbling in agreement, Kinsey nodded and sighed. "Exactly." Like Agatha, she boxed away the awful memory and said, "We should let her sleep." She smelled Agatha's displeasure about leaving so soon.

"I like her hair." Agatha folded her arms and leaned into her sister. "It's different from the other Alphas."

"Yes." Kinsey chuckled and nudged her sister to the open door, but she hesitated when she heard a familiar voice.

"Here comes Father," Agatha muttered.

Before Kinsey or Agatha could leave, their father entered the room and dominated the space. He placed his hands on his hips and studied his daughters. "It is getting late and supper will be soon."

"We're sorry, Father." Kinsey smiled in hopes to disarm the hint of annoyance she smelled on him. "I wanted to show Agatha the Alphas you brought me."

Wilmont stood behind his daughters, blocking the exit. His attention flickered to the Alpha behind them, who remained passive and silent. He rumbled low and asked, "Did you explain to her—" he nodded to Agatha—"why this Alpha is a *degen*?"

Kinsey clenched her jaw and sensed where her father's questioning might go. "Agatha knows why." She was grateful that her sister started bobbing her head. "Just like I do," she said, not being able to keep the edge out of her voice. As a child, she only knew of Alphas and Omegas being a certain way. Later in life, she had learned that there were other breeds of Alphas and Omegas who didn't conform to the majority. This was the first time that Kinsey had met the special breed of Alpha.

"But you have not seen what makes her or others like her a degenerate." Wilmont turned to the slave and ordered, "Remove your bottoms."

"Father, is this really necessary right now?" Kinsey glowered when she looked from her father to the Alpha, who was already untying the pants' string. Grabbing her sister, she shoved Agatha behind her back and blocked her view of the Alpha dropping her drawers. She should have looked away herself, but her curiosity won out and caused her grip to loosen on her sister.

Below the shirt's hem, the Alpha's toned stomach ended where muscular thighs began, and between them was a penis about the length of Kinsey's hand. It wasn't the first time she'd seen someone's penis, having accidently walked in on her parents at an early age. But she had seen—and even touched—a Beta's dick, which was similar in size to the Alpha before her. Typical Alphas were bigger than Betas and degenerate Omegas.

A soft set of giggles cut through Kinsey's appraisal of the Alpha. She growled at Agatha, who had stepped out from behind her. "Go wait outside." With her hand, she covered her sister's eyes.

"Kinsey," Agatha whined and struggled to pry Kinsey's hand from her face. "It's just a penis."

Wilmont grunted and folded his arms, but he allowed Kinsey to shove Agatha out of the room. He then remarked, "A little one with no balls."

Kinsey heard it and glanced over at the slave, who retained a stoic face. She suspected the Alpha had grown a thick skin over the years from other Alphas, like her father, mocking her.

"Are you sure you wish to waste time on a *degen*?" Wilmont asked. "She's more useful mucking stalls."

Crossing the small distance, Kinsey neared the Alpha and kept her eyes above her neckline. Kinsey raised her hand but refrained from touching the Alpha, who smelled of tension and caged anger. After a sigh, she whispered, "Put on your bottoms." She stepped aside when the slave bent down to pick up her clothes. Returning to her father, she paused in front of him and said, "Don't be envious that her breasts are bigger than your balls, Father." Patting him on the stomach, she exited the room. "Are you hungry, Aggie?" Behind her, she heard her father's rumbles about her joke, but she shrugged it off. She and her father had struck a deal that they both had to honor. Kinsey retained the right to choose any Alpha who'd provide for her—and it included the rare Alpha.

"I like her even if she is a *deg*—"

"Agatha," Kinsey whispered.

Gerald and Huxley fell into step, shadowing them out of the west wing.

"Even if she's different," Agatha attempted, sighing after her sister gave her a slight smile. "Did you see the freckles on her face?"

"Yes. I like them." Kinsey slid her arm across Agatha's shoulders and continued their walk through the castle. Behind them, their father followed at a distance and allowed them their time together, knowing it would end someday soon. "What do you think of the others?"

"I really like the first Alpha."

"And the second one?" Kinsey probed, valuing her sister's insight.

"I like him the least. He kind of smelled funny."

Kinsey leaned in and whispered, "Like our father?"

Agatha laughed and nodded a few times. "Two of them did, I thought." She crinkled up her nose and mirrored Kinsey's gagging look.

"What about the third one?"

Agatha was quiet and reflected on the question before replying, "Maybe I like him the best. I'm between him and the first." She hesitated, seeming to have a thought. "But I think the last one is the best." Pausing, she leaned in and whispered, "Best for you."

Kinsey snorted and asked, "Why?"

"Because you hate Alphas, and she's not a real Alpha."

Kinsey rolled her eyes at her sister's assessment of the four Alphas. "She's more Alpha than you or me."

Agatha laughed loudly and smiled at her sister.

Kinsey echoed her sister's laughter as they went down the steps and entered the great hall. Their mother was already seated and waiting for them. She kissed her mother on the cheek after Agatha, then sat down in her usual spot. Wilmont sat at the head of the table, and Sir Philip and Aerin joined as well.

Aerin and Wilmont mostly chatted about political nonsense. At times Kinsey spoke with Sir Philip or her mother Agnes who mentioned she had seen the four Alphas. Agatha was the first to finish her meal and excused herself, most likely having a game of cards left to finish. Eventually Wilmont invited Philip and Aerin to join him in the cabinet, which was Wilmont's private sitting room.

Kinsey finished her drink and waited for her mother to speak now that they were alone, with the exception of the servants and the guards.

Agnes was eating the last bit of fruit in a bowl, saving the sweetest piece for last. "Your father showed me the four Alphas." This conversation was not unexpected.

After signaling a servant, Kinsey waited until her cup was full before she responded to her mother. "Yes. What did you think?" She leaned to one side, allowing the servant access to the dirty plates in front of her.

"All of them appear to come from good stock."

"But?" Kinsey sipped on the mild wine and waited for her mother's honesty. Even though her little sister was named after their mother, Kinsey was a duplicate of her mother, except for her blue eyes; those were from her father.

Agnes set aside the empty bowl and ordered the servants to finish clearing the table. "There is no 'but,' dear."

Kinsey weighed her mother's smile and decided it wasn't forced at all. "Father doesn't like the…." She hunted for a less harsh word.

"Degenerate," Agnes supplied and shrugged at Kinsey's sour look. "Call it what it is."

Kinsey didn't approve of the slur. She still had trouble finding a better word and had never heard of anything else. After a sigh, she argued, "She's still an Alpha."

"I didn't say I disapproved," Agnes countered.

Kinsey rumbled low and considered her mother's angle, even though they had an arrangement. "I didn't say she was the right Alpha."

Agnes pursed her lips and remained quiet for a moment. "Hopefully not, dear."

There's her opinion. Kinsey had waited for it and chose to ignore the prod. "What did you think of them?"

"The Alpha in the first room has everything you're looking for."

Kinsey rumbled and leaned against the table for support and then eyed her mother. "I do fancy him. But I still must get to know their personalities."

Agnes chuckled and said, "All Alphas are the same." She nudged out the bench and stood up. "There are little differences you'll find between them."

"Grandfather Randall was different," Kinsey argued, thinking back on her mother's father. As a child she spent quite a bit of time with him and her grandmother, both teaching her how to read at an early age. Since then, Kinsey's experience with most Alphas never played out well. Prior to her brother's death, she had almost been betrothed to an Alpha prince, who promised her that his claim over her would mean locking her in a castle.

"Your grandfather was a kinder Alpha in his later years." Agnes sighed and whispered, "Those are few and far between, love." She came around the dinner table and asked, "Do you have time to spend with your mother?"

Kinsey took the invitation and left the great hall for the ladies' chamber, where the fire had already been started by a servant. They sat in chairs across from the fire, played a board game, and chatted further about the Alphas. Tomorrow morning Kinsey would spend a few hours with her tutor, then meet with her father and begin the process of choosing an Alpha. The day would be busy and tiresome but necessary for the kingdom's future.

After leaving her mother's sitting room, she returned to her bedchamber in the north wing. She welcomed the warmth from the fire in the fireplace. After preparing for bed, she sat in front of the fire, brushed her hair, and considered the four Alphas. None of them were poor quality, but she could only choose one.

With the kingdom's future having shifted since her brother's death, Kinsey sensed the mounting pressure upon her shoulders. Devon had died three years ago and left the large role to be filled by Kinsey. She missed her brother greatly and hoped he was well in the afterlife. But his early passing also placed a mountain of responsibility on Kinsey that she never expected. Oftentimes she imagined a simpler life, but that was a fairytale.

Chapter 3

allory finished washing her face and went to the table near the burning fireplace. She studied the porridge that'd been brought to her by a servant this morning. Next to it was a smaller bowl of fresh fruit and vegetables. Picking up the larger bowl, she sniffed the contents and noticed a maple scent. A pleasant rumble shook in her chest at the prospect of eating something sweet.

Sitting at the table, she paced herself with the porridge, especially since it was still quite warm. A soft knock on the door announced a chambermaid coming in to collect the pot. Mallory watched the shy Beta. Once the maid left, Mallory finished the porridge and ate the fruit and vegetables before the maid returned to collect the dirty dishes.

The maid moved the clay cup of wine off the tray, and took the tray with the dirty dishes. As she lifted the tray, the two bowls shook and rattled together.

Mallory stood up and towered over the Beta maid, who backed up in two steps, then rushed to the door. After a huff, Mallory crossed the room and peered out the small open window that overlooked the west lands. There wasn't much to see besides a mountain range, but the little bit she could see was beautiful. She wrapped her hands around the two iron bars and tugged on them, finding them deeply rooted into the castle wall. Even if she could remove the bars, there was no place to go and nothing in the room to use for climbing. The room was too high up in the castle.

The sounds of voices tickled Mallory's ears, and she looked to the sealed door when she heard a low boom. It was the neighboring Alpha's room. She withdrew from the window when her door's lock clicked free.

The guard entered first, as normal. He scanned the room and eyed Mallory from head to toe before he stepped aside, though he kept his hand on his sword's hilt.

Mallory stood in the same spot as last night when the princess and her sister visited her. As trained by her owners, she stared through them and waited for their command. She choked down a snarl when King Wilmont entered, followed by Princess Kinsey. They were here to tell her why Wilmont purchased her from her former owner. She smelled the anxiousness from Kinsey, who took a position in front of her father. It was an unspoken stance of authority, especially over Wilmont.

"Good morning," Kinsey offered, a faint tremble in her tone.

Mallory remained indifferent, even though she was listening to her new owner. Wilmont and Mallory's dominant scents filled the room, but Kinsey straightened her back and held her ground. *She's an Omega who doesn't automatically bare her neck to Alphas.*

Kinsey cleared her throat once, then said, "There is much to be done in a short time." She paused, as if expecting Mallory to respond to her, but silence lingered for a beat. "You and the other Alphas were brought here to carry out a service for your kingdom."

Mallory clenched her jaw and waited to learn what service she could possibly provide to the royal family. She pictured cleaning cesspools for the garderobes, mining metals, or even tanning rotten animal hides, all in the name of the Kingdom of Tharnstone. With her gaze going through the nobles, she listened for their pending command.

However, Kinsey took a few bold steps closer to command Mallory's full attention.

"Kinsey," Wilmont called and moved toward her until she stared him down. He rumbled and growled but returned to his previous spot.

Mallory was forced to lower her gaze to Kinsey now that they were so close, or else she could suffer punishment for disregarding a noble. Under Kinsey's nervous scent, Mallory also found a measure of fire that was uncommon for Omegas. Perhaps some of Wilmont's warrior blood did flow in Kinsey's veins.

"Starting today, you and the other Alphas have five days to present yourselves to me." Kinsey hooked her hands in front of her body, never breaking her gaze with Mallory. "At the end of those five days, I will choose one, and that Alpha will impregnate me."

Mallory's body jolted to life, and she inhaled sharply. *Alphas don't present themselves to Omegas.* It was tradition for Omegas to give themselves over to a desirable Alpha, never the reverse. Kinsey's distinct scent filled Mallory and left her a bit lightheaded, but she withheld her Alpha's hungry rumble. She huffed low, never breaking her eye contact with Kinsey.

"If the chosen Alpha successfully impregnates me, then they will be awarded their freedom," Kinsey whispered and searched Mallory's eyes.

Mallory tried holding a neutral expression, but her lip twitched a few times. Somehow the proposition seemed like a game or a joke, except Kinsey was stern. Glancing at Wilmont, she confirmed that it was true. The proposition was a rare and strange chance to end a slave's bonds. It also left Mallory with greater doubt about her future if she failed to be selected. Even if she could outmatch the better qualified Alphas, she still had to impregnate Kinsey.

In the end, she only cared about what would happen to the Alphas who failed to be selected, because that was her fate. However, Mallory remained silent and stared into Kinsey's intense blue eyes.

For a moment, Kinsey shifted on her feet and appeared unsure of herself, until she straightened her back. Few people knew how to handle silence, especially from an Alpha. Kinsey nodded once, then said, "We will begin today." She departed the room first.

Mallory tracked Kinsey's exit, then returned to staring straight ahead.

Wilmont narrowed his eyes at Mallory and rumbled before he left. The guard was the last to leave, securing the door behind him. Mallory released a large sigh and returned to the window, seeking fresh air after the disturbing news about her future. First and foremost, she was a slave to be used as her master saw fit. In this case she was a potential stallion meant to breed the princess of the Kingdom of Tharnstone.

The entire proposal was bizarre and ludicrous. Why wasn't Kinsey being wed to an Alpha of another kingdom?

Such a noble Alpha would have a royal cock that could produce an entitled offspring. What was the value of a bastard child to the House of Wymarc?

Grumbling, Mallory clutched the two bars, pulled on them, and allowed her frustration to bleed out the more she put her strength into it. She growled and pushed off the bars, stomping over to the locked door. Baring her teeth, she considered taking the door off its hinges. Her rage was enough to do it, but once she was free then the guard would gut her. At least he would try, until Mallory pounded him into the wall; then the next guard might get her.

Mallory exhaled loudly and snarled again before starting to pace the room from one end to the other. It was one thing to be a slave, tied to a single, meager duty for the rest of her life. But now she was a slave and a prisoner in the Tharnstone Castle, with some obscure proposal that she would undoubtedly fail to achieve.

As her muscles began to loosen, she formulated a plan to escape the castle and her ugly future. If the selection process was five days, then she had four days to work out an escape. First, she needed to focus on the castle and what she had learned about its layout. She'd have to hope an opportunity to escape might present itself. Once beyond the city, she could be a free Alpha on her own terms, not those of a twisted noble's scheme.

* * *

Mallory kept her eyes down as the guard finished locking the shackles around her wrists. Her ankles were left unchained, however.

"Let's go, *degen*," the guard ordered and stepped out of the room.

Mallory departed the bedchamber, sandwiched between two Beta guards. Most royal families were Omegas and Alphas, while soldiers, guards, and armies were comprised of Betas. Similarly, most of the common folk were Betas with a few rare Alphas and Omegas being born among them. If an Alpha or Omega wasn't a nobleman, then they were often a slave.

The path Mallory followed twisted and turned through the castle; she paid attention to the details, looking for hidden alcoves, dead ends, and exits to freedom. The more the guards walked around her, the quicker she learned their sounds as metal and leather slapped together. Even their Beta scents were distinctive.

The leading guard went through an open doorway, but Mallory paused in the warm, golden light streaming through the doorway, inviting her to enter. After a week of rain and dampness, the sun was a welcomed sight.

"Move, *degen*." The rear guard shoved Mallory through the opening.

Outside, Mallory placed her foot onto a smooth stone that wasn't as cold as the castle's floors. Her other bare foot landed on soft, inviting grass. Gazing up, she admired the sun high up in the blue sky, but she looked over at the guards.

"The princess will be here soon," a guard said.

Mallory looked away and scanned the garden that was coming back to life after a harsh winter. Her curiosity drew her deeper into the garden; there were a few servants cleaning and pruning the different beds, trees, and shrubs. The guards didn't seem concerned about her escaping, and she wondered why until she scanned the layout.

The garden was on the east side and followed the curtain wall of the castle, until the curtain wall bumped out to connect to the north and south ends. The curtain wall ended where the great ravine started. In the garden, there were two paths, both leading north and south, one closer to the wall and one closer to the ravine's edge.

Mallory wandered to the edge and peered over the side, barely able to see the river at the bottom. She frowned at the distance and listened to the soft roar of the rushing waters.

"I don't suggest that way for an escape."

Mallory turned and studied Princess Kinsey.

"It'd be terribly painful," Kinsey added, also gazing over the edge. "Also, the water is quite cold at this time of the year when the snow is melting from the mountain tops." She peered up at Mallory, holding her gaze. "The undercroft is really the best place to find a way out."

Mallory lifted an eyebrow at Kinsey, who probably knew the castle from top to bottom. She pictured Kinsey as a little girl exploring every tiny nook of the Tharnstone Castle.

"That's if you can get across the bridge," Kinsey whispered, then grinned at Mallory.

After a rumble, Mallory withdrew from the edge and returned to the garden, observing the nearest statue. Kinsey followed alongside her and whispered, "That's my brother, Devon."

Mallory had heard of the former prince who died in the last great war that King Wilmont had waged and won. Glancing at Kinsey, she caught the sorrow on Kinsey's face, but she refused to give a damn. After all, it was King Wilmont's victory that had turned Mallory into a slave.

Farther down the path, Mallory paused in front of a beautiful tree that had buds at the ends of its twisty branches.

"It's a curly willow," Kinsey said and studied the tree.

Mallory had seen willows in the past, but none with such twists and turns in its branches.

"It came from a kingdom far to the east," Kinsey whispered. "It was a gift for good fortune to my grandmother. I suppose it worked, since she died at the age of eighty-one."

Mallory rumbled low after hearing the story. Everything in the garden seemed to hold the House of Wymarc's history. To have old possessions passed through the family was a strange idea to Mallory.

Kinsey shifted her gaze to Mallory and asked, "What is your name?"

Clenching her jaw, Mallory replied, "Whatever you wish it to be."

"I wish it to be the name you were given," Kinsey said.

Mallory kept her attention on the willow tree but said, "I am called Mallory."

Kinsey stared for a long moment at Mallory's profile before she nibbled on her lower lip.

She knows it's a slave name, Mallory concluded. She withdrew and followed the path, heading north. In the distance the mountains towered up beyond the castle. The terrain was dangerous but also safer than the gorge and rushing, cold water. Her stroll was cut short by Kinsey's stepping in front of her.

"I was asking for your birth name," Kinsey said.

"I have forgotten it." Mallory wanted to go around Kinsey, but she didn't want to insult her. Royals tended to have delicate egos when they didn't get their way. The excuse that she had forgotten something often worked best when it was something unimportant. Her birth name wasn't important to anyone, but it was her only personal possession.

"Just as you forgot where you came from." Kinsey tucked her hands into the sleeves of her soft blue dress. Her eyes echoed the dress's delicate shade and made her tempting to Mallory, who looked away. She nodded once and said, "Fine. Then I will call you 'Alpha' until you tell me your birth name."

Mallory huffed and gazed down at Kinsey again, narrowing her eyes. "That is something I am not, as you may recall." She tilted her head when a blush colored Kinsey's cheeks.

"You are more Alpha than I," Kinsey whispered, her cheeks growing redder. "Your scent is Alpha."

Breaking their eye contact, Mallory looked toward the mountain range again. She considered whether there were any exits on the north end of the castle that led to the mountains. There had to be, because the nobles needed more than one exit from the castle than just the bridge into the city. No army would dare travel the treacherous mountains to attack from the north. It was a well-placed castle.

"You're not taking this seriously," Kinsey growled.

Mallory's attention snapped back to Kinsey, and she weighed the danger after disregarding the princess. Even if she was being forced into the proposition, she needed to play along so that she wasn't cut from it too early. With a sigh, she pursed her lips and said, "It is all a bit peculiar." Her honesty could trigger a bad response, but Kinsey's scent wasn't bitter.

Kinsey sighed and gazed back at the garden before she pointed at a stone bench. "Sit with me, please."

Mallory obeyed, more willing after the politeness. Somehow the simple gesture shifted her opinion of Kinsey, who would be frowned upon for being polite to a slave.

Kinsey sat after Mallory took one end. "The whole truth is that one day soon I will be queen of the Kingdom of Tharnstone. But I refuse to marry an Alpha for my king, who would take my power for their own. I will only rule alone."

Mallory stared at her chained wrists, but tilted her head to signal she was listening.

"My father wishes for an heir so that the House of Wymarc will continue after me." Kinsey withdrew her hands from the sleeves of her dress and fiddled with the golden girdle in her lap. "I agreed I would get pregnant from an Alpha ensuring the House of Wymarc will live on. Yes, the child will be a bastard, but I will give him or her the family name."

Mallory considered the details of their arrangement, frowned, and leaned in closer. "Why not bed an Alpha prince?"

Kinsey huffed and gave Mallory a drop-dead look. "An Alpha prince would make claims for the throne."

"But an Alpha slave would be ignored for such ridiculous claims," Mallory concluded aloud.

"Yes." Kinsey stared at her lap, stilling playing with the girdle. "And the payment for the child is the slave's freedom."

Mallory wanted to snarl, but she held it back, except for the vibration in her chest. Her inner Alpha howled at the idea of producing an offspring, then leaving it. *I would rather die than let my child live with these Wymarcs, especially that butcher king.*

"At least you…" Kinsey faltered and said, "At least the slave would know their child is safe and growing up as a noble."

Mallory huffed and restrained her ingrained nature to fight and protect. "The child will ask questions."

Kinsey shrugged, looked at Mallory, and whispered, "Sometimes things are forgotten on purpose."

Mallory gazed down at her own hands, noticing their larger size compared to Kinsey's. Even if she was born an Alpha, she never felt like a true Alpha and had done everything possible to forget her upbringing. But she could still feel her father's belt across her back. For most of her life, she lived without a past and was surviving okay. One day she would die, but she was determined to do so as a free Alpha.

After a huff, Kinsey leaned closer to Mallory and whispered, "You won't be able to escape Tharnstone Castle. It's too well guarded. If the soldiers catch on that you're even thinking of escaping, they will return you to the dungeon until this is over."

Mallory curled her fingers against her knees and peered into blue eyes. "And if I fail to be selected?"

Kinsey sighed and shook her head. "That is up to my father."

"Then I will die," Mallory concluded and smelled a hint of distress from Kinsey. Her Alpha responded with a natural growl, but she tamped it down.

Kinsey shook her head and straightened; a slight shift compared to her open posture earlier. "Your only chance is to present your Alpha to me and convince me you're worthy of impregnating me." She leaned in closer, using her sweet pheromones to taunt Mallory. "Unless you are indeed not an Alpha."

For a moment, Mallory sat stiff and stared at Kinsey, an Omega who just challenged her very nature. Thunder rolled in her chest, then a strain started between her legs. Her Alpha was reacting to Kinsey's call, and she wanted to give into it. She had no other choice, but to answer it.

"What will happen over the next five days?" Mallory asked, her voice heavy and rough from desire.

Kinsey's lips curled into a grin. "Today and tomorrow I spend time speaking to each Alpha. Then on the third day, there will be a contest."

Mallory lifted an eyebrow at the mention of a contest, already guessing what it might be.

"The fourth day a healer will examine each of you to ensure you're in good health." Kinsey bit her bottom lip and whispered, "On the fifth I will select the best Alpha." She used her sweet scent to entice Mallory more, even letting their bodies touch. "By the seventh or eighth day, the Alpha will be released and have their freedom."

Popping up off the bench, Mallory put space between her and Kinsey, allowing the fresh air to clear her mind. But then she smelled Kinsey's sweet scent coming up behind her, and she closed her eyes. "You are challenging me on purpose."

"I think you need it," Kinsey said, coming to Mallory's side. "You've been suppressing your Alpha for a long time."

Mallory couldn't deny the truth and snarled to herself. Already she felt a slight pressure between her legs from Kinsey's presence. She could hold it back for a while, but the longer they remained together it would become difficult. An escape plan required focus and not thinking with her little head. Even as a slave, she managed to have limited sex with other slaves, but only with Betas. Such an option was impossible here in the Tharnstone Castle.

"I do not have the luxury to be an Alpha," Mallory whispered.

"But now is the time to be one." Kinsey watched Mallory's features. "Because there are three other Alphas who want their freedom."

Mallory peered down at Kinsey and narrowed her eyes at the prize being dangled in front of her. She wanted her freedom and her Alpha hungered at the idea of mating Kinsey, who was a beautiful Omega. However, her Alpha's excitement was dashed by the reminder that she was solely impregnating Kinsey, not taking a mate for life. With a huff, she looked away and glared at the mountains. She distantly heard Kinsey's sigh and smelled her retreat.

After a minute, a guard approached her and ordered, "Let's go, *degen*."

Fighting a snarl, Mallory clenched her chained hands and followed the guards through the garden. Even after Kinsey's departure, she could smell the golden scent of an Omega, and the pressure between her legs pulsed in remembrance. The walk back to the bedchamber was torturous; Kinsey's scent drifted everywhere. The guard took even longer to free her wrists, but she was grateful to be alone again.

Mallory was certain she'd find peace in the bedchamber, but that was not to be. Lifting her tunic, she breathed in the very scent that called to her Alpha. She growled at Kinsey's plan to taunt her, purposely allowing her smell to permeate the fabric. Yanking the shirt over her head, she tossed it to the bed and paced topless in the room.

Going to the window, she breathed in the fresh air that soothed her wired body. Her self-control returned, and she leaned her weight against the stone sill. Off in the distance, she could make out the sounds of life from within the inner ward. At this time of day, the castle's inner ward would be bustling with blacksmiths, cobblers, hoopers, billers, and spencers. For a moment, the noise gave Mallory something to focus on rather than her body's need.

In the past, Mallory had been mildly aroused by a few Betas and pursued by curious ones who wanted to see her cock. The initial conversations with her past lovers were always awkward. She smelled and bred like an Alpha, but her appearance resembled an Omega. Most Betas steered away from her, but some of them were curious to have sex.

Mallory slid her hand past her pants' waistline and clutched her cock, feeling the firmness. She ran her thumb lightly over the throbbing tip. Withdrawing her hand, she focused on the exterior sounds rather than worrying about her hard-on.

Soon, it would subside.

* * *

Sunset had been over two hours ago, along with supper. For once, Mallory had enjoyed her meal, which was more substantial than the last ones. This time the plate had half of a chicken, vegetables, and grain. She saved the small dish of fruit with honey for last, savoring the sweetness. After eating, she drank the wine at a leisurely pace and stood by the window, her favorite spot in the room.

Earlier she had hung her tunic over the sill and waited for Kinsey's smell to disperse. Once satisfied, she put it back on and continued to pace the room, working on her future plans. She hated her odds, whether she tried to win her freedom or steal her freedom.

A strong knock caught her attention, so she went over to the table, expecting the handmaiden to pick up the dirty dishes. She swallowed the last of the wine, then put the goblet on the tray with the other items.

The guard entered first, signaling that a noble was coming into the room rather than the handmaiden. He scanned the room, stepped aside, and watched Mallory.

Kinsey came in next and looked to the guard. "You can leave us." She kept her arms behind her back.

The guard looked between his princess and the Alpha slave, not at all pleased by the orders. He stomped out but quietly closed the door.

Mallory remained next to the table, studying Kinsey.

Bringing her hands forward, Kinsey revealed a thick leather-bound book. Its gold leaf letters and designs on the cover caught Mallory's eye. "I thought perhaps you might enjoy this book."

With a frown, Mallory huffed and said, "I cannot read." Like any peasant's upbringing, it didn't include reading and writing or even math. She had learned to count up to a certain number, but only because of time spent with another slave who was a blacksmith for their last master.

"I know," Kinsey said, her tone soft and delicate. She opened the book halfway, turned its pages to Mallory, and said, "But it also has illustrations."

Narrowing her eyes, Mallory was already intrigued by the images on each page. They were unusual but gorgeous types of birds.

Kinsey adjusted the large book in her hands and said, "Each illustration has information about the animal under it. I thought you could look through it. If there's a particular animal that interests you, I could read it to you later."

Mallory's brow wrinkled. She stared at Kinsey and rumbled for a long moment. "Why?" She smelled a hint of Kinsey's own confusion.

"So your time alone will be less bored."

Mallory pursed her lips, then released a chuff and approached Kinsey but kept space between them. "I meant why would you offer your book to *me*?"

Tilting her head, Kinsey closed the book and ran her hand across the top, a fondness in her features. She sighed and hugged the book against her chest, supporting its great weight. "Because I know what it's like to be a prisoner." She held out the book with both hands, waiting for Mallory to make her decision. "It's not the exact escape you seek, but it might do for now."

Mallory took another step closer and reached for the offering, arm outstretched in front of her. Her fingers brushed the bottom of the book, but she hesitated to take it. Looking from the gleaming cover to Kinsey, she saw hope in the blue eyes, and it encouraged Mallory. Once it was gifted to her, it would weigh a great deal in her hand. Deciding to take the offering, she studied the leather cover and the gold leaf letters that she couldn't read.

"It's called the *Kingdom of Animals*," Kinsey said, smiling slightly when Mallory looked up.

Mallory was unsure what to do with the book at first, never having been responsible for someone's precious object, especially from a noble. She almost placed it on the table but instead went to the bed, still studying the cover. With care, she put it on the bed near the pillows and planned to look at it later. Nearing Kinsey again, she said, "You have not told the guards about my idea."

Kinsey rumbled and folded her arms but shrugged. "I'm just as guilty of wanting the same."

Growling, Mallory argued, "My wants are nothing like yours." Her Alpha clawed in her chest and made her skin itchy.

"Aren't they?" Kinsey closed the distance, crowding Mallory, who backed up from the sudden offense. "What does freedom look like?" she whispered, leaning into Mallory's space.

Mallory was panting and curled her hands at her sides, urging her Alpha to submit to Kinsey's authority as a noble. *I didn't know Omegas could be so fiery.*

Kinsey slipped past Mallory, went to the window, and gripped an iron bar. "Some shackles are invisible."

For a moment, Mallory paused and discerned the meaning in Kinsey's words, her annoyance forgotten. She rumbled low when Kinsey turned and brushed past her.

Holding onto the door handle, Kinsey peered back at Mallory and said, "Goodnight, Alpha."

Chapter 4

At first light, she had spent three hours with her Beta tutor, and they focused on math and politics. Normally she dedicated her entire day with the tutor, but her schedule had changed once her father obtained the breeder Alphas.

Kinsey smiled at Luca, the Alpha she'd been spending the last two hours with. Similar to yesterday, Kinsey would spend most of her day with each Alpha to test and understand them. Tomorrow was the contest.

Before her time with Luca, Kinsey had visited with the other two Alphas, Eldon and Terrel. Eldon was the least interesting to Kinsey, and he was also the oldest of the four. Terrel was the pushiest of them, and Kinsey gave him the least amount of attention. The next time she met him, she planned to have her guard Gerald in the room with her.

Kinsey sipped on wine while she listened to Luca's latest war story from his previous life as a soldier for the Cushar Kingdom. Many times her father had regaled her with his battle stories, and it bored Kinsey. However, Luca's stories were different. Each one was about his daily life as a soldier, and one in particular amused Kinsey, when Luca described falling asleep and falling off his horse.

Shifting on the window bench, Luca mirrored Kinsey's smile and asked, "Do my stories bore you?"

"They are interesting and make me laugh." Kinsey placed the cup on the table. "Most Alphas prefer to flaunt their victories from battle. Or argue about the best way to sharpen their swords."

Luca grinned and folded his hands in his lap. "Yes, from one Alpha to another."

Kinsey appreciated Luca's keen awareness about her dislike for battles and deaths. She gazed about the solar room, enjoying the sunlight that warmed her. "If you had your freedom, what would you do with it?" she asked and peered up at him. "Return to the Cushar Kingdom perhaps?"

Luca folded his muscular arms and leaned back against the stone window frame. "Perhaps." He had a distant gaze that looked like longing. "My wife is dead."

Kinsey choked on her next sip of wine. "W-wife?" She put the glass on the long table next to her and coughed twice.

"Yes." Luca lifted his head off the wall and looked at her. "She was beautiful. You remind me of her."

Kinsey patted her chest, buying more time. *I forget they had lives before being slaves.* "What happened to her?"

"While I was away in the war, she died from the Ravage."

Cringing, Kinsey remembered what she had heard about the nasty disease called the Ravage that plagued several other kingdoms in the past. Once someone contracted the disease, their skin became feverishly itchy, and they scratched until their skin was raw and gone. It was ugly and painful, and the infection led to a slow death. "I'm sorry," she whispered.

"It was many years ago," Luca said.

But Kinsey rumbled in sadness for both Luca and his dead mate, who could have been alone on her death bed. She bit her lip and studied her hands in her lap, unsure what to say.

"It's in the past." Luca turned his attention to the window, gazing out at the world.

Kinsey nibbled on her lip after learning another detail about Luca's past. It was easy to care about the Alphas, especially when they opened up to her. Her father had warned her multiple times to not become attached to any of them. *They're like any other ware from the market*, her father's voice echoed in her head. She was supposed to select the best Alpha so that her child was the perfect heir.

Luca pushed off the bench and took the seat near Kinsey, facing her. He grinned and said, "At least my path has led me to you."

And charming, Kinsey checked that off the list. Unlike her sister, it was difficult to win over Kinsey with flattery, but she wasn't opposed to hearing it. "You're different from most Alphas," she remarked, thinking of her father's boorish behavior. Alphas tended to be headstrong, difficult, and volatile at times. Luca's personality seemed gentler, contrasting to his muscular build. Pieces of him were similar to her grandfather Randall. *A gentle beast, I suppose.*

"Perhaps because my father died when I was a baby." Luca leaned back in the chair. "My mother raised me."

Kinsey pursed her lips and crossed her legs under the soft yellow dress that fell to her ankles. "But your mother had to be tied to someone."

"We lived with my grandparents." It was common for a widow to return home to her parents for support.

Leaving the chair, Kinsey gazed out the window at the distant mountains. The sun had crept into the western sky and sunset would be in several hours. She thought of the one Alpha she hadn't seen today, saving the visit for last. The thought of seeing the female Alpha brought her both excitement and anxiousness.

"Are you all right, princess?" Luca asked and stood up.

"I am." Kinsey turned to Luca and had to crane her neck to see him better. "Perhaps a bit weary."

Luca bowed his head. "Then I shall take my leave."

Kinsey ignored the twinge of guilt at dismissing Luca, who was the easiest Alpha to talk to so far. She rather liked him, but she had to be sure she chose for the right reasons. "Until tomorrow."

Luca lingered for a moment but nodded, then departed the solar room. She heard one of the guards escort him down the hall.

Once alone, Kinsey sank into the same chair and called, "Gerald." After he stepped in, she ordered, "Bring me the fourth Alpha."

"Yes, my princess."

Kinsey listened to Gerald's retreating footfall, sighed, and sipped on the last of her wine. A servant arrived, stoked the fire and delivered finger food and fresh wine. By the time the handmaiden left, Gerald had returned with the last Alpha, who cradled the *Kingdom of Animals* in her left arm. For a moment, she wondered if the Alpha was left- or right-hand dominant.

"Hello, Alpha," Kinsey greeted after Mallory entered the solar room. She wasn't bothered by Mallory's silent acknowledgement, growing rather used to it in a short period. People had a tendency to blather at her and gossip about her family. Mallory's quiet and reserved mannerisms were a blessing to Kinsey.

Mallory studied the room from top to bottom. She appeared awed by the wooden, painted arches overhead that clung to the plaster ceiling. Between the wooden beams were artistic inlays of what the gods' heaven might be like. The back wall had shelves that were lined with pretty books from floor to ceiling. She peered down at the book in her hands and a slight frown pulled at her lips.

Kinsey had risen from the table and moved closer to Mallory. "I actually keep that book in my bedchamber. It was given to me by my late grandfather when I was about four."

Gazing at Kinsey, Mallory held a neutral expression again, but there was a new glow to her eyes. With the sunlight streaming through the windows, the warm golden hue to Mallory's eyes drew Kinsey in closer.

"Did you find any animals you would like me to read to you?" Kinsey asked, refraining from touching Mallory.

"Yes." Mallory held out the book in offer. "Several."

Kinsey smiled and took the book, then signaled over to the long, deep, and cushioned window that had the bench butted against it. "Sit with me." She went to one end and sat in the deep sill with her feet tucked under her. She rested the book on her lap and waited for Mallory to become comfortable.

Mallory took the opposite spot on the cushioned ledge but crossed her legs and leaned forward, her focus locked on Kinsey. "I wish to know about the creatures at the end."

"Ah." Kinsey chuckled and flipped the book over so that the front was against her lap. "The mythological creatures, then."

"Mite-tho," Mallory attempted.

"Myth-o-logical," Kinsey pronounced slower. "It means fairy tale. They're just stories." She grinned and whispered, "As far as we know."

"The big, black creature," Mallory said. "It's like the tattoo on the other slave."

"Luca," Kinsey whispered and flipped to the exact page, knowing it by heart. "It's a dragon." She heard Mallory's low huff and wondered if it was at the mention of the other Alpha, but she disregarded it. "This is my favorite." With a light touch, she brushed her hand over the illustration that had fascinated her since childhood.

Mallory leaned against the window's casing and waited for Kinsey to tell her more about the dragon.

"The dragon is an ancient and legendary creature thought to originate in the old Kingdom of Dilith. They are gigantic, reptile-like creatures that are born from eggs and can grow anywhere from thirty to one-hundred feet long, and they have an incredible wingspan of forty-five to sixty feet." Kinsey paused at hearing Mallory's rumble; she grinned but continued to read the description. "They come in a variety of colors including black, red, brown, grey, violet, blue, and white. Most dragons have the ability to fly and breathe fire or ice. They are believed to choose one mate per lifetime and can lay three to ten eggs per year. The name 'dragon' is believed to mean 'I see' because of their uncanny ability to see during the day and night." She looked up from the book and said, "The dragons went extinct thousands of years ago during an unnaturally long ice freeze across all the kingdoms."

Mallory's chest rolled with deep vibrations, and she had a thoughtful expression. "I would perhaps like to meet one someday."

Kinsey chuckled and propped her head against the window frame. "Yes, so would I and go for a ride."

A frown tugged at Mallory's lips. "From the ground, I would watch it fly."

Still amused, Kinsey studied Mallory, who was stunning in the soft afternoon light. Old scars on Mallory's face stood out to her suddenly, reminding Kinsey that Mallory was a slave. At one time, Kinsey suspected that Mallory wasn't such a submissive Alpha and fought her owner tooth and nail. One day Mallory's Alpha either broke or went into hiding somewhere under all the muscles and power.

"What is the next creature?"

Kinsey looked down, but she had the book memorized and knew what was next without turning the page. But flipping the page, she revealed the sinister and hideous creature that had a female upper body and a snake-like lower half. Her hair was made up of hissing snakes. "It's the gorgon." She shivered and whispered, "I hate snakes." She was startled by Mallory's low snicker.

"But you are not bothered by the dragon."

"Dragons are different. They can fly." Kinsey traded a grin with Mallory, then she read the information to Mallory, who listened with great interest. This went on for a while until Kinsey neared the end of the book, but she closed it and said, "We should save the last few for another time."

Mallory grumbled and studied the thick book in Kinsey's lap. "We have not discussed the real animals."

Kinsey grinned and agreed with Mallory, but she refused to allow all their time to be spent on the *Kingdom of Animals*. "Are you hungry?" Without waiting for an answer, she slid off the sill and collected a plate of cheese, fruit, and bread. She placed it between them on the sill and hoped Mallory would snack with her. "Try some," she said, nudging the plate closer to Mallory.

At first, it seemed as if Mallory would ignore the food, but her stomach growled in interest. She sighed and took a few grapes, hints of enjoyment showing in her features.

"So have you remembered where you are from?" Kinsey asked between bites of cheese. *Are you willing to tell me now?*

Mallory turned a grape through her fingers, possibly deciding whether to sidestep Kinsey's question again. "Lower Light," she whispered, hooded eyes lifting to meet Kinsey's. "I'm from Lower Light."

Kinsey was midchew and paused for a moment before swallowing the food. "You're from the Reninn Kingdom," she whispered.

"Former."

Over the years, Kinsey's father had waged wars against the Reninn Kingdom, tearing it apart limb by limb until he executed the entire House of Frilleck. The ruined kingdom was then merged with the Kingdom of Tharnstone, making it the largest in the lands. To forever commemorate King Wilmont's great triumph, he named his newly born daughter Kinsey, which meant "victory."

Like any war, the losers suffered immense humiliation and years of cruel hardship under their new king, her father. Today, the people from the fallen Reninn Kingdom suffered higher taxes than those in the original Kingdom of Tharnstone. Her father levied a hefty tax against them to keep them poor and unable to rise up against him. It would take generations for the two kingdoms to truly unify before they were viewed as one.

As they sat in silence, Kinsey grasped what might have happened to Mallory, who couldn't be much older than Kinsey. She picked up a piece of bread and played with it before saying, "You were enslaved during or after the war." The dark light in Mallory's features was answer enough.

"After," Mallory said. Her voice held a cutting edge, as if she was close to losing control. "Do you wish to know more, princess?"

Kinsey frowned. By default, Omegas were shielded and coddled from real life because "they were made from glass." However, she had yet to shatter and refused to be treated differently just because of her breed. "Yes." She tore the bread in half, taking her agitation out on it. "How did it happen?" With Luca, it had been easy to get the details from him about his enslavement, but Mallory was different.

Mallory cocked her head and narrowed her eyes, rumbling heavily before she nodded once. The air around her shifted and signaled a slight change in her attitude toward Kinsey. After a chuff, she said, "During the war, my father lost all his crops. They were burned by Tharnstone soldiers when they came to Lower Light."

Kinsey finished her last piece of bread, then lost her appetite. She lifted her knees and pulled them to her chest, anything but becoming of a noble.

"When the war ended, the high taxes started, which my father could not afford after losing his crops." Mallory paused, as if gauging whether or not Kinsey wanted to hear more. "I am one of eight children and the only Alpha in a family of Betas."

Holding her tongue, Kinsey listened to every detail Mallory was willing to give to her freely. The thin trust and openness between them were delicate. Whereas Kinsey could charm the other Alphas into talking, it had been difficult to earn Mallory's confidence.

"One day my father and I rode to the market with an empty wagon to buy food and goods. At the time, I didn't understand how he planned to pay for it, but I often went with him." Mallory uncrossed her legs, stretching her right one near Kinsey while her left leg hung off the sill. "We first went to a home of a rich Beta. I doubt that he was from the Reninn Kingdom."

Kinsey chewed on her lower lip. After the fall of the Reninn Kingdom, many of its nobles were stripped of their wealth and position. It was another step in keeping the people from rising up against the Kingdom of Tharnstone.

"Before I understood what was happening, I was chained and my father had a bag of coins in his hand."

Closing her eyes, Kinsey swallowed down the pressure in her throat and whispered, "He sold you to a Tharnstone noble in order to cover the taxes." She opened her eyes and gazed at Mallory's cool features, knowing under it all there was a girl still in pain.

"I was of no consequence to my father," Mallory said. "I am a degenerate Alpha. He would not collect a dowry on me because no one would marry me."

Kinsey turned her head and stared out of the window, feeling her Omega react to the Alpha's hidden pain. A very natural part of her wanted to comfort the Alpha, who had suffered under her own father's conquest and reign. She sensed her body already emitting a comforting scent that could agitate a proud Alpha, if unwelcomed. "I'm sorry for what happened." She turned her attention back to Mallory. "For what happened to you."

Mallory was silent and unmoving, perhaps lost in the past.

"You must hate my father," Kinsey whispered, smelling the heat of anger rolling off Mallory the longer they sat there. It would be easy for someone like Mallory to seek revenge on King Wilmont by murdering his child, especially the daughter named after his victory.

"You did not cause my enslavement," Mallory whispered. Her lip curled a bit and revealed her sharp canines under the silent sneer. "You do not owe me an apology." Swinging her body, she slid off the sill and paced the length of the long room.

Kinsey remained curled up on the sill and listened to the bitter sounds from Mallory. She flinched at her mistake for bringing up Mallory's past rather than letting it lie to rest.

It made sense why Mallory deflected Kinsey's earlier attempts. *Why give in now?*

Mallory continued to pace the room but couldn't seem to shake the dark energy that now consumed the solar room. Her fists were clenched at her sides, and she gritted her teeth like a caged animal.

Crinkling her nose, Kinsey breathed in the heated scent that might trigger a guard or two to rush in the room any minute. She pushed off the window sill and stepped into Mallory's path, holding up her hands. "You will alarm the guards."

Mallory glared at the sealed door, growling until Kinsey's calming pheromones filled her.

Kinsey withheld from touching the fiery Alpha and watched how her scent eased Mallory's temper. Alphas ran hot and always carried a spicy scent that turned sharp when their rage built up. Kinsey was thankful that her calmer Omega nature helped her relieve the Alpha boiling under Mallory's skin. "Then they'll take you. Maybe to the dungeons until you're not a threat." Her hands still hung in the space between them. "I don't wish for you to end up there again."

Mallory took a deep breath, seeming to feed off Kinsey's comforting pheromones. Her shoulders fell from their tense position, and she said, "Thank you."

Kinsey gave a slight smile and lowered her hands now that Mallory seemed better under control. After a faint nod, she indicated the table and said, "Perhaps a game of draughts will help."

"I do not know how to play." Mallory eyed the board game that was set up at one end of the table.

"Even better." Kinsey chuckled at Mallory's perturbed look. "I may win for once in my life."

Mallory frowned but nodded after a minute. "I will add more wood to the fire."

Kinsey sensed that Mallory needed the task so that the final bits of anger could wear off. While Mallory went to the fireplace, Kinsey took a seat and reorganized the board game for a new match. Once Mallory joined her, they went over the rules and how the pieces moved on the board. The first game required a lot of direction from Kinsey, but Mallory learned quickly.

Their second game was different. Mallory was slow to make her moves, seeming to calculate each one. Kinsey smiled to herself and tried refraining from helping Mallory, who was determined to win. Although they enjoyed the game, Kinsey was pleased by Mallory's ability to learn and think of different strategies. The game was more than simple fun; it was Kinsey's test of Mallory's intelligence. Mallory was the only Alpha of the four who accepted the invitation to play draughts.

More than just an Alpha brute, Kinsey thought. As she peeled back one of Mallory's layers, there were multiple ones underneath. Most Alphas had defined, consistent characteristics that left them simple and shallow to Kinsey. From the first day meeting Mallory, she was different in the way she carried herself. Their precious time together helped reveal why Mallory was unlike the others.

However, Mallory's uniqueness from other Alphas didn't mean she was ideal for Kinsey. Differences bred more differences, which often lead to fear, disdain, and even violence among people. A more traditional Alpha would guarantee an offspring who would be accepted by her people. Such concerns dampened Kinsey's mood and affected her game play, nearly causing her to lose to Mallory by the fifth match.

"You are troubled," Mallory whispered after making the first move of their sixth game. When she looked up from the board, her eyes glowed with rich amber that was inviting and warm. Under the setting sunlight, the freckles on the crest of her cheeks were beautiful.

Kinsey tore her gaze away and studied the board, weighing each of her next moves. "The day is getting late, and this will have to be our last game."

"But that's not what troubles you."

After a rumble, Kinsey moved one of her red pieces and bought time on how to handle Mallory's keen awareness. They were seated so closely that they could scent each other's moods. "Would you return to Lower Light if you were free?"

Mallory touched a piece but paused and whispered, "I would not return there." Her chest rolled with soft thunder. "I was sold for a reason."

"By your father." Kinsey found hard features lifted to her. "Not your siblings."

After a huff, Mallory moved her piece, then said, "I was a wolf among sheep." She leaned back in the chair and folded her arms, causing her biceps to protrude even with the loose tunic.

Kinsey bowed her head and focused on her next move in the game, but she turned over Mallory's response. "Then what would you do?" She had asked the other Alphas, curious about each one's dreams for a future.

"Find a blacksmith willing to apprentice me."

Kinsey's head jerked up at the news. "Blacksmithing?" She smiled at the image conjured in her mind and wondered why Mallory was interested in the trade. Returning to the board, she made her move and waited for her turn again.

"I have learned the basics from another slave." Mallory stretched out both her legs on either side of Kinsey's chair. "What would you do if you were free of your duties as a royal?"

The unexpected question left Kinsey silent for a long beat. Then she noticed that Mallory ignored the game of draughts and waited for an answer. "I…" Kinsey frowned and slumped against the chair's ladder back. "I am unsure."

Mallory chuffed and revealed a faint grin before leaning forward. She placed her hand on the table's edge while her left hand hooked the edge of Kinsey's chair. With only a breath of space between them, she had a wolfish smile and a glint in her eyes. "Show me the way out of here, and I'll take you with me," she whispered.

Kinsey was certain her frantic heartbeat filled the entire room like it did her ears. She was overwhelmed by Mallory's enticing scent that coaxed her to submit, but it was a skill she had learned to resist after being around her father. She licked her lips and noticed how Mallory's eyes dropped for a second. "I promised to rule my people."

"Promises can be broken," Mallory said, voice rumbling with heat. "Come with me, and I'll protect you."

A moan almost escaped Kinsey, but she fought her natural desire to accept an Alpha's alluring protection. Every Omega had a biological need to be mated and protected by an Alpha. Over time, Kinsey had learned how to control that piece of herself and thought she had mastered it, at least around her father, who lorded over his Omega wife and daughters. But Mallory's offer struck a different chord inside of her, and she struggled to find the strength to deny the Alpha.

"You should have a choice about your life," Mallory said. "Come with me."

Kinsey struggled for more space, but Mallory had her blocked. Her mind was clouded by the Alpha's proximity and enticing scent, her Omega desiring more. She snapped and popped up from the chair, fleeing to the other side of the room. The warm fire welcomed her and burned away Mallory's strong pheromones that clung to Kinsey. But then she sensed Mallory's imposing presence nearing her, and she turned her head sidelong. "You don't understand what you're asking me to do."

Mallory remained several steps away from Kinsey, but her dominance crept over to Kinsey. "I'm asking you to help free both of us." She struggled to keep her voice down, or the guards would hear their conversation even through the closed door.

Crossing her arms, Kinsey half turned and looked at Mallory. "I can't abandon my family."

"What kind of family forces you into pregnancy and ruling if it's not your desire?" Mallory hissed, then a snarl started deep in her chest. "How often do you get outside these walls? Once or twice a year?" She puffed up and shook her head before she closed the distance again. "You said yourself you're a captive."

Kinsey trembled and shook her head against Mallory's reasoning. Long ago she had accepted her fate as a noble and found a flicker of freedom at the thought of becoming queen one day. At least as a ruler, she could have more choices, even if she was tied to a throne. Unlike her father, she planned to be a just ruler and redeem the House of Wymarc. "I can't leave," she said, renewed determination in her tone. Her finality closed the door on the argument, and her features stoned over. "It is your choice to attempt an escape, but I don't recommend it. I can't halt what they will do to you when you are caught." She wanted to implore Mallory continue with the competition rather than risk losing her life. At the end of the competition, Kinsey vowed to plead with her father to not slaughter the remaining three Alphas.

Mallory reeked of bitter Alpha pheromones. "What is the point of this game?" She crowded Kinsey but never touched her, even though her dominance controlled the room. "We all have cocks, so choose one and fucking get on with it, princess."

Kinsey was flushed from the crudeness but turned her head away in submission, needing it to cool Mallory's anger. However, the imposing pheromones vanished, and Mallory's bare feet slapped against the stone floor. Kinsey looked over as Mallory wrenched open the door and vanished without a second glance.

As the fresh air rushed around her, Kinsey stumbled over to the nearest chair and fell into it just before someone hurried into the solar room.

"My princess, are you safe?" Gerald asked.

"I'm fine." Kinsey met his worried features and said, "I promise."

Gerald shifted on his boots, then nodded once and asked, "Is there anything I can do?"

Kinsey offered him a reassuring look and shook her head. "Thank you, Gerald, but I am fine." She sighed and added, "I need a few moments alone, then we'll go to supper."

"Of course." Gerald bowed and stepped out of the room, leaving the door open.

Kinsey slumped against the chair's back and stared up at the beautiful ceiling. The earlier argument should have been enough for Kinsey to take Mallory off the list for mating. But her Omega whined in protest, and she was too weak to deny herself Mallory's company. Many times in the past, she had feared her father's rage whenever their fights boiled over. Mallory was far more controlled, perhaps due to her time as a slave.

Tomorrow would be the day of battles between the four Alphas. Her father was looking forward to it, but Kinsey had disagreed with the idea until her mother pointed out that the fights would reveal the Alphas' true personalities. The rules would be simple but also telling if an Alpha broke any of them.

After a deep breath, Kinsey straightened up and reached for the *Kingdom of Animals*. Her fingertips traced the golden letters that were losing their brightness from years of Kinsey's touching them. She frowned, pulled the book to herself, and hugged it against her body.

* * *

Kinsey adjusted the heavy fur around her shoulders after Agatha crawled under it with her. They were standing out on the balcony under the moonlight, watching the stars crawl across the dark blanket above their heads. Since childhood, they cherished their alone time together and even more as Kinsey grew older. As kids, Kinsey told her sister different stories about the constellations in the night sky. Sometimes Agatha pleaded to hear them again as a teenager, but they often talked about their daily lives and futures.

"How do you like the Alphas?" Agatha asked, leaning more into her sister's taller frame.

"I like them." Kinsey nibbled on her lip, then rested her chin on Agatha's head. "All but one."

"All but Terrel," Agatha guessed and chuckled when Kinsey sighed in agreement.

"You know me well, little sister." Kinsey moved her head and rubbed her temple against Agatha's own, needing their closeness after today's argument with Mallory. As Omegas, they found and shared comfort especially during stressful times.

Agatha chuckled and nuzzled her sister back before cocking her head. "Which Alpha do you like the best?"

Kinsey frowned and looked out at the dark world. The real answer was complicated, but the right answer was the important one. "Luca is the most promising one."

Agatha responded with a gentle rumble and asked, "He was in the first bedchamber?"

Kinsey hummed in agreement, then rested her chin on Agatha's head. If she chose Luca, the child would be perfect, whether an Alpha or an Omega. Luca was a healthy Alpha in his prime and had a better temperament than most Alphas. However, the only hurdle was Kinsey's lack of attraction toward him. Luca was the epitome of handsome and powerful, but Kinsey's Omega didn't respond to his call.

"What do you think of the *degen*?"

Kinsey's troubled thoughts were pierced by her sister's slur. "Agatha," she warned.

Agatha grumbled a few times, then asked, "What shall I call her? She has no name."

"Her former master called her Mallory." Kinsey squeezed Agatha tighter, considered Agatha's question, and whispered, "Call her Mallory or She-Alpha."

Agatha sighed with exaggeration, but tilted her head back and asked, "Do you know what that name means?"

Kinsey canted her head, silently prompting her sister, who loved to learn the meaning of names.

"It means ill fated," Agatha said. "Quite fitting for a degenerate Alpha who's a slave."

Frowning, Kinsey struggled with the uncomfortable twisting in her gut. She now wanted to forget the name, but it was too late after learning the meaning of it. The only thing that could erase the slave name's brutal history was Mallory's birth name. Mallory's previous master was cruel and had a sick sense of humor.

"What do you think of the She-Alpha?" Agatha asked and wiggled her eyebrows. "Do you think she's as handsome as Luca?"

"In a different light, yes." Kinsey pursed her lips and nuzzled her sister, who playfully growled at her. "I like her the most."

Agatha jerked back and smiled until it reached her ears. "I knew it." But her sister's dismay caused her to sigh. "But you won't choose her?"

"I can't, Aggie." Kinsey bit her lip, trying to reason with her own struggles. "I'm not even sure father would let me. I believe he only allowed her to humor me."

Agatha rolled her eyes, shifted, and rested her head on Kinsey's shoulder. She was quiet for a while but eventually said, "Because she's a degenerate Alpha." After Kinsey's agreeing sound, she sighed and argued, "But if that's whom you choose then—"

"The child could be a She-Alpha too."

"Oh."

Kinsey closed her eyes and breathed in Agatha's familiar scent that calmed her tense body. She then whispered, "Or it could be an Omega or Beta. But it's a greater chance that the child would be like her." Their father wouldn't stand for a degenerate Alpha in the family line, much less allow Kinsey the chance to be bred by one.

"Why are they even called degenerates?" Agatha's question held a lost note in it. "Even the He-Omegas are called degenerates."

"I'm not sure," Kinsey replied. "Perhaps because they are rare and misunderstood. There are so few of them, even fewer of them than Omegas and Alphas." Betas were the majority in the population while the Alphas and Omegas were the second largest population. It was normal for Beta parents to birth an Alpha or Omega at times, but it was rare for Alpha and Omega parents to have Beta children.

"It seems strange," Agatha whispered.

"Yes, it does." Kinsey closed her eyes and continued to think about Mallory... and their fight. Even now she struggled with what her head told her to do and what her Omega truly wanted her to do. She had thought picking an Alpha would be simple math. It was a matter of adding up each Alphas' scores from the tests and having one night with them. But Mallory complicated it, because Kinsey's Omega was responding to her.

"Even if her penis is a little smaller, I think it's about how well she can use it."

"Agatha!"

Agatha puffed up and turned in her sister's arms. "I'm not naive about Alphas."

Kinsey huffed and rumbled a few times. "That may be so, but I don't wish to discuss such things with my baby sister."

"Please." Agatha snuck out of the fur and said, "In a year or two, I'll be wed to handsome Alpha prince from another kingdom."

If Kinsey was the queen by then, she would ensure it didn't happen, at least not without Agatha's consent. Even if it happened after her crowning, she would do anything in her power to ensure Agatha was well cared for by her Alpha husband. "I know, but it doesn't mean I want to hear that language coming from my sister's mouth."

Agatha snorted, reached through the fur, and patted her sister's cheek. "Do you prefer I use cock instead of penis?"

Kinsey blushed at her sister's crudeness and replied, "How about you use none of it?"

Agatha laughed and shook her head. "Don't be such a prude." She pecked her sister on the cheek. "I'm going to bed."

Kinsey turned her head as Agatha left the balcony and headed into her bedchamber. "Good night, Aggie."

"Night, Kins." Agatha hung onto the drape and held her sister's gaze. "Don't stay up late thinking about Alpha cocks."

"Agatha Wymarc!" Kinsey fumed and huffed as her giggling sister escaped, slamming the bedchamber door for extra effect. She blew out a breath and adjusted the fur against her body, blocking out the cool night. Her face was still flushed from the earlier conversation about Alphas. How had her day started with educational topics like math and politics, then ended with the discussions about Alphas and their penises?

Kinsey wasn't a prude, at least she didn't think so. She was simply focused on her studies and teachings so she could be a well-educated queen. As far as the Alphas went, they were undeniably handsome and attractive, in the mathematical sense if Kinsey were to rate them on a scale. All four of them were rather muscular, confident, and attractive. It was their personalities that differentiated them, not how well endowed they were between their legs.

But she had seen Mallory's lower attributes and agreed with Agatha about length versus skill. Just the memory of Mallory standing confident without her pants on was seared in her mind. If Kinsey was being honest, Mallory hadn't been hard—for obvious reasons—and therefore wasn't showing off her full length. Biting her lip, Kinsey tried guessing how much longer Mallory might be once she was excited or even in a rut.

Do She-Alphas even have ruts like the other Alphas?

As she recalled, the He-Omegas had heats just like any Omega. It was reasonable to believe that Mallory would have ruts. If that were true, then Kinsey wondered if Mallory's cock was any larger during her ruts. It was true of regular Alphas, who also developed knots during their ruts to help ensure pregnancy. Every biological piece of an Alpha and Omega centered on having offspring. They were designed to ensure their race continued each generation, whether the Alpha or Omega wanted it or not.

With a sigh, Kinsey returned to her warm bedchamber and adjusted the heavy curtain that kept the chill out of the room. She considered undressing and going to bed, but her mind wandered back to Mallory and their argument. If Mallory had made up her mind to attempt an escape, Kinsey was sure that it would fail and Mallory's life would be forfeited. She trembled at the idea of Mallory being beheaded in the inner ward. If Mallory attempted an escape, then she would need help, but Kinsey could not help.

After she deposited the fur on the bed, she cracked the door open and called, "Gerald?"

"Yes, my princess?" Gerald appeared near the door. His armor reflected the flickering lamp lights in the hallway.

"Come inside." Kinsey opened the door wider, then closed it after he joined her in the bedchamber. She paced a few times and put together the plans.

"Is everything all right?" Gerald rested his hand on the sword hilt at his hip.

Kinsey suspected he noticed her anxious scent. Since childhood, she had developed a fondness for Gerald, who returned the sentiment. After Devon died in the wars against the Reninn Kingdom, Gerald filled much of the gap left behind by her brother. "Yes." She stopped pacing and stood in front of him, then walked away, then turned toward him again. "Not quite."

Gerald frowned and approached Kinsey, but never too close. "What can I do?"

Kinsey folded her arms against her body and sighed. Her personal guard's loyalty would never falter, and she adored him for it. "It's the She-Alpha."

Gerald's features darkened, and his hand twisted against the hilt until his knuckles turned white. "Did she harm you this afternoon?"

"Nothing like that." Kinsey moved closer even though they usually kept a certain distance between them. "She's thinking about escaping Tharnstone Castle," she whispered. She almost laughed at Gerald's big eyes. "But she will be caught and beheaded for it."

"Yes." Gerald cocked his head, which caused his dark brown eyes to shine in the firelight. Over the years, his features had filled out as he aged. He had short, brunette hair that had become a bit long. His goatee now had a few streaks of gray after he turned forty last year. "Should you not report it to your father before it's too late?"

"I considered it, but I don't wish to." Kinsey returned to pacing and said, "She became a slave because her father sold her for gold coins. He needed the money to pay the high taxes after my father conquered the Reninn Kingdom."

Gerald responded with an acknowledging sound and continued to listen.

"I wish to help her escape." Kinsey was near the foot of the bed and stood beside the wooden chest. She sighed, spun on her heels, and said, "But it's really you who can help her." Seeing Gerald's confusion, she walked back and whispered, "You're the only one who can take her to the undercroft and to the hidden passage."

After a rumble, Gerald rubbed his goatee and had a distant expression. "It will not be easy."

Hearing Gerald's unspoken acceptance, Kinsey blew out a breath and said, "Perhaps you can escort her to the dungeon. The undercroft is on the way there."

"It may work." Gerald hooked his hand into his belt and studied Kinsey. "Why do you wish to help the Alpha? You feel responsible for your father's actions?"

"You know I always have." Kinsey closed her eyes against the sting. Once becoming a young teen, she was able to grasp what her father had done to become king of both the Kingdom of Tharnstone and the Reninn Kingdom. So many lives had been impacted by her father's hunger for power. "But it's...."

Gerald remained quiet and waited for Kinsey to speak her mind.

"I'm unsure what it is." Kinsey toyed with the girdle around her waist. The evening she first met Mallory, she'd been infatuated by the Alpha's unusual nature. In a short period, their time together had become special and different from what Kinsey was used to in an Alpha. In truth, she wanted Mallory to stay even though Mallory's chances were slimmer compared to the other Alphas, who were the purest in her father's eyes. The best option was for Mallory to escape and regain her freedom than to remain here and probably lose her life.

"You do not have to explain," Gerald said, bringing Kinsey back to the present. "If you wish for her to escape, then I will assist."

Kinsey shut her eyes and held down a whimper but gazed back at Gerald's confident features. "Thank you." She released the girdle and whispered, "I must to talk to her, then." She went to the table in front of the fire, collected the *Kingdom of Animals* to use as an excuse, if necessary. She and Gerald journeyed through the lit castle and greeted a few guards along the way. Once entering the west wing, she left Gerald, passed the first three guards, and asked for the last guard to open Mallory's door. When it was safe, she entered to see Mallory's back to her.

Mallory was bent forward, hands on the window sill, and staring out at the dark world. The only recognition she gave to the newcomers' presence was a faint tilt of her head.

"Face your princess, *degen*," the guard ordered.

Kinsey held out her hand at the guard, then said, "You can leave us."

The guard puffed up and prepared to protest before he received a dark glare.

Kinsey had learned from the best, her father, how to take control, even being an Omega. She watched the guard leave the room, closing the door behind him. Now alone with Mallory, she lost a measure of her conviction because the powerful Alpha still didn't acknowledge her. "You forgot the book," she said, frowning at how weak her voice sounded. She squared her shoulders, neared the bed, and placed it on the foot of it.

Mallory remained statue-like other than a faint huff.

Kinsey folded her hands in front of her and watched Mallory's body for any signals. "I could stop you from attempting to escape, but instead I will help you." Somehow taking the choice from Mallory felt wrong, even if it could end in Mallory's death. On some level, she related to Mallory's stolen freedom and having the chance to take it back. "My personal guard will take you to the hidden tunnel in the undercroft."

When Mallory stayed silent, Kinsey rumbled and sighed at her failed attempt to get a response from Mallory. "He will come for you tonight under the guise that you are being taken to the dungeon." She pursed her lips and whispered, "It will be your chance."

Mallory's only slight movement was the tilt of her head.

Kinsey forced herself to go to the door, but she hesitated to leave. Deep inside, her Omega was clawing at her, and she fought to remain in control. The sheer idea that Mallory would be gone in hours took the air from her lungs. Never had she experienced such a reaction, and she struggled with the strength of it. Turning back to Mallory, she whispered, "You should return to Lower Light, to your family." She bit her lip when her voice shook, but she said, "Sometimes family is all we have left."

Turning to the door, Kinsey accepted that she had done all she could. She exited the room and passed the four guards until she was beside Gerald, who followed her out of the west wing. Kinsey slowed until Gerald was closer, then whispered, "It is done."

Chapter 5

"Come, daughter," Wilmont ordered. He stood beside the closed door of Kinsey's bedchamber with his arms crossed, impatient as ever. In twenty minutes, the contest between the four Alphas was expected to start. Wilmont had chosen the contest and argued that it was a perfect way for Kinsey to determine the best Alpha.

Kinsey had other opinions about the contest, but she agreed to her father's wishes. She was allowed to control the rules of the contest. After hours of consideration, she settled on a few but important ones. She was expected to stand before the Alphas and explain the contest to them. As Wilmont rumbled and huffed, Kinsey finished preparing for the day and thanked the servant. Nearly ready, she put on her bright blue surcoat that hugged her wide hips. "Thank you," she whispered to the handmaiden.

The handmaiden smiled, then stepped around the folding screen and waited for Kinsey.

Coming around the screen, Kinsey cooled her irritated father with a warm smile. "I'm ready, Father." She noted that he hadn't moved from his spot since his arrival ten minutes ago. She forwent the bonnet, not wanting to delay any longer. "We should hurry."

Wilmont grunted and yanked on the door's heavy iron ring. "Your sister and mother are waiting on us."

"Of course." Kinsey exited the bedchamber and frowned when Gerald wasn't in the hallway. She worried her lip for a moment and wondered why her personal guard hadn't returned this morning. Had he left with the She-Alpha last night? Or had they both been caught? If something had gone wrong, there would have been news about it. With a sigh, she followed her father through the castle until they arrived at the inner ward, which was set up for the contest.

The castle's walls were decorated with flags of the House of Wymarc. At the center of the inner ward, a square battle ground had been set up with temporary fencing. At the south wall, a tiered stage had been fashioned, and the four thrones were set on top. Standard chairs had been placed below the thrones for other nobles of Coldhelm.

People from the city had already begun to gather around the inner ward and chatted about the upcoming battle. The air was charged and citizens turned their attention to King Wilmont and his daughter. Beside the stage, Aerin and

Sir Philip waited for the royals, both brightening at Wilmont's approach.

Agatha beamed at her sister and left her mother's side. "Are you ready?" she asked, leaning in close and hooking Kinsey's arm.

Kinsey whispered, "No." She and Agatha shared a quiet laugh, then she greeted her mother, who kissed her on the cheek.

"Did you rest well?" Agnes asked after withdrawing from her daughter.

"Mostly." Kinsey turned when her father called her name.

"We should begin." Wilmont pushed between his family and climbed the stage to his throne, which was black and laced in gold. On its back were golden crests of fallen noble families that Wilmont had defeated over his lifetime. At the top of the back, the crest of the House of Wymarc, a mountain lion, roared down at the fallen crests. Like the king, the throne was large and aggressive with its sharp lines, clawed feet, and iron arms. Wilmont filled it with power, and only the crest of the House of Wymarc could be seen above his head.

After brushing her dress, Agnes took the smaller throne beside her husband. Her violet attire was embellished with golden tassels, a girdle, and a bonnet. She was the extreme end to King Wilmont and every bit the dutiful Omega.

Agatha went to her seat next to her mother while Kinsey sat behind her father's right side. Kinsey folded her sweaty hands in her lap and struggled to ease her heart's wild beat. Scanning the area, she grumbled and knotted her fingers until she saw Gerald pushing through the crowd. She fisted her hands and fought the urge to rush to him, demanding to know what had happened to the She-Alpha.

Gerald neared the stage, but stayed off it and stood next to Huxley. There were plenty of guards and soldiers throughout the inner ward, and he would only ascend if he were ordered by the king or queen. He remained at the ready with his hand on the hilt. His bronze armor reflected the midmorning sunlight.

Kinsey willed her personal guard to peer up at her. When their eyes met, she sighed and mouthed her question.

Gerald shook his head and had a displeased look about him. His attention shifted to the battle ground when the growing crowd cheered at the arrival of the Alphas.

Kinsey straightened up and leaned forward to get a better view. She spotted a handful of soldiers shoving people out of the way to create a path. Next, the Alphas filed out of the open door from the far wall, each one ducking out of its dark mouth. They were chained together and walked in single file through the opening. People cheered or shouted at the slaves, some even throwing rotten food. One Alpha barked at them after a tomato hit him in the face.

As the Alphas neared the battle ground, their faces became distinguishable. In the lead was Luca followed by Eldon and Terrel. At the end, Mallory's distinct features stood out among the Alphas. Several people jeered and called her a degenerate, but her attention remained forward.

Why did she stay? Her demand was screaming through her head, and she jerked her attention to Gerald, who shrugged in response. Kinsey's Omega buzzed with life, and a slight burn started between her legs at the idea that Mallory stayed for her.

One by one, the Alphas climbed over the waist-high wooden fence and were ordered to stand in the center in a line. The Alphas stood shoulder to shoulder and held their hands in front of them, gazing toward the nobles seated on the stage.

King Wilmont rose from his seat, and in a heartbeat his people fell silent. He flashed a toothy smile at the crowd, and when he spoke his deep voice broadcasted throughout the inner ward like a drum. "Today I give you a tournament between some of the best Alpha slaves in the Kingdom of Tharnstone!" He paused while his citizens cheered for the excitement; then he turned to his daughter.

Kinsey understood the signal and took her father's side. Her voice couldn't compare to her father's, but she gathered the strength from deep in her gut. Even though she wasn't an Alpha, she would soon be a ruler, and a powerful voice was expected of her. "The tournament will be made up of seven rounds, and there will be only one winner." She studied the crowd before she lowered her attention to the four Alphas, directing her words to them. "The rules are simple. For the first three rounds, you will be given ten points, and every strike against you will be subtracted from your score. The first opponent to reach zero is the loser. For the remaining four rounds, you must defeat your opponent by keeping them down for five counts."

Luca and Eldon were moving their heads in understanding while Terrel and Mallory remained motionless.

"You will have a choice of weapons," Kinsey announced, triggering a few soldiers to roll the weapons rack from the open door behind the crowd. "The last rule is that you may *not* kill. If you kill, then your life will be forfeited." *A chance to show restraint*, she silently told them. One of the soldiers was instructed to secretly keep track of how many injuries each Alpha inflicted on the other.

Wilmont rumbled and ordered, "And the prize, daughter."

Kinsey cleared her throat and nodded. "The winner of the tournament will be guaranteed their freedom." The people's excited uproar made her chuckle. She signaled the soldiers to handle the tournament's process. Her father had made the captain of the guards in charge of it, and he was already snapping orders at the Alphas. Once settled into her seat, Kinsey watched Mallory, who marched with the other Alphas to the far side of the battleground, where the soldiers had brought the weapons rack.

With a grumble, Kinsey shifted several times in the chair and never found a comfortable position. A heavy stone settled deep in her belly, but all she could do was watch the tournament unfold before her. "The gods keep her safe," she muttered.

* * *

Like the other Alphas, Mallory held out her arms and waited until the shackles were undone then taken from her. She rubbed each wrist for a moment while listening to the captain bark out opponents for the first three rounds. Luca and Eldon would be the first round, then she would battle

Terrel for the second round. Afterward, the two losers would fight in the third round.

"Get over the fence and pick your weapon," the captain told them. He stepped aside when the Alphas climbed over and went to the rack.

Mallory waited for the other three to make their selections. As she stood there, she hooked her hands over the leather cuirass that covered her chest but stopped short halfway down her stomach. Her leather skirt wasn't much better, protecting a portion of her thighs. Her battle attire had been given to her like the others, except the other Alphas had full cuirasses, gauntlets, and boots with leg guards. For the tournament, someone decided her bare midriff was somehow an advantage, but it was an attempt to sexualize her so the people forgot her degenerate nature.

After the three Alphas chose their weapons, Mallory went to the rack and eyed what was left. The selection was decent and each one enticed Mallory as she walked down the rack. For a moment, her hand rested on a spear, but Terrel had already taken one. Luca had a sword and Eldon took a spiked mace. The weapons they chose were all designed to kill without mercy, which went against the tournament's major rule.

Near the end of the rack, Mallory fingered a quarterstaff that had no blades of any kind. She ran her fingers over the wrap and considered pulling it from the rack.

"Hurry up, *degen*," a soldier snarled.

Mallory ignored him, hardly pressured by a Beta. Throughout her life she had little experience fighting, other than a few fist fights and wrestling, both playful and from arguments. She suspected the other Alphas had advantages over her, whether it was strength or skill, or even both. Dropping her hand, her attention shifted to the last weapons, which were a pair of hammers. Mallory shifted closer to them and recognized them as blacksmith's hammers, except they were made from one solid piece of metal. In recent years, she had worked several months alongside a blacksmith, who was a slave to the same master as she. The blacksmith had taught her basic skills that included using the tools of the trade. Somehow seeing the finely-crafted blacksmith hammers gave her a new fire.

Mallory yanked the hammers off the rack and spun the one in her right hand. When Terrel snickered, she flashed him a wolfish smile.

"The first match will be between Alpha One and Alpha Two," the captain said. "Then Alpha Three and Alpha Four will be the second round."

Luca and Eldon climbed over the fence, then faced off in the center of the battlefield. They readied their weapons and assessed each other until the captain bellowed out for the fight to begin.

Mallory placed one boot against the lower rail of the fence and watched the two Alphas battle each other. It was apparent that Luca had formal training; perhaps he was a soldier at one time. Eldon was sloppier, but he held his ground with each swing of his mace. Their metal weapons clashed and caused the people to cheer and hoot.

Lifting her gaze, she studied the stage that held a variety of nobles, who were adorned with their brightest and wealthiest attire. At the top were the immediate members of the House of Wymarc, but Mallory was only interested in the princess.

Kinsey appeared calm in her seat, situated behind King Wilmont. She wore a fine blue dress that had a soft golden pattern stitched into the chest and torso. The different hems at her wrists and edge of the dress all tied into the golden pattern. Like other times, her dark hair had a braided strand that started at her temples and wrapped around to the back. She was as gorgeous as the blue sky and as bright as the sun.

Off to the right of the stage, Gerald stood at attention with keen interest in the tournament. Late last night he had come to Mallory's room and offered to take her to the undercroft where a hidden passage would lead Mallory into the mountains. He even had a few minor supplies prepared for her so that she could hope to survive the journey.

Mallory had been flipping through the pages of the *Kingdom of Animals*. She peered up from her spot on the floor and declined his offer. Gerald had sputtered and insisted that Mallory come with him, declaring that it was Kinsey's wish. Mallory refused again and watched Gerald stomp out of the room.

At the time it felt like the right choice. She could have been free but instead was waiting her turn to battle Terrel in front of a hungry mob. Now the choice felt utterly foolish, until she looked at Kinsey. Mallory had wanted to escape Tharnstone Castle but with Kinsey. Nothing about it was logical, and it could get her killed in a few days. For some reason, the Alpha inside Mallory held her here in Tharnstone Castle. She wanted to believe it was her pride or the need to dominate the other Alphas, but the deep rolling thunder in her chest warned her that it was more.

Mallory dug her nails into the hammers' metal shafts and felt the rumble deep in her gut. She stared across the field, and her heated gaze met Kinsey, who was the only person in Mallory's view. Even from such a distance, Kinsey's eyes caused Mallory's skin to burn and blood to rush through her veins. She felt the strain between her thighs, and her teeth craved to sink into soft flesh. Each day her Alpha strained harder against the chains she had wrapped around it. The more it howled at her, the closer she grew to breaking for her Alpha. She was tired of wrestling it and holding it in check. From her first day of birth, she was told her Alpha was perverted and abnormal. At first, she was instructed to keep her Alpha at bay so attention wasn't drawn to her family. After being sold into slavery, her Alpha was beaten down, deeper and deeper until she disconnected from it.

But since her arrival in the Tharnstone Castle, her Alpha broke back and new life breathed into her. Mallory tried denying that it was happening, until Kinsey's refusal to escape with her had released a wild storm. Her Alpha snarled and chomped at her to take Kinsey with her, and Mallory could only heed it. Somehow, she would win Kinsey over.

Eldon's sharp cry jerked Mallory's attention to the ongoing match. People's cries exploded, and Mallory cringed from the sound. She smelled the sweat of a beast, then the strong blood from Eldon's arm injury.

"Four!" a soldier called. He appeared to be one of the judges that kept count of the strikes for the first three rounds.

So far Luca had seven points left, while Eldon was down to four. They circled each other, then Luca charged and landed another blow to Eldon's side, causing the soldier to cry out: three points remaining. Eldon managed a kick to Luca's chest and sent him down, taking a point from Luca, who was angry now. Once on his feet, Luca made short work of Eldon and won the match.

Glancing at Terrel, Mallory prepared to take on the other Alpha, who met her glare. At the same time, they hopped over the fence and went to the middle, while Luca and Eldon left the battlefield. Facing each other, Terrel tossed the spear between his hands, then settled it into his left hand. Mallory grinned at the fact he was left-hand dominant.

Hunched forward, Mallory raised the hammers and prepared for the first time she could fully unleash herself in a fight. She was a master at self-control, and so she waited, knowing Terrel would make the first move.

Terrel spun the spear in front of him, showing a measure of finesse. He halted, then swiped at Mallory, who jumped backward and sucked in her stomach for good measure. Terrel hissed and brought the spear tip around again.

Mallory ducked under it, popped up, and kicked Terrel in his side as he twisted from his swing. She sent him down onto his back. In the distance, she heard the soldier cry out the loss of a point for Terrel. She attempted rushing him, but the spear's butt end landed solidly in her stomach and sent her stumbling back, almost to her knees.

Terrel flipped onto his feet and readied his spear that doubled as a staff. He growled and taunted, "Degenerate."

After hearing the slur all her life, Mallory was well armored against it and smirked in response. Terrel's rage erupted, and he came at her with careless technique. She needed to get past the spear before getting close enough to strike him. Once within range, Mallory landed both hammers into his side.

Terrel growled and stumbled away, almost dropping his spear. He failed to recover in time and Mallory was on him again. She slammed the head of one hammer into his gut, all her force into it. The shockwave went through his cuirass, and he grunted while trying to grab her with his free hand.

Mallory rammed her elbow into his head and forced him onto his hands and knees. She wanted to land a blow to his head, but it could kill him. Instead, she kicked under his stomach and sent him onto his back.

"Five points remaining for Alpha Three!" a soldier announced, which triggered the crowd to chant.

Fueled with fire, Mallory lifted her foot and brought it down, aiming for his gut. But he snared her heel and tossed her backward. A yelp broke from her lips as she collided with the solid ground and smacked her head. Her vision swam and grew darker while the pounding in her ears exploded like a cannon. A hard boot landed in her exposed midriff, and she curled up on her side, gasping for air. Another blow struck her in the stomach and radiated pain up her spine.

"Six points left for Alpha Four!"

Mallory sensed that Terrel might keep kicking her until all her points were gone. He pulled his leg back farther than last time. Gritting her teeth, Mallory lifted her upper body with one hand and hooked her other hand around Terrel's ankle. She yelled, yanked him toward her, and grew smug as he fell back into the ground.

"Four points left for Alpha Three!"

After gulping air, Mallory forced herself to get up, and managed to grab Terrel's spear and toss it out of reach. She forewent her hammers and used her bare hands, grabbing him by the collar of his cuirass. From a crouched position, she lifted his upper body and punched him in the face. The blood from his nose covered her knuckles, and he growled at her but was unable to stop her. She wanted to pummel him into submission, make him fall to her and beg her. But she controlled her Alpha needs and instead stood up with him in her hands.

Terrel tried to regain his footing, but Mallory shoved him, then kicked him in the chest. He toppled again and stayed up on his hands and knees, gasping and coughing while blood fell from his face.

Mallory stalked over to him and slammed her boot heel into his padded side.

"One point remaining for Alpha Three!" the soldier cried out.

Terrel was on his back and glaring up at Mallory, but he had already given up.

Mallory growled and almost slammed her boot into his throat. After a huff, she placed her foot against his chest, held him down, and looked to the soldier standing by the captain.

"Alpha Four is the winner of round two!"

Walking away from Terrel, Mallory collected the hammers in one hand, grabbed the spear, and returned to her fallen opponent. "Get up before I drag you," she ordered him.

Terrel stood up, wiped the blood from his face, and glared at Mallory. He stretched his back, which popped a few times, then retrieved the spear Mallory held out to him.

Mallory climbed over the fence while Eldon hopped over to start round three with Terrel.

"Not bad for someone who doesn't fight," Luca remarked.

Mallory was given a waterskin from a soldier and sucked it down before responding to Luca. "Thanks." She looked over at Terrel and Eldon, who were sizing up each other.

"Why the hammers?" Luca indicated a blacksmith's trademark tool, that in Mallory's hands were weapons. "Something familiar?"

Mallory canted her head toward him but didn't reply and watched the fighting. Already Eldon had lost three points to Terrel, who still had his ten.

"Terrel will win," Luca said and leaned against the fence post. "He's had some formal training."

Mallory suspected that Luca and Terrel had spoken in the past, perhaps during the journey here. For most of the trip, she had kept to herself, while the other Alphas whispered amongst each other. She had learned their names, but none ever asked for hers.

When Terrel and Eldon circled each other again, Luca pointed at Terrel and explained, "Whenever Terrel thrusts or swings with the spear, he exposes his flank for an attack." He leaned toward Mallory and whispered, "Terrel also has a habit of dropping his front and exposing his back."

Mallory eyed Luca for a moment before she looked at Terrel with a different eye. One of Eldon's attacks with the mace confirmed that Terrel had a habit of bending forward exposing his shoulders and the back of his head.

"Two points left for Alpha Two!"

Rumbling, Mallory was certain that Terrel would win. Eldon was the oldest of them, and he seemed tired after being beaten by Luca earlier. She had hoped Eldon would advance, but as Terrel landed the final strike, her mood darkened.

Luca straightened from his spot against the post and picked up his sword. "I imagine we're next."

Mallory was curious how the next few rounds worked, especially since it required the loser to stay down for five counts. Luca was correct; they were next, which allowed Terrel a break. Together, they hopped over the fence and spun their weapons on the walk to the center of the field.

Terrel glared at them both but departed the field.

Luca flashed a toothy smile at Eldon, who was limping back with his weapon. Once in the center, Luca and Mallory faced each other. "Don't get yourself hurt, kid."

Mallory puffed up her chest and rested one hammer on her shoulder. "Don't hurt yourself on the sword, little man." Luca was oddly short for an Alpha, but still taller than Omegas and Betas. She was a few hands taller than he.

Luca snorted and raised his sword, preparing for the fight. He attacked first and smiled when Mallory parried his swing.

The fight against Luca was different from the one against Terrel. Where the first fight had been filled with anger and rage, this fight was closer to a dance that made Mallory's blood sing. She deflected his attacks and went on offense between each of his attempts. None of them were brutal or harsh, but more a persistent style to outlast the other. If Mallory went down first, it would only take a count of five for her to lose.

Luca's attacks became feverish, and Mallory struggled to keep up with him. Unlike Terrel, Luca was determined to win by merit rather than force. Mallory returned his kindness by landing lighter blows that caused him to grunt or growl rather than take him down. Somehow the fight had turned into a teachable session for Mallory.

By the end, Mallory had won the fight after taking Luca down onto his back. She expected him to get up and continue their battle, but he stayed down for the entire count. Her win felt hollow when he stood without any trouble and grinned at her.

Mallory walked off the field and saw Terrel coming out to fight Luca next. Peering over her shoulder, she noticed how Luca stiffened up and took on a more aggressive nature. *Did he go easy on me just to save his energy for Terrel?*

Once on the other side of the fence, Mallory watched the first blows exchanged. They were brutal and ugly. After a huff, she gazed across the tournament field and studied Kinsey, who appeared calm, until she shifted in the chair several times.

Mallory wondered what Kinsey was feeling and thinking as Luca and Terrel battled each other. She suspected that Kinsey liked Luca, who appeared to be a gentler Alpha than the normal. Even Mallory admitted that he was likable, but everyone had their dark side. From the way Luca fought, he appeared to have formal training at one time, which meant he may have been a soldier and had the ability to kill. Every Alpha was bathed in dominance, but some were better at hiding it than others.

Terrel yelped after Luca's sword sliced into his left bicep. He backed away from Luca and switched the spear to his other, less dominant hand.

Luca planned that, Mallory concluded. She propped up a foot on the fence and studied the last moments of the fight. Luca defeated Terrel after a few more strikes and taking him facedown.

Luca backed off after the captain declared the win. He approached Mallory, who was climbing over the fence. They exchanged nods, a silent promise to finish Terrel.

For a moment, Mallory glanced toward the stage and held Kinsey's gaze. She could feel the princess's worry and questioning even from a distance. Maybe if she survived the tournament, she could explain herself to Kinsey. Looking at Terrel's dark features, she prepared for the worst and hoped she could beat him again. If she did, then he might be done for the rest of the tournament, along with Eldon.

Mallory gave Terrel another minute, allowing him to breathe before he started his next round. She spun the iron hammers in her hands and bent her knees. "Anytime you're ready," she taunted.

Terrel roared and charged her with the spear pointed at Mallory's chest.

Mallory gawked at Terrel's rage and jumped to the side as he barreled toward her. As he charged, she swung the hammer, scoring a direct hit to his chest, sending him back... for only a beat. He quickly returned with stabs, but she dodged every one. Exhaustion wanted to seep into her bones, but she rallied and crossed the hammers when the spear's butt end neared her neck.

Their battle was frantic, desperate, with pure adrenaline rushing through her as they growled and struck each other. At one point, Mallory broke through his defenses and swiped at him, exposing his neck. She could have ended him with a hammer to the back of his head, but she slammed her elbow between his shoulder blades instead. With her foot, she tried to keep him down for the count, but he rolled out of the way.

Terrel was slowing down. Her chance to beat him grew closer, but his spear's edge sliced her bare arm and clawed into her bicep. Mallory snarled and jerked back, tearing the spear from her muscle and skin. She seethed at Terrel's gloat before she redoubled her efforts, refusing to lose to the asshole.

Terrel lunged with the spear but missed his mark, then was stunned when Mallory dropped her hammers and grabbed the spear's shaft with both hands. He tried jerking it free, but Mallory only strengthened her grip.

Bracing herself, Mallory began to spin them in a circle and increased the speed until Terrel was about to fall back. But she released the spear, pushing him back. Dancing on his feet, Terrel stumbled, dropped the spear, and hunched forward. He cupped his head and groaned as he clutched his stomach.

Mallory scooped up the iron hammers and sprinted toward Terrel. She held her right hammer low, dashed up to Terrel and swung upward. The hammer collided with Terrel's chin and launched him a few hands into the air before he hit the ground.

Mallory backed off and listened to the soldier hollering the count. She waited for Terrel to get up, but he moaned and rolled to his side.

"Five!"

Declared the winner for round six, Mallory lowered to one knee and inhaled a deep breath. In the background, she heard the people cheering and yelling for her.

"*Degen, degen!*" the crowd chanted in exhilaration.

Mallory grumbled and huffed, knowing they'd have chanted for her with disdain if she had lost. She stood and stretched her sore body, unsure if she could handle another round.

Terrel staggered to his feet and used the spear for support. He remained rooted, breathing hard, and his face twisting with hate. Scanning the chanting crowd, he centered his focus on the stage where the nobles were clapping. King Wilmont was on his feet, seeming mildly impressed by a degenerate Alpha's abilities.

Mallory frowned at Terrel's stormy features and waited for him to leave the field. From the corner of her eye, she saw Luca lifting himself over the fence for the last round. Then Terrel's unexpected movements sent a chill down her spine, and a charge bolted through her entire body.

Kinsey!

Terrel hefted the spear, raised it above his head, and started dashing toward the stage. His roar was mighty and pierced the crowd's cheering.

Mallory dropped the hammers, sprinted in front of Terrel, and tracked the spear that he launched at the royal family. She had no idea the intended target and reacted to the threat that could befall Kinsey. As the spear sailed into her view, she lunged into the air and struck it with her hands.

The spear altered course and went spinning into the ground about twenty steps from the base of the stage, narrowly missing a noble's foot.

Mallory crashed face first into the grass and groaned from the harsh impact. When she had her hands under her, a boot slammed into her right side. Terrel's growls filled her ears, but a foot connected with her face. Her head rolled with the strike; then before the darkness claimed her, she heard Terrel's last words.

"You fucking degenerate bitch!"

Chapter 6

Mallory groaned and moved her hand off her stomach, but her entire body felt heavy. There had to be iron weighing her down, except something felt soft and warm under her. Testing her eyes, she flinched from the golden firelight that pierced her vision. She groaned and rolled her head away from the light.

After her initial attempt, she adjusted and discovered she was back in her bedchamber. Her memories were foggy, then came back in a rush. Terrel had attempted to kill someone in the royal family, but Mallory had intercepted the spear in time. Rubbing her throbbing head, she recalled Terrel's attack before she blacked out.

"Fucking bastard," she muttered and propped up her body with her arms. She scanned the room, realizing it was dark. Someone had been in the room recently, because the fireplace was burning fresh wood, keeping the chill at bay. Next to the fireplace, the table had a tray of food and drink. She was hungry, but she needed to go to the garderobe first, if she could manage it.

Taking a deep breath, Mallory pushed her aching limbs and climbed out of bed. Once her bare feet were on the cold stone, she stood, stretched her tired muscles, and noticed the wrap on her shoulder under the clean tunic. Peeking through her tunic, she confirmed that her wound had been cleaned as well.

Mallory limped a few times to the door, then knocked on it to get the guard's attention. In a second, the guard opened it and gave her a wary look, but he seemed to understand her need without asking. He stepped aside and allowed her to go first. With a straight posture, she exited the bedchamber and didn't allow her pain to show. She grunted as they passed Terrel's room, knowing he was either in a cell or dead.

After a short walk through two hallways, she arrived at the garderobe and went to the bathroom. Upon her return to the bedchamber, she frowned at the newcomer waiting for her. Behind her, the door closed but didn't lock.

"How are you feeling?" Kinsey had her back to the window.

Mallory huffed and went to the table, needing a drink to ease her dry throat. She filled the goblet with the small pitcher's contents, then swallowed a mouthful. The cool wine soothed her throat and would later ease the strain in her muscles. She studied the food but hesitated to eat in front of Kinsey, whose soft footfalls drew closer.

"Thank you for what you did today," Kinsey whispered.

Mallory stared into the fire, then placed the goblet on the tray next to the plate of food. She turned around and rumbled seeing the glistening in Kinsey's eyes.

"If you had done nothing, my father might be dead right now." Kinsey swallowed, then her voice trembled when she spoke again. "I know you loathe him, like so many others."

Mallory breathed in Kinsey's beautiful scent, which comforted her uneasy mind. Since she woke up, she felt disoriented and unsure about the future. "I didn't do it for him."

"I know," Kinsey whispered and shifted closer, easing into Mallory's space. "You did it to protect me."

Mallory looked over Kinsey's head and struggled to hide the truth. When Terrel had prepared to throw the spear, she had no idea who his target was, but her first instinct was to protect Kinsey. She remained silent while the memory played in her head but stiffened when Kinsey pushed against her. Her Alpha was stirred by the rare contact, and she craved more of it, so much more.

"Thank you," Kinsey whispered, a soft purr behind her appreciation. She placed a hand against Mallory's stomach and gazed up, willing Mallory to look at her.

Unable to resist, Mallory met the gorgeous blue eyes that were framed by pale features and dark hair. She breathed in the sweet, enticing scent that was all Kinsey. Her tongue hungered to taste it on Kinsey's skin. In seconds, her penis hardened between her thighs, and she was certain Kinsey might see or even feel it.

After a swallow, Mallory nodded, grabbed the edge of the table, and dug her nails into the wood. When Kinsey withdrew her hand, Mallory's skin was burning from the delicate touch.

"I'm sorry." Kinsey stepped back once, and lines creased her brow. "You've had a long, difficult day." She indicated the tray of food behind Mallory and said, "If there isn't enough, please tell the guard." Retreating to the door, she hesitated with a hand on the knob and glanced back. "Rest well, Alpha."

"Au-Aubrey." Mallory swallowed, then gasped after her birth name tumbled from her lips. For a moment, she stumbled over her birth name's pronunciation, having nearly forgotten how to speak it. But saying it aloud for the first time in fifteen years freed an iron anchor that'd been strangling her

Alpha. When Kinsey faced her, Mallory puffed up her chest and declared, "My name is Aubrey."

Kinsey smiled for the first time since their visit in the solar room and whispered, "Rest well, Aubrey." She slipped out of the room, and the door's latch sealed behind her.

Finally shedding her slave name, Aubrey collapsed to the chair beside the table and released a pained breath that she had held while Kinsey was near her. Her body buzzed with soreness from the fight and heat from Kinsey; she was unsure which one was stronger. She grabbed her crotch and felt her hard cock through the fabric. A groan escaped her while she squeezed the swollen head that was mildly mild throbbing. She had no memory of the last time anyone affected her this way.

How can she do this to me?

With a sigh, Aubrey looked at the tray full of food, which was double the amount she'd received so far. She wondered if her reward for saving the king would be more than extra food. But the meal was welcomed, and Aubrey was famished from today's tournament. After supper, she returned to bed and exhaustion claimed her, allowing her to ignore that tomorrow was the last day of the contest.

* * *

"Is she well?" Gerald asked once he and Kinsey departed the west wing.

Kinsey slowed her pace and allowed her body guard to near her. "She appeared fine." She tilted her head and whispered, "Perhaps in some pain." *And on the verge of a rut*, she recalled after being drawn in and wanting to inhale every spicy, sensual scent.

"A good night's rest will help." Gerald put space between them as guards patrolled past them in the halls.

Gerald was right. Tomorrow some of Mallory's minor wounds would heal, and any strains and aches would start to recede. *Aubrey*, her mind whispered as a reminder. She banished the old slave name from her mind, leaving it to die. Since meeting Aubrey, she had doubted she would ever learn the She-Alpha's birth name. Tonight, it had been gifted to her, like a rose blossoming in snowy winter.

The name Aubrey was unusual but not unheard of in their lands. What struck Kinsey as odd about the name was that it was traditionally given to regular Alphas. Perhaps Aubrey's parents gave her the name under the pretense that Aubrey was an ordinary Alpha. As Aubrey aged, her physical attributes and features would have later altered from traditional Alphas. Regardless, the name suited the She-Alpha, in Kinsey's opinion.

Arriving at her mother's ladies' chamber, she rapped on the door; after her mother called out, she entered. Her mother was reading a book in front of the fire, but she set it down and greeted Kinsey. Taking a seat by her mother, Kinsey poured hot water into an empty cup, then added tea herbs into it from the small box on the table.

"How is the *degen*?"

Kinsey struggled with a natural growl after her mother's use of the slur. After blowing out a breath, she replied, "The She-Alpha is fine." She couldn't fault her mother, at least not entirely. Her father's prejudices had a way of seeping into others. "She will recover."

Agnes closed the book but left it on her lap. "She performed a brave action today that most in her position would not have done."

Kinsey wasn't about to explain that Aubrey's actions were to protect Kinsey, who could have been the target. The truth would remain between her and Aubrey, like the discussions about Aubrey escaping from Tharnstone Castle. Earlier she had wanted to question Aubrey about why she didn't go with Gerald last night, but it could wait until tomorrow.

"What does Father make of it?" Kinsey asked after a quiet moment.

"Wilmont has not spoken of it." Agnes rested her head against the back of the chair and looked over at Kinsey. "I believe he is still thinking through today's events."

Long ago, Kinsey had learned her father was a slow thinker, but he did weigh things, unlike most Alphas. He had become king because of his ability to think, plan, and scheme, while other Alphas fell a step behind him.

"Will you choose the *degen*?"

Kinsey frowned and stole a moment to think of her answer while she sipped on the tea. She cupped the hot mug in her lap and whispered, "I do not know."

"She is nearly flawless," Agnes said.

Kinsey pursed her lips and stared into the steaming mug. Aubrey was, in fact, a near perfect Alpha specimen, except being a socially unaccepted breed of Alpha.

"Degenerate breeds tend to sire more degenerate breeds," Agnes uttered, gazing over at Kinsey's hard profile.

"I know." If Aubrey impregnated Kinsey, then she stood a higher chance of having a She-Alpha or even a He-Omega. The child would face a lifetime of hardships like Aubrey. It was quite possible that the child could be born an Alpha or Omega but certainly not a Beta. "Does Father know this?"

"I believe your father is aware." Agnes placed the book on the table, then made herself another cup of tea from the last of the hot water.

"I am also very fond of the first Alpha." Kinsey had formed a bond with Luca over the last few days. She had rooted for him during the tournament, just as she did for Aubrey. After the incident with Terrel, she was grateful to Luca, who had stopped Terrel from further hurting or even killing Aubrey today.

Agnes rumbled low and said, "He is a wise choice." She sipped on the tea, humming from its flowery taste.

"Tomorrow the physician will examine the three Alphas," Kinsey said.

"Perhaps they should have been examined prior to the testing."

Kinsey shook her head and lifted the mug closer to her lips but explained, "Father thought they would be more docile after the tournament."

Rumbling low, Agnes drank more tea. "Indeed." She and Kinsey continued their discussion about the three Alphas. She attempted to push Kinsey toward Luca, who had also caught Wilmont's eye. Kinsey was fond of him, but her attraction toward him was minor. Luca greatly reminded her of her fallen brother Devon. There were days she still cried for him, even though he had died in battle almost three years ago. Her mood grew solemn as the evening wore on, and after a game of backgammon, she said goodnight to her mother.

As always, Gerald silently greeted her in the hallway, and they returned to Kinsey's bedchamber. She thanked him before he finished for the night, and a guard was posted at her door. Inside the warm bedchamber, Kinsey prepared for bed, but her mind was busy with concerns. Tomorrow's choice not only affected her future, but also her child's fate.

* * *

"We'll start with the first Alpha," Wilmont told the physician, Orman.

Orman nodded and adjusted his dark grey robe that had red and gold accents. He went to the empty table and placed his bag on it.

Wilmont turned to his daughter and said, "Orman started as a surgeon in our army, but he recently finished medical school."

Kinsey recalled the details about Orman's history as a physician. She studied the empty flasks that Orman pulled out one by one, lining them up. "How will he proceed?"

"First I will examine each Alpha's body," Orman replied, nearing them again. "Then I will check their fluids. If there are any defects, I will report my findings."

Kinsey nodded at the thorough exam and hoped none of them revealed underlying issues. Behind her, Gerald stood in a corner and kept a watchful eye over her. To their left, the heavy wooden door opened to the solar room, and two guards entered with the first Alpha.

Luca's wrists were chained, but the shackles were removed after he was guided to the table. He rubbed his wrists and watched the guards stand by the wall closest to him.

"Remove your clothes," Orman ordered.

Luca took a deep inhale and stared hard at Orman before his attention cut to Kinsey.

Offering an assuring smile, Kinsey nodded at Luca to follow Orman's wishes. She sensed Luca distrusted Orman, who had a peculiar scent, even for a Beta.

After a huff, Luca removed his tunic, then his pants. Even though he was bare of clothes, his confidence wasn't stripped away. He rumbled a few times while Orman started looking over his body but touched little.

Kinsey kept her line of sight above Luca's shoulders. He held her gaze from across the room, as if signaling his pride as an Alpha.

"He is an excellent choice," Wilmont stated, his voice firm.

Kinsey chewed on her bottom lip. Luca was both an excellent and wise choice among the three remaining Alphas. Her offspring with him would be a strong Alpha or a fertile Omega, both pure breeds that would carry the House of Wymarc for generations. However, her Omega was left unaroused by Luca, even though she was intrigued by him. But did she need sexual attraction to complete her arrangement she'd made with her parents? When their conversations first started, Kinsey hadn't placed desire on the checklist for the best Alpha.

"He was a soldier for Cushar Kingdom," she whispered to her father.

Wilmont canted his head, then peered down at Kinsey. "Oh?"

"A captain, I believe," Kinsey said, meeting her father's gaze.

Wilmont folded his arms and pursed his lips before he rubbed his goatee. "He fought well in the tournament."

"The best," Kinsey whispered. Whereas Luca fought with skill, Aubrey had fought with passion. The tournament had given Kinsey plenty of insight about the four Alphas' personalities. Of the four, Aubrey had the most control and landed the fewest number of blows to the other Alphas. Luca had been the strongest one and showed compassion toward Aubrey. Terrel and Eldon were the least exceptional, especially Terrel. Kinsey refused to ask her father what happened to him after the tournament ended abruptly. Without question, she knew he was dead.

After the tournament, a winner hadn't been named since the last battle between Aubrey and Luca never took place. Wilmont considered completing the tournament with a wrestling match between the two finalists, but Kinsey denied it. She was certain Luca would win and insisted that she'd seen enough from the tournament. Wilmont accepted his daughter's wishes.

When Orman finished with Luca, he asked the guards to return him and bring in the next Alpha. Orman set aside the samples he'd retrieved from Luca and prepared flasks for Eldon. Before the Alpha arrived, Philip and Aerin arrived and greeted their lord.

"How goes it?" Philip asked and took Wilmont's side. He had a beaming smile and clasped his hands in front of his leather cuirass-padded front.

"Well," Kinsey replied. "We are waiting for the second Alpha."

"Will you make your selection today, Princess?"

Kinsey nodded, then looked at Aerin, who was next to her. "Yes, I will decide today."

Aerin rested his hands on his belly and smiled big at Kinsey. "This is exciting, my princess."

Wilmont grunted, then looked at the second Alpha. Like the others, he watched the proceedings as Orman inspected Eldon from head to toe and took samples. He continued conversing with Philip and Aerin while Kinsey observed Orman and Eldon.

Orman scratched several notes in a book as he studied Eldon. He flipped a sand clock and held Eldon's wrist, then jotted down his findings in the book. Much of his inspection was visual, especially of Eldon's face and neck. He took the same samples from Eldon as he had from Luca.

Eldon put on his clothes after Orman was finished, then was escorted from the solar room. The guards returned later with the last Alpha, who looked less worn out than last night.

Kinsey clenched her hands in front of her body when her Omega stirred awake from Aubrey's spicy scent filling the room. She fought the flush that crept up her neck toward her cheeks.

Orman had a startled expression and said, "I was not aware that one of them is a degenerate Alpha."

A snarl climbed up Kinsey chest, but she cut it short before it was too late. She huffed low and asked, "Is that a problem?"

Wilmont had his mouth half open, prepared to respond to Orman, but he looked at his daughter. Hints of pride showed in his features, and he grinned at her.

"Of course not." Orman spoke faster as the last Alpha was brought to him. "I have never seen one in person."

One of the two guards unshackled Aubrey, then joined the other guard near the head of the table.

Orman walked a full circle around Aubrey and breathed in her scent, perhaps convincing himself that she was real.

"Get on with it, then," Wilmont ordered.

Orman nodded. "Takes off your clothes, *degen*."

Aubrey narrowed her eyes at him and huffed loud enough for everyone to hear. After a rumble, she grabbed the hem of her tunic and lifted it off her body. She stepped out of her pants next and placed both items on the table near Orman's equipment. The only material left on her was the wrap over her right shoulder that needed to be changed. Kinsey made a mental note to do so after their time with the physician was done.

"Fascinating," Orman whispered. He stood in front of Aubrey, blocking Kinsey's view. "Can you impregnate Omegas?"

"I am an Alpha," Aubrey replied, a bite to her tone.

Orman fidgeted, then looked over his shoulder at his king, who chuckled at the exchange. "Yes, of course." He shifted to her side and leaned toward her injured shoulder.

Kinsey held Aubrey's gaze and offered a soft smile in hopes to ease Aubrey's tension. Her attempt seemed to help as Aubrey's shoulders lowered a fraction. When Orman went behind Aubrey, Kinsey's gaze dropped to Aubrey's muscled abdomen. As her eyes roamed, she couldn't help staring at Aubrey's penis. With the other two Alphas, Kinsey had been respectful about not looking, but her interest in Aubrey's genitalia was different. Her Omega's response was sudden and sharp, spurring a hot flash through her body.

"Fascinating," Orman repeated yet again. He jotted down a few things in his book, then came back with a tiny flask that had a red ring on its neck to distinguish it from the other samples. The first sample he took was Aubrey's blood, then he used the larger flask to collect some of her urine.

Orman set aside the samples and stood in front of her. "How often do you go into a rut?"

Above Orman's head, Kinsey made out Aubrey's darkened features and flinched at what the question might have provoked in Aubrey. *Can no one else smell the onset of her rut?* Her father, another Alpha, seemed unaffected by Aubrey's approaching rut. She found it strange when it was so obvious to her. But it wasn't unheard of for Alphas and Betas to miss the signals of a pending rut until it was in full force.

"Enough," Aubrey replied, her tone leaving no room for more questions.

Orman puffed up and argued, "It is important that the king and princess—"

"Her answer is plenty," Kinsey cut off, struggling to keep the edge out of her voice. She wanted to shove Orman away from Aubrey and end the inspection, but everyone would frown upon her reaction. "Have you finished?"

Wilmont shook with silent laughter and had a proud smile.

"Yes, Princess." Orman stepped back and neared the table with all the samples from each Alpha. "I will need some time alone to finish my assessment."

Kinsey rumbled, then signaled Aubrey to put on her clothes. "You will have your time, but Father and I will be expecting to hear from you."

Orman bowed his head, but his attention remained on Aubrey, who was pulling on her pants and tying them off. He pursed his lips and leaned near her.

With all her self-control, Kinsey did her best to remain still rather than attack Orman. Her Omega loathed how he invaded Aubrey's space and how infatuated he was with her. She released a strained breath after the two guards escorted Aubrey away from Orman and left the room.

"She is the most handsome of them all," Aerin whispered.

Kinsey canted her head after his remark and nodded.

"A perfect specimen, if I may say." Aerin winked at her, then went over to Philip, and they left together.

Kinsey hoped that Aerin hadn't picked up on her defensive nature over Aubrey. If he had, then her father also knew it, and she wasn't ready to face his disapproval about Aubrey.

"I'm going to go to the garden, Father. I need some time."

"Of course." Wilmont turned to Orman, who was already going over his notes and samples. "A guard will find us when you are ready."

Orman nodded and returned to his work.

Kinsey exited the room with Gerald behind her. She took the nearest stairwell, went to the ground floor, and out the garden entrance. Gerald took post by the doorway and allowed Kinsey her personal time.

Her first visit was to Devon's shrine, and she spoke to him, hoping he'd somehow reply to her. Once she was done, she took a seat on a stone bench and called to Gerald. "Can you bring me the She-Alpha?"

Gerald followed his princess's wishes and returned awhile later with Aubrey. He freed Aubrey's wrists and pointed to Kinsey on the bench.

"It is a cold day," Aubrey said. Even with spring on the way, the days were still chilly. Kinsey was wearing an ankle-length soft blue dress with long sleeves.

"I'm warm enough." Kinsey couldn't bring herself to tell Aubrey that she was warm ever since Aubrey had been brought to the solar room. "How do you feel today?"

"Better." Aubrey stood a few steps to the right of Kinsey, minding their space. "You smell anxious."

"It is the final day." Kinsey rose from the bench and neared Aubrey. "I must choose one." She folded her arms and looked off to the right. "In days, I will be with a child." Her heart raced at the thought, and she prayed she could be both a good mother and queen all at once.

Aubrey's chest vibrated with soft thunder. "What will become of the last two Alphas?"

Kinsey bit her lip, then met Aubrey's intense gaze. "That is up to my father." She shifted on her feet and whispered, "But I will do my best to influence his decision." She had already planted one seed for Luca, who held value as a former soldier. Eldon might be of use to someone else, if he could be sold off again. Aubrey had a possible skill set as a blacksmith, if she could convince her father of it. Maybe Aubrey could work for her freedom as blacksmith's apprentice somewhere in the city.

"Have you already chosen?"

Kinsey indicated the bench behind them and said, "Sit with me." She sat first and waited until Aubrey was next to her. She noted how Aubrey sat with her legs spread open for the first time in each other's company. "It will not be Eldon."

Aubrey said nothing, but her eyes held a glint in them.

"The choice between you and Luca is a very difficult one." Kinsey stared at the grass under her feet and thought about the future. In truth, her Omega had already made a choice, but she needed to use strong reasoning skills. Omegas were considered soft and emotional creatures compared to their Alpha counterparts. However, Kinsey didn't believe it was true, after growing up with an Alpha father and brother, along with an Omega mother and sister. She'd learned the differences between the two natures and felt Omegas' coolheaded minds prevailed over the Alphas' reactive tendencies. She believed an Omega queen could fare better than an Alpha king.

"Do you wish for me to choose you?" Kinsey asked, coming out of her thoughts. Every fiber in Kinsey already sensed that Aubrey wanted to bed her. The longer they spent time together, the stronger Aubrey's scent grew, as if attempting to reel in Kinsey.

Aubrey clenched her hands and leaned forward, her biceps strained against her tunic's sleeves. "No."

Kinsey gasped and nearly crumbled after the cutting answer. If she hadn't been seated, her weakened legs would have put her on the ground. "N-no?" Her Omega's pained howl forced her voice to quake, and she fought the sting in her eyes.

"I do not wish to sire a child whom I will never raise." Aubrey turned her head to Kinsey, and fire was bright in her golden eyes.

Kinsey lowered her head and blinked back the tears, but her chest was heavy. She closed her eyes and whispered, "Then why did you stay?"

"To convince you to flee with me."

Kinsey covered her face when a few droplets made it past her eyelids. She gritted her teeth, then pushed off the bench and faced Aubrey. "I have told you that I must stay." Her pain twisted into rage, and it burned in her cheeks.

Aubrey stood and towered over Kinsey yet didn't impose herself. "The only thing we must do in life is die." She narrowed her eyes and growled before she said, "Everything else is a choice with consequences."

With a shake of her head, Kinsey whispered, "My answer remains the same." From Aubrey's stance, she could tell that she hadn't convinced Aubrey. *Alphas are ridiculously stubborn*, she seethed.

"There is still time," Aubrey argued, her chest puffing up.

Kinsey shook her head, stomped off, and stood by the curly willow. She tried to grasp how Aubrey could refuse to bed her when every signal from Aubrey's body told her differently. However, the Omega in her adored Aubrey even more for wanting to raise and care for a child. Most Alphas placed the offspring in the Omega's care while they left to earn a wage. An Alpha's interaction with their offspring was often minimal, other than in farm families.

"But perhaps my answer will now make your choice easier," Aubrey said.

Looking toward the tree, Kinsey weighed Aubrey's remark. She was still torn between Aubrey and Luca. She was certain that she could convince Aubrey to bed her. Luca had no qualms with taking Kinsey for himself. Tabling her worries, she turned and said, "Come with me. I want to change your bandage."

Aubrey frowned but nodded after a moment. She followed Kinsey out of the garden and into the castle. She remained a respectable few steps behind Kinsey. Farther behind them, Gerald followed like a silent shadow and with a hand on his sword hilt.

Kinsey arrived at the top of the steps of the third floor and looked to Gerald. "Take her to her room. I will be there momentarily."

"My princess—"

"I'll be fine." Kinsey waved him off and left him to carry out his duty. She traveled through the castle until she reached her bedchamber. Once inside, she collected the few medical supplies she kept from her lessons with the city's top-rated healer. The bag's contents had bandages, herbs, and salves that she learned how to administer. Early on her mother had insisted that Kinsey have basic medical knowledge. At first the idea seemed silly, but as she aged, she realized the knowledge had served her well when it came to her sister's rough playfulness, Gerald's battered body after practices, or her mother's few ailments.

Going to the west wing, Kinsey entered the bedroom alone. She closed the door and found Aubrey seated at the table with the *Kingdom of Animals*. With a slight smile, she placed the bag on the table and opened it. "How does the wound feel?"

Aubrey closed the book and left it in her lap, while she watched Kinsey unwrap the bandage. "Sore." She grabbed her tunic and pulled it off, exposing her injury and upper body.

Swallowing, Kinsey forced her mind to remain focused on the task. "Any pain?" After Aubrey's headshake, Kinsey studied the exposed wound, which was angry but not infected. The marred flesh around the entry point appeared normal rather than dying or pussy. When Aubrey had been brought to the room yesterday, she had observed and helped the healer, Lind.

Aubrey tilted her head when Kinsey dampened a cloth with liquid from a clay flask. She crinkled her nose at the pungent scent that was laced with wine. "What is that?"

Kinsey gently pressed the soaked cloth against the wound and replied, "It's a combination of vinegar and wine to sterilize the wound."

After a huff, Aubrey asked, "You are a healer?"

"A bit." Kinsey leaned in closer to Aubrey's shoulder. "I was schooled by the city's best healer." She reached into her bag and pulled out a fresh wrap. "Tonight I will put salve on it so that it heals properly." After she finished wrapping the injury, she closed up the bag.

"Thank you," Aubrey whispered.

Kinsey cleared her throat and stepped back, fiddling with her bag. "Of course." From the corner of her eye, she watched Aubrey put on her shirt, and it was easier for Kinsey to refocus. "After what you did yesterday…."

Aubrey rose, lowered the book to the chair, and placed her hand against Kinsey's bag, halting her fidgeting. "Make a different decision from what's expected of you." She closed the distance and pressed her body against Kinsey's side. "Come with me tonight."

Kinsey clenched the bag with both hands and bowed her head, breathing harder the longer Aubrey remained against her. Her rational mind warred with her body's response to Aubrey's closeness and Alpha influence. She shoved down her Omega's desire to pack a few things and vanish in the middle of the night with Aubrey. "I-I...."

Dipping her head, Aubrey started to breathe in Kinsey's scent and rumbled low. "I'll keep trying until you change your mind."

So will I, Kinsey's Omega swore back. When Aubrey pulled away and walked to the window, Kinsey choked on fresh air after being enthralled by Aubrey's spicy scent. She peered over her shoulder and studied Aubrey for a moment before closing the bag and slipping out of the room, needing the distance to think more clearly.

* * *

"They are all in excellent health," Orman reported from his seat by the table.

Kinsey was seated at the head of the table while her father stood behind her. "What of Eldon's age?"

"I estimate that he is between fifty-five and sixty." Orman glanced at his open book and checked his notes. "He is in good health. Even Alphas at his age can produce strong offspring."

"And the *degen*?" Wilmont asked.

Orman's interest was piqued again at the mention of Aubrey. "Yes, she is in excellent health like the other Alphas."

Wilmont rumbled and placed a hand on the back of Kinsey's chair. "Can she reproduce?"

Orman flushed and looked from Wilmont to Kinsey, uncertain about how to proceed with the topic.

"Speak freely," Kinsey ordered, but she noticed he only did so when Wilmont nodded at him. She grumbled at people's needs to always default to an Alpha's approval

"I conferred with my books," Orman said. "We discussed degenerate Alphas in medical school, but there are still many unknowns about their kind."

"Can they sire children?" Wilmont asked, a twinge of frustration in his tone.

"Yes, most certainly." Orman folded his hands in his lap and looked between both nobles. "Like normal Alphas, their best chance to sire a child is during their rut when they can form a knot."

Kinsey was flushed in the cheeks, again but remained focused on the conversation. The other half of the equation was that the Omega should be in heat to optimize pregnancy.

"Will she breed another degenerate?" Wilmont inquired.

Orman frowned and leaned against the chair. "That is where the texts become confusing about degenerate Alphas and Omegas. There is no proof that a degenerate will sire only degenerate offspring or what the chances are." He looked from Wilmont to Kinsey and added, "But the old wives' tale about their kind is that degenerate begets degenerate."

"An unnecessary risk," Wilmont concluded aloud.

Orman nodded several times before he smiled at them. "In my professional opinion, the first Alpha is the best specimen of them."

Wilmont touched his daughter's back and asked, "Do you have any other questions before Orman leaves?"

Kinsey shook her head, already lost in her thoughts.

Orman stood and took Wilmont's hand for a shake. He bid good-bye to them and collected his things. Once he closed the door, Wilmont took his empty seat and studied his daughter.

"I know your choice, Father." Kinsey eyed him and waited for him to speak his mind, like always.

"You would be wise to pick him, Daughter." Wilmont rested his arm on the table and played with his goatee, while holding Kinsey's stare. "Is it the second Alpha too? He is rather old, however."

Shaking her head, Kinsey said, "It's the last Alpha."

Wilmont grunted and whispered, "I should have had the *degen* killed at the start, then your decision would have been done by now."

Kinsey swallowed after hearing her father's wishes for Aubrey. She looked away and stared out the windows of the solar room, studying the distant mountains.

"If I spare the *degen's* life, then will you bed the first Alpha?" Wilmont lowered his hand to the table and leaned closer to Kinsey, trying to push his authority onto her.

Used to the tactic, Kinsey ignored it and whispered, "I don't know." She bit her lip and continued staring out of the window. "I feel nothing sexual for the first Alpha."

Wilmont slammed his fist against the table and caused Kinsey to jump in reaction. "You need not feel anything at the moment. Once your heat is induced, you will take to him."

Well educated on the topic, Kinsey hated the plan that she would have to take an herb to trigger her heat. It was the best way to ensure her pregnancy, but the idea didn't settle well with her. As a teenager, her first heat had been scary and confusing. Her mother had been with her the entire time, while Gerald had protected her until it came to an end. Outsiders were forbidden to come to the castle that week or any week that Kinsey or her sister went through a heat. Since then, Kinsey had heats twice a year, as expected, and had learned how to cope with them.

"If I choose the She-Alpha, what will happen to the others?"

"You will not choose the degenerate!" Wilmont smashed his fist again and bared his teeth.

Kinsey popped up from the chair and put space between them before she kneeled to his demands. "We agreed that I could make the choice." She folded her arms and stood next to the burning fireplace. "That I could bed the one I feel most comfortable with."

Wilmont growled and stood, causing his chair to fall back. "Kinsey, I will not let a degenerate—"

"You agreed," Kinsey argued, then turned to face him. "Please, Father keep your word." Wilmont's face was bright red, and his growls made Kinsey's knees shake. For a long minute, she fought to submit to his will, since she always gave into him.

Wilmont huffed loud enough to almost shake the sealed doors, then approached Kinsey. His voice came out calmer than his features looked. "If the child is a degenerate like her, then I will forbid it to carry the family name of Wymarc."

Kinsey held her tongue, even though the anger poured off her. Once her father passed, then she could ensure the child carried the family name. She held her ground and ignored her father's imposing attempt. "If she hadn't stopped that spear, you would be dead right now." Leaning toward her father, she whispered, "She is more Alpha than most."

Wilmont rumbled and straightened up after he failed to influence Kinsey. "I will give you until sunset to reconsider your choice." He folded his beefy arms and allowed his dominant pheromones to wash over Kinsey. He growled, flung open the door, and stood in the doorway. Before he departed, he whispered, "If your final decision is the degenerate, then I pray for the future of my kingdom."

Chapter 7

Aubrey continued to pace the room, from the door to the window. She carried her hands behind her back and wondered when she would know her fate. Sunset had been a few hours ago, but she hadn't heard any news.

Coming back to the open window, Aubrey paused in front of it and allowed the cold air to wash over her. It relieved the heat radiating throughout her body that had started after Kinsey left the room this afternoon. Aubrey was convinced that her shoulder wound was infected and had triggered a fever. As a child she had once cut her calf open on her father's rusty sickle, when she was horseplaying with Corin, one of her brothers. Her mother had halted the bleeding, but Aubrey fell ill for several days.

With a frown, Aubrey grabbed a bar and pulled on it, but it didn't budge. She still held hope that Kinsey would sneak out of the castle tonight with her. They both deserved freedom rather than fighting iron or golden chains. However, her mood dampened the longer she reflected on their conversation in the garden. Kinsey had been devastated by

Aubrey's answer about their having sex. Aubrey was generating attractive pheromones that called to Kinsey, contradicting Aubrey's wishes. She refused to sire a child with Kinsey when neither she nor the child could be hers.

After their conversation in the garden, it was likely that Kinsey would choose another Alpha, like Luca, who was more than willing to impregnate Kinsey. Even now it was possible that Luca was fucking Kinsey in her bedchamber. The forbidden images of Luca mounting and knotting Kinsey attacked Aubrey's mind. She snarled and growled at the sheer idea of Luca bedding Kinsey, who was the first person to acknowledge Aubrey's existence.

Her Alpha grew and swelled in her chest, making her see red. Aubrey wanted to grab something and smash it, but she clung to the bars harder and wrenched them. Even though she had rejected Kinsey's offer, she wouldn't allow another Alpha to touch Kinsey. None would please or care for Kinsey, not like Aubrey. Barking with anger, she slammed her palm against a bar and stomped over to the door, prepared to tear it off its hinges and find Kinsey.

Aubrey huffed and glared at the door, then took a deep breath. She waited until the trembling in her body died down before she returned to the window for some cool air. After a grumble, she lowered her sweaty forehead against the bars and closed her eyes. The fever was playing with her mind, and she tried to calm herself, but forbidden images of Kinsey touching and kissing her toyed with her. Aubrey groaned from the strain between her legs; then her sensitive nipples hardened against the tunic. Just as she prepared to reach in her pants, the sounds of the guards stopped her.

A guard snapped at someone, then she heard a soft boom. Next, the exterior bolt on Aubrey's door slid open, and two guards entered the room.

Aubrey faced the two guards and narrowed her eyes at them. With fists at her sides, she resisted the urge to attack and break them in half. Over the years as a slave, she had never felt such a surge of superiority and need to dominate others who controlled her life. She had learned how to suppress her Alpha, but today it was rising to the top.

"You are to come with us, *degen*," a guard ordered.

The other one stepped back into the hall and kept a hand ready on his sword hilt.

Aubrey snarled once but walked past the first guard and entered the hallway. To her curiosity, the other two Alphas were being rounded up too, but Aubrey was escorted out of the west wing first. She peered over her shoulder and watched Luca being led down the stairs. Not far behind him, Eldon was guided in the same direction. Aubrey was the only one who remained on the third level and continued to the other side of the castle. They came to a different set of stairs than the ones Luca and Eldon went down. Once on the second floor, the guards commanded her to go to the right, then they turned left into a short hallway that ended with two wooden doors.

One guard stepped past Aubrey and pushed the right door open, revealing a much larger bedchamber. The fireplace was burning, heating the room and welcoming Aubrey into it. In front of the fireplace lay a fur rug, four chairs and a table with a few items. Directly ahead of her was a grand bed.

Turning to the guards, Aubrey wanted to know what was happening to her, but they had already exited the room. After the door shut, a heavy bolt was set in place, effectively sealing Aubrey into the larger, comfortable prison.

After a chuff, Aubrey approached the fire and lifted an eyebrow at the bowl of fruit, cheeses, and bread. She considered eating an apple but walked away from the sitting area and went to the window that had iron bars like the old room. To the left was a small room that had a garderobe, wash basin, and a short bench.

Aubrey was drawn back to the doors when heavy, muffled voices sounded, followed by the bolt sliding free. She breathed in deeply and caught King Wilmont's distinct scent, causing her to growl.

The right door crept open, and the two guards entered; then King Wilmont, a stranger, and three more guards came in next. The spacious room was tight and choking, filled with a mix of Beta and Alpha scents all trying to compete for dominance.

"Move her to the bed," Wilmont ordered and snapped at the guards, who danced on their feet to obey their king.

Aubrey growled when the five guards surrounded her in a U-shape. She bent her knees and prepared to drive them back, baring her teeth at them. Two guards rushed her, then a third followed. Aubrey punched one and shoved another back, but three guards swarmed her, and the two previous ones returned. They overwhelmed her and pushed her toward the bed.

"Hurry up," Wilmont barked. "Get her on the bed!"

Yelling, Aubrey kneed one guard in the gut, but a solid blow landed to her temple. She collapsed to her knees and saw the guard had used a sword pommel on her. Two guards hooked her under her arms and dragged her backward. She was lifted and tossed onto the bed.

"Get the serum ready." Wilmont neared the bed and crossed his arms. To his right, the stranger placed a wooden box on the table, opened it, and started rummaging through the items.

Aubrey groaned and rolled her head away from Wilmont when cold metal closed over her right wrist. She strained to lift her head and felt an iron shackle clamping around her ankles. The same cold metal clamped around her ankles and left wrist. Turning her head toward Wilmont, she watched the guard step back after shackling her.

"Is it ready yet, Lind?" Wilmont turned to Lind, who was an older Beta.

Lind adjusted the glasses on his nose and leaned over the glass tubes nestled upright in the box. "Not quite, sire." His hand shook as he touched each tube. "But close."

Wilmont huffed and stomped off to the foot of the bed.

Aubrey cleared her throat and watched Lind touch a corked vial then glance at Aubrey. He had a thoughtful expression and rumbled softly. As if making a different decision, he picked the tube behind it and poured the contents into a stone mortar. Aubrey caught an aromatic, sharp scent as Lind used a pestle to crush the items together.

"What are you...." Aubrey groaned, her head foggy from the hit.

Lind paused, then finished his work and poured the contents into another bowl that had a spout. "I will need assistance."

Wilmont returned to Lind's side.

Lind held the bowl and raised it over Aubrey's face. "Lift her head."

After a grunt, Wilmont placed one hand under Aubrey's head and his fingers twisted painfully in her short hair.

Aubrey gritted her teeth and held her mouth closed when the bowl's spout came near her lips. She growled at both of them and jerked on the chains.

Snarling back, Wilmont grabbed her jaw with his meaty hand and forced her mouth open. He smirked at her continued thrashing against the chains.

With care, Lind started to pour the contents into Aubrey open mouth.

Aubrey fought against Wilmont, but his grip was too strong. She gagged on the initial part of the oozing liquid.

Lind slowed the rate and said, "I suggest you drink it."

With eyes screwed shut, Aubrey forced down the harsh serum and felt it slide all the way down to her belly. The earlier putrid smell was a hundred times stronger on her tongue, and it clung to her mouth after Lind finished. She coughed and rasped once Wilmont released her.

"By sunrise, it will take full effect." Lind put away the items and closed up the box. "I will go see the princess next."

Wilmont grunted and thanked Lind; once he was gone, Wilmont ordered the guards, "Remove her clothes."

Aubrey clenched her teeth and jerked on the shackles that bound her to the bed. She glared at the guard's blade, but he ignored her and started cutting the tunic off first and then the pants. The clothing was pulled away and left her fully exposed to everyone. Only the wrap around her shoulder remained. She wanted to claw off the few smirks on the Beta's faces, knowing they were amused by her inferior size.

Wilmont was the only one who remained indifferent and commanded the soldiers out of the room. He departed last, after a final glance at Aubrey.

* * *

The knock startled Kinsey, but she hurried to the door. She smiled at the familiar face and welcomed Lind into her bedchamber. "Is she all right?"

Lind stroked his white beard and hobbled over to the nearest chair with Kinsey's help. "I'm sure she has suffered worse in her time." He sighed in relief once seated, placed the box in his lap, and opened it. Again, he rummaged through the items until he had what he needed for Kinsey.

"Did you give her the stimulant?" Kinsey could hear her own heartbeat.

Lind pursed her lips and whispered, "No. I gave her a sleeping sedative to ease her." He hesitated and peered over at Kinsey. "I pray your father does not find out."

Kinsey latched onto Lind's forearm and squeezed it. "He will not find out." She leaned over and kissed his temple. "Thank you."

Lind sighed and patted Kinsey's cheek but hesitated for a moment. He rumbled and stroked her damp cheek before retrieving a pouch from the box. "Mix it with hot water. Take it tonight before bed and then another in the morning." He handed the mixture to Kinsey. "However, I do not believe you require it."

Kinsey toyed with the sealed herbs and whispered, "I can feel the early onset."

"The timing of your heat is uncanny." Lind stroked his beard a few times and eyed Kinsey, as if willing her to speak.

"It is." Kinsey held up the pouch and said, "Thank you for this too."

Lind bowed his head, closed the box, and flicked the hasp. With shaky legs, he stood and said, "I should be going."

"I'll have Gerald walk you home." Kinsey followed him to the door.

"That won't be necessary." However, Lind looked pleased look with Kinsey's offer.

"Nonsense." Kinsey opened the door and called to her personal guard. "Gerald, can you please escort Lind home."

"Of course, my princess," Gerald stepped back and waited for Lind to join his side.

Kinsey watched them depart, then hid away in her room with the pouch still cupped in her hand. She considered whether to take it or not. But as Lind discovered, her body was already building up toward a heat. Wiping her forehead, she rubbed the sweat between her fingers and groaned at the pending future. By dawn, Kinsey expected to be in full heat with little to no rational thought other than to seek out the only Alpha worthy of her.

Leaving the pouch on the nightstand, Kinsey prepared for bed and attempted to rest for what might come tomorrow. At first, she had started under the furs and blankets, but within hours her body boiled over. She thrashed and turned on the bed, whimpering at times. At some point, she must have cried out because her mother hurried into the room well before dawn.

"Kinsey," Agnes whispered and held her daughter's shoulders. "Wake up."

Jerking back, Kinsey sat up and stared in shock at her mother. "W-what?"

Agnes wiped the damp hair from Kinsey's face and said, "You're in heat." She climbed onto the side of the bed. "The stimulant must be working already." Cupping Kinsey's cheeks, she leaned in and studied Kinsey's features. "Have you slept much?"

"Barely," Kinsey replied with a rough voice. She was panting and clutching her mother's hips for support and comfort. "I-I need…." At a loss, she fought to wrap her hazy mind around the heated hum in her body.

"You don't have to do this, Kinsey." Agnes stroked her child's sweaty cheek. "I will talk to your father and—"

"No," Kinsey whispered and leaned into her mother. "I'll be fine." She clenched her teeth and took a deep breath, which helped sooth her racing heart. "I need the Alpha."

Agnes bit her lip but turned and called, "Gerald?" When he stepped into the room, she ordered, "Kinsey needs help getting to the Alpha's room."

Gerald nodded and neared the bed, offering a hand.

Agnes moved off the bed and stood aside while her daughter took Gerald's assistance. She followed them to the door and said, "Gerald will stay near."

Kinsey nodded and offered her mother a reassuring smile before she departed the bedchamber. Her steps were small and slow the entire journey, but the stairs to go to the second floor were the most difficult. She leaned against the wall at the top and stared down at the flickering stairwell.

"If I may, my princess." Gerald pressed into Kinsey's side and lifted her arm over his shoulder. He crinkled his nose, now so close to Kinsey and her wired scent.

With the extra support, Kinsey went down the steps with ease and made it to the second floor, but lost her sense of direction.

"This way," Gerald whispered. He guided her to the left and then made a right down a short hallway.

Kinsey moaned at the musky smell that saturated the hallway, knowing who it was that was so close. *I need the Alpha*, her mind whispered. "I need *my* Alpha," she muttered and moaned when pain pulsed low in her gut the closer she came to the double doors.

"Open the door!" Gerald snapped at the two guards.

Kinsey clutched her stomach and dragged her slipper-covered feet a few times. Gerald had most of her weight, and he carried her into the bedroom after the door opened for them. Once inside she was overpowered by Aubrey's rich and heavy scent that overwhelmed the bedchamber. She heard Gerald choke, but he continued to aid her.

"Chair," Kinsey whispered. In a few seconds, she was lowered to the chair but her eyes searched the dark room for Aubrey. She could hear the harsh breathing off to her right, near the window. Gerald's movements distracted her, yet the fire's warmth and light were welcoming.

Gerald reemerged and knelt in front of Kinsey. "I will dismiss the guards, but I will stay on duty until you are done." He placed a hand on Kinsey's covered knee and squeezed it.

Kinsey nodded, then glanced toward the bed. She pursed her lips and frowned at the shackles around Aubrey's ankle. "Why is she chained?"

Gerald peered over his shoulder at the shackled slave and replied, "For your protection." He clenched her knee harder. "Don't forget how dangerous Alphas can be in ruts."

Blinking, Kinsey lowered her gaze to Gerald and parted her lips.

"Don't trust her, my princess." Gerald sighed, then stood up. "Just take what you need from her." His unspoken words told her that an Alpha would take what they wanted from an Omega, without regret.

Once alone, Kinsey hobbled over to the bedside, placing her hand on the edge for support. She gasped at Aubrey's nude form chained to the large bed.

Aubrey was coated in sweat. With closed eyes, she thrashed her head and pulled at the arm shackles in her sleep.

Kinsey inhaled Aubrey's scent, which filled the bedchamber and indicated that Aubrey was close to a full rut. She raked her eyes down Aubrey's body, her mouthwatering upon seeing the hard nipples. Aubrey's stomach was plated with muscles that Kinsey had craved to touch since the first day they met. But Aubrey's penis caused her to suck in a breath. The story that a She-Alpha had a larger penis during her rut was true. The proof stood proud and tall in front of Kinsey, encouraging her to touch it. In the firelight, a few droplets reflected and clung to the swollen head. Kinsey felt the urge to crawl onto the bed and stir Aubrey from her sleep, but the low growl made her stumble back.

Placing a hand over her racing heart, Kinsey watched Aubrey fight in her sleep and pull against her restraints. Stepping back until her back was against the wall next to the door, Kinsey slid down, balled herself up on the floor, and cradled her head between her knees. She had no idea how long she remained there until twilight glowed in the barred window.

* * *

Aubrey groaned and opened her eyes to the dimly lit room that was also hotter than hell. She was coated in sweat, and her itchy skin made her want to claw, but not as much as the chains holding her to the bed. She growled, twisted her head, and pulled her arms against the iron chains. They held tight, and she jerked against them. A soft roar broke free from deep in her chest. However, the chains refused her demands, glinting back at her in the dying firelight.

She arched her back and took a deep breath, soothing the caged beast in her chest for the moment. Then the throbbing between her legs took precedence, and she lifted her head from the pillow. With narrowed eyes, she stared at her cock standing erect between her thighs. She couldn't recall ever seeing the head so pronounced or angry red. Aubrey clenched her teeth and dug her heels into the bed, wishing she could fuck someone. In truth, she didn't want to fuck just anyone, but she wanted to rut into the princess of Tharnstone. Her teeth hungered to claim, and her cock needed to knot.

After a growl, Aubrey clawed the bed and gulped the air, trying to regain control. However, a very sweet scent invaded her mind and body, calling to her Alpha. She jerked against the chains and followed her nose's direction until her eyes zeroed in on the form huddled on the floor beside the doors. Breathing harder, she caught the blue orbs peeking out at her. Aubrey fought the shackles again, more determined than last time.

"Stop."

Aubrey heeded the command, and silence lingered in the bedchamber, other than a soft crackle from the fireplace.

"You'll hurt yourself," Kinsey whispered from her spot.

Aubrey panted, clawed the bed, and listened to Kinsey's soft breaths. "Free me," she ordered. After a long silence, she snarled and pulled at the iron chains that held her against the golden fur under her. She closed her eyes and raged harder against the restraints until a burning hand pushed against her chest, taking away her strength.

"Stop." Kinsey stood next to the bed and held Aubrey's gaze. "It's not safe."

Aubrey was compelled to listen to Kinsey, and the pheromones eased her anxiety until her cock's needy demands pulsed again. She groaned when Kinsey's fingertips blazed a trail between the valley of her breasts and paused over a stomach muscle. For a moment, she could see the dark circles under Kinsey's eyes and damp spots in the nightgown.

Aubrey took a deep breath and consumed Kinsey's distinct, honey-like scent that she wanted to taste. "Free me."

Kinsey cupped one of the stomach muscles and caused Aubrey to groan. "I can't." Her gaze traveled lower, but she stared at Aubrey's breasts. She massaged the muscle under her hand before her eyes skipped down to apex of Aubrey's abdomen.

Aubrey smelled Kinsey's arousal and pictured it smeared all between her thighs. Lifting her eyes from Kinsey's crotch, she saw how Kinsey was staring at her cock that twitched in reaction to the appraisal.

Kinsey withdrew her touch, which caused Aubrey to whimper. Grabbing her nightgown, Kinsey pulled it over her head and dropped it to the floor. Her skin was pale and her petite frame was perfect. Kinsey whimpered and clutched her lower belly, causing her to bend forward.

Aubrey had learned what pain Omegas could suffer in their heat, but it was the first time she had witnessed it. Her Alpha gnarled and howled to the point she lunged, until the chains jerked her back into the fur. "Free me."

Panting like Aubrey, Kinsey came to the bed, climbed onto it, and crawled on top of Aubrey. She straddled Aubrey's hips and sank down until her dripping sex smeared over taut muscles.

Aubrey growled and bucked her hips, causing the tip of her cock to brush Kinsey's ass. She dug her nails into the blanket, pulling against the furs. Her heart thundered against her chest while her Alpha raged inside of her. Her body ached to knot and claim Kinsey, but her mind still clung to a measure of resistance. All she could picture was the birth of a child who would never be hers.

"Don't," she rasped to Kinsey. "Don't," she repeated again.

Kinsey whimpered and lowered until her front molded against Aubrey's. She braced both arms on either side of Aubrey's head and buried her face into the side of Aubrey's temple. "Don't make me go to Luca." She tangled long fingers into Aubrey's sandy blond hair and whispered, "I want you. Please, Aubrey."

Even with her eyes closed, Aubrey felt the tears escape and roll down her cheeks. As Kinsey's legs tightened around Aubrey, more tears fell and salted her lips until she realized the tears weren't just hers.

"Please, Aubrey. Don't make me go," Kinsey rasped and trembled. "I *need* you." Her fingers twisted harder in Aubrey's short hair, and she buried deeper into Aubrey's larger body. "I swear you'll see your child."

Aubrey pushed against the bed, but the shackles chewed into her wrists and ankles. Her freedom was denied again, but Kinsey's calming pheromones settled her Alpha. She twisted her head and pressed her nose into Kinsey's hair, inhaling her scent. "Free me, and I'll knot you." She wanted Kinsey and the child for herself, but the promise that she could see them at all was a start. Regardless, her Alpha wouldn't dare allow Kinsey to be touched by Luca or any other Alpha.

Kinsey scraped her nails against Aubrey's scalp and nuzzled her ear.

"I'll take care of all your needs," Aubrey whispered, her chest vibrating with a rumble. When Kinsey lifted her head, Aubrey frowned at the red puffiness around the blue eyes.

Kinsey whined and nuzzled Aubrey again before pulling back. She rested on her haunches, staring with a peculiar expression at the shackles on Aubrey's wrists. Huffing low, she grimaced, then crawled up Aubrey's body.

Aubrey was given an eyeful as Kinsey's breasts filled her view. She bit her tongue to keep from sinking her teeth into the pert nipples daggling above her.

Kinsey toyed with the left shackle first, growling at it. A soft curse filled the air and sent a shock through Aubrey, who had never heard swears from the princess. There was a pop sound, then a triumphant huff from Kinsey. She removed the loosened shackle from Aubrey's wrist, then moved onto the next one.

Aubrey groaned at being able to lower one shoulder, and the next metal pop gave her more relief. With both arms free, she tested her wrists and shoulders until her arms felt better. When Kinsey spun around and crawled down the bed, Aubrey sat up and lifted an eyebrow at the round ass in front of her.

Stretched forward, Kinsey manipulated the first ankle shackle and was faster at it than last time. After tossing the shackle to the floor, she crawled on her elbows until she had the final restraint in her hands. She struggled with the rusty pin, leaned forward more, and stuck her ass up higher.

Aubrey bent her right knee, now free from the chain, and watched Kinsey struggle with the last shackle. The polite thing would have been to help Kinsey, but Aubrey's attention shifted to Kinsey's round ass cheeks. Her cock throbbed with need.

With a snarl, Kinsey yanked the unlocked shackle and freed Aubrey from the irons. She attempted backing up to her original spot, but her ass bumped Aubrey's stomach.

Aubrey had both her legs bent and sat upright. She rumbled low when Kinsey's round ass pressed into her lower stomach, but she controlled her immediate desire to knot Kinsey. Instead she hooked an arm under Kinsey's stomach and pulled her into her body.

Following the command, Kinsey was drawn into the larger body that enveloped her and fit like a puzzle piece in Aubrey's lap. She whimpered and relaxed her head back onto Aubrey's uninjured shoulder.

"Thank you," Aubrey murmured and rubbed her nose against the shell-like ear. "I have to go to the garderobe first." She grinned at Kinsey's whine. "I won't be long." She dissected herself and vanished into the garderobe for a minute. Upon her return, she discovered Kinsey in the center of the bed, moaning, and touching herself.

Kinsey sensed Aubrey and jerked her hand away from between her thighs. Still on her back, she scrabbled to the far corner of the bed.

Aubrey stood next to the bed and appreciated Kinsey's soft form in the early dawn light from the one window near the bed. She moved forward, bringing her first knee to the bed and remaining upright on her knees. Frowning, she watched Kinsey crawl farther away and shrink herself with her legs drawn toward her chest. Aubrey rumbled and said, "I won't hurt you." She smelled the fear laced in Kinsey's scent, which triggered Aubrey's low growl until Kinsey whimpered in submission.

Huffing and taking a deep breath, Aubrey settled her dominant nature and frowned at their situation. She glanced at the iron chain that hung from the bed post and gritted her teeth. Even through the fogginess in her mind, she realized why they had chained her like an uncontrolled beast. Kinsey was probably told wild stories about untamed, rutting Alphas, who were rapists who defiled Omegas. They weren't untrue, but Aubrey was far from one of those demons.

Then a second thought blindsided Aubrey when she looked at Kinsey's huddled form. *She's a virgin, like me.* Aubrey had experimented with two Betas, but it was limited. She had never been in a rut until now. Unlike Aubrey, this might be Kinsey's tenth or so heat, but it was her first real sexual experience. Her Alpha swelled with pride at being Kinsey's first.

"Have you been with anyone before?" Aubrey asked. She trained her voice to be soft, inviting Kinsey's Omega to her.

"No," Kinsey whispered.

Aubrey rumbled in pleasure and accepted the delicate situation. The original plan had been for Aubrey to remain chained and give Kinsey the control she needed to take Aubrey's knot and seed. But now that Aubrey was free, it changed everything for Kinsey. Aubrey didn't want to break Kinsey's trust, regardless of how much her cock pulsed with demand.

Fisting her hands at her side, Aubrey rumbled low while she spoke in a gentle tone. "Have you touched an Alpha before?" Fighting a growl, she asked, "Or anyone's penis?"

Kinsey shook her head and continued holding Aubrey's gaze from her safe spot.

"Do you want to touch me?"

Kinsey licked her lips and cut her eyes to the erect penis that protruded from Aubrey's hips. "Yes," she whispered and fascination showed on her face.

Aubrey revealed a toothy smile and gave off more inviting pheromones that she hoped eased the Omega's distress. "You can." She didn't notice the sharpness in Kinsey's scent anymore and the Omega started calling to Aubrey's Alpha again. With an iron grip, she remained in control and waited for Kinsey to come to her.

After a moment, Kinsey crawled over and sat back on her heels. "I can touch you?"

Aubrey heard the Omega's submission in Kinsey's question and frowned at it. She had grown accustomed to

Kinsey's more driven personality, but their heat and rut had tilted the power between them. With a steady voice, she replied, "Yes, touch me."

Kinsey dropped her eyes to the long shaft that was unsheathed and glistening in the morning light. She was breathing hard and hesitated to make the first move.

Reaching out, Aubrey cupped the smaller hand in hers and directed Kinsey to her cock. She rumbled from the trembling in Kinsey's hand, but the first touch would break through Kinsey's anxiety. Together, she closed Kinsey's fingers and palm around the center of her cock. She grinned when Kinsey sucked in a breath.

"How do you get so hard?" Kinsey flushed and tried pulling her hand away, except Aubrey stopped her.

"You," Aubrey replied, her voice rough and growly.

Kinsey looked away until Aubrey started dragging their hands down the length. She was staring at their hands and gasped when they touched the swollen head. "Does it hurt?"

"It hasn't before," Aubrey whispered.

Peering up, Kinsey frowned and asked, "Is this your first rut?"

Aubrey flushed in response and closed her eyes until she heard a giggle. She growled and said, "I haven't been around an Omega before you." But this rut wasn't natural, it was induced by a bizarre drug. She tried not to brew on it or else her temper would flare up. Her memory from last night was cut short by Kinsey's thumb rubbing her cock's tip.

"Did you know you would get bigger during your rut?"

Aubrey grunted and huffed at the question. "I wasn't sure." However, her Alpha was proud of the development, and she loved it too. She sucked in the next breath when Kinsey squeezed the head of her penis. Letting her hand fall away, she allowed Kinsey to explore and test by herself.

Kinsey scooted closer, now in front of Aubrey. Using her right hand, she ran her thumb along the rim of the head, then went underneath, tracing a vein to the slit. After a few droplets weeped from the tip, she smeared it over the head. "I've heard She-Alphas can get pregnant too."

Aubrey rumbled and nodded. "I'm similar to Omegas in some ways." She caught Kinsey's wrist again. "I'll show you." Guiding Kinsey's hand, they reached underneath her cock, past the base. "Do you feel that?" She and Kinsey pushed their fingers past small folds, teasing Aubrey's entrance.

Sucking in a breath, Kinsey looked up and replied, "You are like me."

"A little bit," Aubrey said, grinning at Kinsey's keen interest. She encouraged Kinsey by cupping her hand and pushing a finger inside. She groaned at the slight pressure against the sensitive bundle just past her entrance.

Kinsey grabbed onto Aubrey's hip, trembling some. "You're so wet." She blushed when Aubrey smirked at her, then she pushed in a second finger. Kinsey rubbed the sensitive spot that sent shocks through Aubrey's stomach and made her cock throb even harder. When Aubrey growled in response, Kinsey yanked her hand away, as if burned by the new experience.

Aubrey groaned and grumbled after losing the pleasurable contact. With her jaw locked, she did her best to control her growls, concerned it would deter Kinsey. "It's okay." Perhaps later, Kinsey would explore her again, after they built up more confidence and trust.

Kinsey gripped Aubrey's cock and slid her fisted hand up the full length. Aubrey moaned and rumbled from the wonderful sensation. Then Kinsey paused and rubbed the ring that had formed at the base. Aubrey noticed that Kinsey's arousal had returned, the sweet, tasty smell pulling at her senses. She revealed a hungry smile and asked, "What do you need?" Her voice was coarse and heady, drawing a moan from Kinsey.

Blushing from her chest up to her cheeks, Kinsey gazed up and moved her hand to Aubrey's hip. She crawled closer on her knees until Aubrey's cock was pushed between their bodies. She hooked her hands behind Aubrey's neck and requested that Aubrey bend down to her.

Following the command, Aubrey bent over until their lips brushed against each other. She could recall two or three kisses from her past, but none were so delicate as this one. The chaste kiss continued until Kinsey's hands slid to Aubrey's face, cupping under her jaw. Kinsey pushed up and pressed their lips harder, asking for more.

Aubrey whimpered and parted her lips, and Kinsey did the same but remained uneasy. Taking control, Aubrey slid her tongue into Kinsey's mouth and tasted the Omega she'd wanted for days. She groaned when Kinsey's nails dug into her stomach muscles and caused her skin to burn. Her cock jumped and throbbed for Kinsey, but she held control over her Alpha.

At the end of the kiss, Kinsey traced her thumb across Aubrey's swollen bottom lip. She was breathing hard and clawed Aubrey's stomach with her other hand. "I-I want...." Her flush returned brighter than last time.

"It's okay," Aubrey whispered. "It's okay to want this."

Kinsey lowered her eye contact, then her right arm dropped and went across her stomach. Pain danced across her features, and Aubrey grabbed her hips to hold her up. "It's never been—" She groaned louder and clutched Aubrey's arm. She hissed and jerked her head up, showing her clenched teeth. "Aubrey, please."

Growling, Aubrey took control again and pushed Kinsey to the left, then down onto the bed. She lowered herself between Kinsey's legs as they settled across the furs. She rumbled when Kinsey hooked her legs around Aubrey's waist and back.

Kinsey whimpered and ground her pelvis against Aubrey's lower stomach, smearing slick all over. "I n-need...."

Aubrey braced her arms on either side of Kinsey's head and pushed her hips down, allowing Kinsey to grind hard onto her. "Need what?" She loved how Kinsey moaned and arched against her.

Kinsey opened her eyes, showing off the brightness in her eyes. "I need you." She latched onto Aubrey's shoulder and cut her nails into the skin. "Please, Aubrey."

With a growl, Aubrey pulled back on her heels and grabbed the underside of Kinsey's thighs. She separated them, then grabbed her swollen cock. Wiping more of Kinsey's fresh slick down the shaft, she centered herself over the princess.

Kinsey sucked in a breath when the tip brushed over her clit, rubbing it. "Oh gods!" She loosened her legs more, then her body jerked after the tip swiped under the hood of her clit. "Aubrey," she begged with both need and uncertainty.

Aubrey snarled and grabbed Kinsey's ass and moved her cock to nudge Kinsey's slippery entrance open. She gritted her teeth and held back from violently plunging into all the tight, wet heat inside of Kinsey. Her Alpha craved to claim the Omega, but this was Kinsey's first time. Glancing up, she captured Kinsey's gaze and saw readiness and anxiousness written on pale features.

"It might hurt at first," she warned Kinsey.

"It can't hurt more than I do now," Kinsey whispered, a plea in her tone.

Aubrey rumbled; the confession reinforced why Omegas' heats needed to be sated by Alphas. No longer withholding from Kinsey, she urged her hips forward and allowed the swollen head to spread open the first bit of Kinsey, who sucked in her next breath. At a delicate pace, Aubrey pushed a little until Kinsey stiffened, then relaxed again as Aubrey broke past the entrance.

Kinsey lifted her back and gasped when Aubrey paused near Kinsey's G-spot. She panted several times, then grabbed Aubrey's knee. "Don't stop."

Freeing her hand that buffered her cock, Aubrey adjusted both hands under Kinsey's ass and focused on fulfilling Kinsey's needs. She continued the careful pace and pushed her hips forward, easing the heat wrap around her length. Her Alpha howled at the wonderful sounds coming from the Omega.

"Ooooh!" Kinsey's voice held amazement, until it was too much. She tensed and grabbed at Aubrey to stop.

With a huff, Aubrey paused and waited for Kinsey to adjust to the new sensation. Once she sensed her lover had settled, she pulled back part of the way, then pushed in again but not as deep. She smirked at Kinsey's surprised gasp and continued the soft strokes. Her cock throbbed and urged her to rut into the Omega, but she kept an iron lock on the need. Aubrey focused on Kinsey first, swearing to please her.

"I-Is there more?"

Aubrey chuckled, hearing the tremble in the question, and pushed back in before she lowered Kinsey's butt to the fur. "Let go of me." After Kinsey unraveled her legs, Aubrey shifted and placed her palm flat against the bed near Kinsey's forearms. With most of her weight on her knees, she softly drove deeper into her lover.

"Oh gods!" Kinsey latched onto Aubrey's biceps and bit her bottom lip.

Growling at the tight heat hugging her cock, Aubrey wanted more and worked her hips faster, testing Kinsey's desire. She grinned when Kinsey raised her ass in response to meet the next drive. "Is it hurting?"

"N-No!" Kinsey held Aubrey's gaze and said, "It feels good."

Aubrey lowered her head and nudged Kinsey's jaw. "Spread your legs wider for me." She basked in the Omega obeying her, opening for her and giving more to her. Not wanting to disappoint, Aubrey worked her hips harder and started soft but fast thrusts.

Kinsey arched her back and tilted her head back. "Oh gods, Aubrey!" She pulled on the biceps wrapped under her fingers, then rocked her hips into every thrust. Her cries grew louder and her bent legs were spread all the way.

Grunting and growling, Aubrey pumped faster and met Kinsey's needs. Each thrust went deeper until Kinsey's entrance brushed the knot at the base of her cock. She wanted to push it through, but Aubrey knew Kinsey wasn't ready for the experience. She increased the pace, reveling in the wet muscles clamping around her cock. The sensitive head throbbed and pulsed against the tightness, sending shocks up Aubrey's spine. Her Alpha wanted to fuck Kinsey and make her scream so that everyone could hear them.

With a snarl, Aubrey clamped down on her Alpha's desires and looked at Kinsey writhing under her. She felt Kinsey building toward her first orgasm, shuddering from every pump of Aubrey's hips. Her focus was on satisfying Kinsey first, and she tried holding back her own climax.

"Don't stop, please!" Kinsey twisted her head back and stiffened with Aubrey's next thrust. Her cry was louder this time. She arched her back up, pressing their fiery skin together.

Kinsey's arousal enveloped Aubrey, who lowered her head and kissed her lover's sticky skin. She moaned at the sensation of the walls fluttering along the length of her cock, begging for her to release inside Kinsey. She promised Kinsey that she would soon. Their time together had only just begun.

Kinsey licked her dry lips after lowering her back to the furs. She was breathing hard but satisfaction was written on her flushed face.

Smug, Aubrey started to unsheathe her cock from inside Kinsey until nails cut into her biceps. She halted and raised an eyebrow at her lover.

"Stay for a second." Kinsey glanced away in embarrassment.

Aubrey chuckled and lowered down to her elbows, which caused her cock to sink back into Kinsey. She rumbled from Kinsey's long moan and whispered, "As long as you want, Princess."

After a swallow, Kinsey brushed her nose against her damp temple and said, "Kinsey."

Jerking her head back, Aubrey stared at Kinsey and remained tongue-tied by the request.

"You can't call me 'princess' after how you just made me feel."

Aubrey bit her lip and smirked at her lover's shy smile. "And how was that?"

"Like an animal."

Aubrey pushed a few, short blond strands from her face. "Like an Omega getting what she wants?" She rocked her hips to emphasize her point.

"Yes." Kinsey moaned and mimicked Aubrey's motions. "Gods. You smell so good." She lifted her head until her nose brushed the upper part of Aubrey's neck where the scent was the strongest. "How can you smell so good?"

Aubrey growled and argued, "It's your scent that's driven me mad." At the thought of it, she decided it was time she had her taste. She planned to lick and suck Kinsey's clit until she had her coming in her mouth. "And I'm going to finally have you."

Chapter 8

Kinsey yelped when her Alpha lover lifted her and propped her back against the headboard. Her legs were balanced on Aubrey's broad shoulders while her ass was seated in strong hands. She held her breath as Aubrey buried her face between her thighs, inhaling her scent. "W-What are you doing?" Aubrey's answering growl caused the slick to thicken and ooze out from her.

"You've been teasing me with your scent since the first day." Aubrey's voice rolled with hunger and desire. "You've made my cock hard *for days*." Her face moved in closer, and her hot breath brushed across Kinsey's pulsing sex.

With wide eyes, Kinsey watched Aubrey's mouth press against her sex, and her body jolted when the Alpha's hot tongue brushed between her slit. She sucked in her breath, and Aubrey did it again but slower to make her gasp louder. The third time was even slower, tasting and savoring her sweet slick. Kinsey moaned at the deliberate taunting, but it felt so damn good. She dropped her head back against the headboard and grabbed it with both hands.

Aubrey withdrew some and kissed Kinsey's inner thigh. "You want more," she said, a pleased rumble vibrating against Kinsey's leg. There was no question or debate in her statement, only a cocky Alpha's conclusion.

"Yes." Kinsey offered herself by scooting forward and opening her thighs. "I'll come for you," she whispered, sensing her words would encourage her Alpha lover.

Aubrey nipped at Kinsey's tender skin and smirked at her. "What other foul words do you know?" She rumbled with amusement after Kinsey flushed. Leaning in again, she took Kinsey's invitation.

Her first licks were light, testing Kinsey. But then Aubrey ran the flat of her tongue across Kinsey's throbbing clit. Kinsey moaned at the pleasure shooting up her stomach. She had to have more, so much more. She started to rock her hips to get friction until Aubrey snarled, then sucked on the swollen clit and made Kinsey's voice echo through the bedchamber. The Alpha released the hard bud and flicked her tongue over it, urging more slick from Kinsey. Aubrey drew circles with the tip of her tongue around Kinsey's aching clit, teasing her again. Kinsey snared Aubrey's head and caused

Aubrey to rumble in pleasure. But Kinsey dug her nails into her lover's scalp when her clit was sucked on.

Every movement of Aubrey's tongue was maddening. Kinsey cried out louder the faster Aubrey fucked her. Her right hand gripped the headboard while she pulled on Aubrey's blond hair with her left. Lifting her head, Kinsey watched how the big Alpha cradled her and drank her like the finest wine. Sharp excitement shot up Kinsey's spine, but she refused to close her eyes; she loved watching the Alpha work her toward an orgasm.

Then her stomach clenched up when Aubrey flicked the tip of her tongue against Kinsey's hard clit. She screamed, and the buildup struck a wave of pleasure that left her driving her sex deeper into Aubrey's sucking mouth. Sweet slick rushed out of her, but none of it was lost. Kinsey slumped against the headboard but jerked from a few final licks.

Aubrey nuzzled Kinsey's thigh and rumbled in satisfaction before she nipped the tender flesh. She chuckled at Kinsey's hiss, then scooted closer and pulled Kinsey's hips to hers. Having Kinsey securely in her arms, Aubrey turned them and laid down the opposite way on the bed. She adjusted Kinsey's tiny frame against her muscular body.

Still panting, Kinsey regained her bearings and started to kiss the hot skin in front of her, earning happy rumbles.

Weeks ago, she wouldn't have believed she would adore such a sound from an Alpha, but it was a magical noise. For a moment, peace settled over her while she remained nestled in Aubrey's arms.

I was only supposed to get pregnant.

The laid out plan had been simple. Kinsey would select the best Alpha, who would be a boorish brute and unattractive to her. Using herbs, Kinsey would induce her heat early so that she had the best chance of becoming pregnant. Then the Alpha would be chained to the bed to ensure Kinsey's safety. Her mother had told her to simply mount and ride the Alpha, then the knot would slide in fine. The Alpha would come inside Kinsey, and they would be tied for a short period. Once undone, Kinsey would leave, and the Alpha would be free to go in two or three days.

Aubrey, however, was more than a prized Alpha.

Kinsey closed her eyes tighter at her error, but from the first day, it was too hard to ignore the charge between them. She was still certain that after Aubrey finished satisfying her heat, Kinsey would leave the room. Aubrey would have her freedom, and they would part ways, for the most part. She had promised Aubrey that she could see their child.

At the thought of a child, her Omega swelled with pride. Their union would create a healthy child, who would be strong and gorgeous. For the first time, she smiled at the thought of raising an Alpha or Omega of her own. But first, she needed Aubrey to knot her.

Kinsey snaked her hand down and found the hard length between their bodies. She felt the warm slick coming from the tip and touching her stomach. Aubrey had plenty to give her.

After a soft growl, Aubrey tilted her hip back and gave Kinsey better access. She moved her head down and sought out Kinsey's lips, kissing her.

Whimpering, Kinsey gasped after the kiss and whispered, "You can't mark me." She dropped her eye contact when Aubrey puffed up and growled at her. "My father… he'll…." Closing her eyes, she trembled at the thought of his hurting Aubrey, who had saved his life. But if Aubrey marked his daughter, his tiny thread of self-control would snap. Kinsey had won him over in allowing her to breed with Aubrey, but marking Kinsey was another matter. King Wilmont would never approve of his daughter being forever tied to a degenerate Alpha.

"I would—" Aubrey lost her threat against Kinsey's sudden kiss. She rumbled, then pushed Kinsey on her back and climbed over her, clasping both her hands and raising them above her head. Bowing her head, Aubrey brought her nose to Kinsey's exposed neck and inhaled her scent.

Kinsey twisted, but Aubrey pinned her down. She should have been outraged and fighting for release. Instead, her body betrayed her and slick coated her thighs. Her arousal encouraged Aubrey to growl more. She at least wasn't wriggling under the Alpha, but her Omega wanted to.

Aubrey licked the spot on Kinsey's neck where she could seal their futures together if she bit down. There was nothing stopping Aubrey from making Kinsey hers, for forever. "I could mark you as mine." Nipping at the spot, she rumbled from Kinsey's moans. "It would keep us together."

Kinsey bit her lip but a whimper escaped. Her Omega craved the Alpha's claim, but she couldn't afford it. As the future queen, she couldn't be bound to anyone or she would lose her power.

Still biting and licking at the spot, Aubrey rumbled and whispered, "Mine."

Closing her eyes, Kinsey stifled her plea of agreement and reminded herself that it was her heat making her irrational. She wriggled under the firm body pressed against her. Then two sharp teeth clamped down on her neck, freezing Kinsey. She gasped and waited for the canines to break her skin, tying her to Aubrey, a perfect Alpha to her Omega.

Aubrey's breath was hot against her skin. Her teeth poised to change the plans for the Kingdom of Tharnstone.

Aubrey would have me and a child, finally a family that's all her own. But the seconds stretched into a long minute, then the pulsing flesh slipped free from Aubrey's canine teeth.

Kinsey deflated and opened her eyes to find the same hurt in her chest reflected in Aubrey's eyes. She wanted to scream at the betrayal her Omega felt after being unclaimed. But all she was given was a nuzzle and a broken whisper.

"You're not mine to take."

No no no! Kinsey's Omega howled in protest, and she felt warm droplets under her nails from tearing into Aubrey, who released her wrists. She rolled onto her stomach and hid her tears. Behind her, she felt muscles and a hard penis pressed into her. Then Aubrey was nibbling at Kinsey's ear and rocking her hips into Kinsey's ass.

Aubrey's next rumble was long and strained with emotions. She nudged Kinsey's temple and whispered, "My knot is for you to take." She nipped an earlobe and earned a hiss from Kinsey. "If you still wish."

Kinsey smeared her salty tears into the fur and took a deep breath that eased the last of the strain in her chest. She nodded and turned her head to one side. "Will it hurt?" She was educated by her mother on how sex worked between an Alpha and an Omega. Knotting often hurt but was also pleasurable for the Omega. Somehow hearing it from an Alpha made it real.

"It can for a moment, I've heard." From Aubrey's curious tone, it sounded new to her too. The idea that Aubrey hadn't knotted anyone made Kinsey feel good. Already the conversation about knotting caused more slick to spread between her legs. She wiggled her ass against Aubrey's front.

"The best position for knotting is if you're on your hands and knees," Aubrey whispered into Kinsey's ear. Her voice was growly and hot.

Kinsey felt a shock tear through her and settle low in her gut. "Y-you mean you would mount me." She wanted to melt when Aubrey's throaty chuckle echoed in her ear.

"Almost, Princess." Aubrey nudged her hips and pushed her shaft against Kinsey's ass cheeks. "You on your hands and knees. I will be upright on my knees, driving my cock into you until you're ready for my knot."

Kinsey was breathing heavily and clawing the fur under her hands.

Aubrey traced the tip of her nose along the rim of Kinsey's ear. "If you want more, you lower your upper body, and I'll get on my feet, bend my knees, and then mount you." She licked her lips and whispered, "I'll fuck you and knot you."

Clenching her lip between her teeth, Kinsey tasted a tang of blood but failed to hold down her moan. Once before, Aubrey had been crude with her, and like last time, it made her weak.

"Does the princess of the Kingdom of Tharnstone want to be mounted, fucked, and knotted by an Alpha?" Aubrey licked Kinsey's nape and whispered, "Tell me, Princess." She pushed her hips forward, demanding an answer.

Kinsey gasped and turned her head to give Aubrey better access to her neck. "Yes." Already her mind was wild with images of Aubrey behind her, taking her. "I want all of it." She blushed when Aubrey chuckled in her ear. But her clit pulsed with greed, and her walls were clenching with anticipation. Embarrassed or not, she wanted to have Aubrey behind her, her hips clutched, and their skin slapping.

With a pleased rumble, Aubrey lifted her body off Kinsey and sat back on her heels. She waited for Kinsey.

Closing her eyes, Kinsey took a deep breath, then moved her legs and arms until she was on her hands and knees. Her heart slammed against her chest, but her sex was hurting while she waited for Aubrey to take control. She twisted her head around and noticed that Aubrey was stroking her cock. In this position, she was every bit the Omega presenting herself to the Alpha, who would satisfy and knot her. Kinsey moaned and caught Aubrey's attention.

Aubrey tugged once on her cock, then scooted closer and reached between Kinsey's legs. Her fingertips grazed Kinsey's clit, then searched for her entrance.

"W-What?" Kinsey whimpered when a finger pushed inside her. Her walls fluttered and tightened, trying to draw in Aubrey.

"You're very slick." Aubrey took a huge inhale and growled as she pulled away her hand. She clutched her penis, then Kinsey felt her rub it between her wet folds, encouraging her to rock her hips.

"Oh gods." Kinsey dropped her head and moved her body so that the friction hit the right spot on her clit. She could have orgasmed from it, but Aubrey moved her cock. Choking on a protest, Kinsey sucked in her next breath when the tip circled her entrance. Unable to wait any longer, she pushed back and smirked at Aubrey's soft hiss of surprise.

Then Aubrey growled and asserted herself again, pushing her cock into Kinsey. She grabbed Kinsey's hips and went deeper at a gentle pace, then paused. "More?"

Kinsey was panting and whispered, "You feel so big." She turned her head back to see her Alpha lover. "I want more." She rumbled at Aubrey's care; it was agitating her Omega. "More," she repeated, her tone clip and hungry. A deep growl sent a shiver down her spine, but her demand was met with a sudden thrust. Kinsey screamed and twisted her fingers into the furs.

Aubrey jerked Kinsey back on her cock as her hips slapped against Kinsey's ass. All the tenderness was forgotten as her hard length pumped in and out of her lover.

Kinsey rocked her body to the harsh rhythm, claiming and taking whatever Aubrey gave her. She cried out each time Aubrey's cock reached a bit deeper through her clenching walls. The fullness inside her was beautiful and perfect. Every thrust brought them closer. Kinsey needed Aubrey to knot her and give her a child who would bind them, with or without the mating bite. She sensed Aubrey holding back, not ready to give her the knot that slapped against her entrance.

With a snarl, she turned her head to one side and demanded, "Fuck me and knot me like an Alpha, or get off." Her heart slammed against her chest when Aubrey paused.

Kinsey yelped when Aubrey shoved her face first into the furs with one hand. Kinsey gasped after she turned her head, but excitement speared her in the belly, and anticipation pooled between her legs. Aubrey was mounting her, and her strong hands clutched Kinsey's sides for a solid hold.

Now atop Kinsey, Aubrey's thrusts were harder and deeper. She grunted with the punishing drive of her hips, filling Kinsey whole.

"Fuck!" Kinsey cried out louder. With Aubrey over her, the knot seemed bigger and maybe even impossible. For a second, she thought it would be too much for her, but her Omega craved the connection. Whatever pain might follow, she didn't care because she would have it and take it. Aubrey would give it to her this time.

Kinsey screamed while Aubrey grunted between pants. Her thick cock satisfied every piece of Kinsey's Omega. As her walls tightened, she sensed she was close and Aubrey was shuddering above her. "Aubrey," she said between growls, "knot me!" Her Alpha lover snarled and latched onto Kinsey's right shoulder. The next thrust was the hardest, and Kinsey's muscles spasmed with heat and pleasure.

Aubrey echoed her lover's scream and urged her hips forward, her knot stretching Kinsey's entrance. It was so swollen, but Kinsey needed it in her. As Aubrey's knot split her open, a slick, hot wave of cum filled Kinsey for the first time. Aubrey grunted and clawed Kinsey's shoulder but continued pushing her knot past Kinsey's tight entrance. A soft, wet pop sounded from between their bodies, then Kinsey gasped from the final connection.

With a snarl, Aubrey rocked her hips against Kinsey's ass and encouraged another shot of cum inside of Kinsey, whose walls locked around the throbbing length inside her. Every bit of Kinsey was full with the cum sealed in her. The knot's girth just past her entrance ensured they would stay joined for a while so that Kinsey would become pregnant. She melted from Aubrey's proud snarls behind her at finally knotting her Omega lover.

Kinsey whimpered when Aubrey nudged her cock again, rubbing the swollen head against Kinsey's muscles. Then Aubrey lowered onto one knee, hooked Kinsey's waist, and picked her up. Their union didn't break as Aubrey changed their position. Now on their backs, Kinsey rested on top of her Alpha lover and remained filled, even though some of the slick and cum slid free.

"I'm going to knot you again," Aubrey whispered, her lips brushing Kinsey's ear. "Then again."

Kinsey moaned and grabbed onto Aubrey's hands that lay on her thighs. She wanted it over and over, until she was too sore. A twinge of shame settled in her chest and caused her to whimper. Strong arms snaked around her chest, and Aubrey nuzzled her.

"It's okay to want this," Aubrey whispered. A purr started in her chest and soothed Kinsey's disjointed emotions. "For it to feel so good."

"I'm a hypocrite," Kinsey confessed, her throat raw and chest tight. "I detested Alphas and swore I'd never let one really have me." She turned her head away from Aubrey and closed her eyes. "But now, I'm begging and demanding an Alpha to knot me." Swallowing, she choked and whispered, "I was wrong."

Aubrey rumbled, then brought Kinsey's head back to her. She nudged her temple with her nose and continued rubbing Kinsey's side with her hand. "It's okay to change your mind and learn what you want."

Kinsey huffed and argued, "I've been unfair."

After a rumble, Aubrey kissed on Kinsey's jaw and cheek. "No." She sighed, then ran her nose along the outside of Kinsey's ear. "But I can understand disliking Alphas because of your father." With a grumble, she whispered, "And the ugly stories about Alphas." Her chest filled with a growl that lasted for a long moment.

"But you're nothing like those examples," Kinsey said. "You make it so easy for me to let go."

Aubrey nipped at the rim of Kinsey's ear, then trailed her hand up to a hard nipple. "Don't be ashamed about what you feel." She rolled the nipple between her fingers. "Or how many times you want my knot."

Kinsey tightened her eyelids as her chest felt heavy, even though Aubrey played with her breast. *I want her mating bite.* However, she strangled down her Omega's need to be claimed by the Alpha. Aubrey's knot had to be enough, and she rocked her hips in reminder. But still, there was a different kind of hollowness hidden in Kinsey at the unwanted truth that soon she would be alone again.

Covering Kinsey's pert breasts with her hands, Aubrey moved her hips down and allowed her shrinking knot to wiggle out of Kinsey. She and Kinsey both moaned at the soft sound of the knot coming free. Lowering her hand, Aubrey pulled out her cock the rest of the way and wondered at all the slick that dampened the fur under them.

Turning over, Kinsey rested on top of her lover and rolled her hips against Aubrey's stomach. "Have you knotted someone before me?"

Aubrey shook her head, then whispered, "I haven't been inside anyone before you."

Kinsey drew back as her brow knitted together. "You mean you haven't fu—" She flushed at almost using the curse word, again.

Aubrey chuckled and threaded her fingers into Kinsey's dark hair. "No." Her amusement fizzled away until a frown marred her features. "I have been with two Betas. Both were too eager and fascinated with me having a penis. I couldn't...." Her eyes cut away from Kinsey, who felt guilty for being so pleased that Aubrey hadn't fucked another before her. "I just used my hands or mouth," she whispered.

"But you were okay with me?" Kinsey asked, worry filling her mind and body. But she chided herself because of the ridiculousness of the past five days. A contest between the four Alphas, their quality, and conversation about their cock sizes. She groaned at the possible damage done to their relationship and how screwed up her father's entire scheme was from the beginning. "I'm sorry. I shouldn't...." She muttered, "What am I doing?" She lifted off Aubrey, but nimble hands grabbed her, pulled her back, and settled her stomach on Aubrey's front.

"I made my decision after you let me have a choice," Aubrey said. She rumbled and sniffed the thick air between them. "You could have taken what you wanted without my consent, but you didn't."

Kinsey groaned and settled on top of her lover.

"You gave me a chance to leave, but I stayed," Aubrey whispered.

Kinsey played with Aubrey's hair, admiring its shortness and how straight it was compared to her own wavy locks. "Why?" She cut her eyes back to Aubrey's soft features, noticing the fine scars from being a slave. "Why did you stay?"

"I thought I could convince you to come with me."

Kinsey sensed the same determination humming inside Aubrey, and her Omega savored it. She admired Aubrey for her persistence to change Kinsey's mind, even if it was impossible. Tracing Aubrey's jaw, Kinsey revealed a sad smile and whispered, "Thank you for trying." She traced her finger along Aubrey's ear and followed the outer rim before threading her fingers into blond strands.

"You are close to your family," Aubrey said. "That is something foreign to me that I may never have or understand."

Kinsey whimpered and lowered her head, touching their foreheads. "You'll have it one day." She was certain that Aubrey would find someone who would love her without limits or restrictions. Someone would give Aubrey everything, unlike Kinsey, who was bound to her people. As she gazed into Aubrey's eyes, she saw the new dreams and a new vision for her life that made them glow. Days ago, Aubrey had been an empty shell of an Alpha, but Kinsey had witnessed the subtle changes the longer they spent time together.

Aubrey parted her lips, about to speak, but the sound of the door's groaning open grabbed their attention.

Kinsey released a yelp when her world turned upside down for a second. Somehow Aubrey had extracted herself, jumped out of the bed, and stood a few steps in front of her. Gathering the nearest fur, Kinsey pulled it up her body and went wide-eyed as Gerald entered the room. Next a handmaiden took a few cautious steps into the room but hesitated and looked between Aubrey and Gerald.

The room smelled of sex and pheromones from their first time together. The handmaiden grew redder by the second, and her hands trembled with the tray of food. It took a moment for Kinsey to figure out why until Aubrey's threatening growls demanded that the intruders surrender to her.

Gerald held his position and fingered his sword hilt. He didn't back down from Aubrey and hoarsely ordered, "Put the food on the table by the fire."

Kinsey cut her attention from the frightened handmaiden to her snarling Alpha lover, who was protecting her. She slid off the bed with the fur against her body and hooked Aubrey's wrist. "It's okay."

Aubrey huffed and went silent, other than a soft rumble. Her attention was locked on the handmaiden, who hastened to the table. She shifted her head and looked to Gerald, who met her silent challenge with a hard stare.

Kinsey rubbed her thumb over Aubrey's burning skin, soothing her. But in truth, her clit throbbed in reaction to Aubrey's aggressive display. Her Omega basked in Aubrey's posturing, but she managed to halt a moan.

The handmaiden hurried from the room, then Gerald backed up and held eye contact with Aubrey the entire time. Before he closed the door, he looked to Kinsey, who nodded and confirmed she was safe. Gerald bowed out of the room and resealed the door.

After a huff, Aubrey turned around and studied Kinsey with her darkened eyes. Her earlier agitation about the intrusion had wired her Alpha senses and left her muscles straining against her skin. Alphas were natural protectors, especially when their Omegas were in heat.

Peering down, Kinsey raised an eyebrow at the erect penis and the glistening head. She grinned and let the fur fall from her hand, feeling relief from the cool air against her burning skin. Her body begged for Aubrey to take her again, and Aubrey responded with a growl. Kinsey gasped when Aubrey grabbed her hips, lifted her and pulled their bodies together. This time, there was no conversation or concerns about what they each wanted from the other.

Kinsey sat on the edge of the bed and spread her legs while Aubrey balanced one knee on the bed. She plunged into Kinsey and grunted in sync with each of Kinsey's screams. Kinsey rocked her hips and dragged her nails into Aubrey's back muscles, encouraging her lover to fuck her harder. Grabbing the back of Aubrey's head, she wrenched Aubrey down for a feverish kiss with their tongues clashing and teeth scraping for dominance.

Aubrey tore her lips free and bit into Kinsey's neck, holding her still under her. She growled as Kinsey whimpered in submission. Her knot banged against Kinsey's greedy entrance, ready to take it when they neared their orgasms. Kinsey cried out when the pace turned almost violent, making her walls flutter against the hard length driving into her. Aubrey's raw power over her was something she had craved without knowing it until now.

Kinsey *loved* it.

Then their orgasms hit simultaneously, and they screamed as the first shot of cum filled Kinsey. With a growl, Kinsey snapped, "Fucking knot me!"

Aubrey grabbed Kinsey's ass cheeks and jerked her down onto her swollen knot in a single thrust. Kinsey cried out but groaned and dropped her head back, offering her neck to Aubrey. It was so natural to her and the craving so strong to be marked by her Alpha lover. There was nothing else she wanted more right now than Aubrey to be her Alpha.

Rolling her hips, Aubrey encouraged another wave of cum and groaned with pleasure. She lowered her head and scraped her teeth over the sensitive flesh that waited for a biting mark. With a hiss, she licked the spot several times and nipped at it. Her entire body shook, perhaps from the fucking's pleasure or from the pain of not marking Kinsey.

Kinsey dug her nails in deeper into Aubrey's shoulders and whimpered at the rejection. How many times would they have sex and knot without every trading the bite mark? She was unsure her heart could handle it, but her body would demand that she keep having sex until her heat was satisfied by the only Alpha that her Omega deemed worthy.

Chapter 9

Aubrey nudged Kinsey with her nose, then offered her the handful of grapes to nibble on. The lovers were nestled together by the fire, hidden under a large fur. Earlier Kinsey had checked on Aubrey's shoulder wound, concluding that it was okay to take off the wrap. The dark, scabbed wound would heal in time. Sunset had been over an hour ago, and they'd shared the supper the handmaiden left. Kinsey was tucked in Aubrey's lap, safe and secure from the world.

Kinsey ate the grapes one at a time, plucking them from Aubrey's cupped hand. She tried offering one, but Aubrey refused with a headshake.

Aubrey pursed her lips and watched with fascination as Kinsey enjoyed the sweet grapes. A soft thunder started deep in her chest after the grapes were gone. She stretched to her left and grabbed a few sliced pieces of green apples that had honey drizzled on them. Again, she offered them to Kinsey, who ate without any restraint. The sweet food seemed especially attractive to Kinsey tonight.

With her right hand, Aubrey covered Kinsey's belly and considered whether or not a baby was developing inside or if it was too soon. Omegas were known to have keen instincts about their bodies, especially when their heats were near and if they were pregnant. As heats or pregnancies neared, their habits changed and even their dispositions as their natural need to produce an offspring became a priority. A pregnant Omega was a different kind of Omega than one who had no children.

"Are you tired?" Aubrey asked after plucking more fruit from the table near them. They had napped on and off, in between their sessions of knotting, fucking, and screaming.

"Full but not tired." Despite her statement, Kinsey continued to snack on whatever fruit Aubrey offered her. "Are you?"

Aubrey leaned her temple against Kinsey's head and whispered, "No." She should be more worn out, but her body was still full of rutting energy and fiery need. By tomorrow, most of her rut would slow down, and she wouldn't feel like she was coming out of her skin. Her mind would be less hazy, and she could think of other things than just knotting her Omega lover. Not that she didn't love every minute of today, but her future was confusing. She wasn't prepared to face it once she left the bedchamber.

"Good." Kinsey twisted her head up and whispered, "I'm not finished with you."

Aubrey lifted an eyebrow and watched Kinsey's eyes darken with need. "Yes, Princess." She grinned at Kinsey's eye roll, but her cock started to harden just from the thought of knotting again. "How do you feel?" Her question slowed Kinsey's desires for a moment.

Kinsey placed her hand on top of Aubrey's that rested on her stomach. "It's too soon, but I'll know."

"How will you know?" Aubrey whispered.

Kinsey smiled and replied, "I will *know*." She squeezed Aubrey's hand, then plucked the last apple from Aubrey's palm. "But until then, we need to make sure." Her tone was playful in between the soft chewing. When Aubrey reached for more fruit, Kinsey snared her wrist and said, "I want something different."

Aubrey drew back and flashed a wolfish smile. The head of her cock started to twitch with anticipation. "What do you want?" She slid her left hand under the fur and snaked it down to the open space between Kinsey's thighs. With two fingers, she dipped into the wet heat that waited for her.

Moaning, Kinsey moved her hips and rubbed her clit against Aubrey's fingers. "I want to fuck myself on your cock." She shrank into herself when Aubrey growled in response.

Aubrey swallowed the next snarl and eyed her lover, who appeared small and unsure of herself now. She nudged Kinsey with her nose, encouraging her to look at Aubrey. "How do see yourself doing that?" Biting her lip, she waited for Kinsey to confess her latest fantasy.

Kinsey pushed her ass into Aubrey's lower gut and whispered, "You lay on your back, then I straddle you and put your cock in me."

Aubrey was reminded of the start of their day when she woke up, bound, and Kinsey on top of her. But this was different, and Kinsey was asking her for the control. Most Alphas disliked the few positions that gave the Omega a chance to control the speed and angle. But Aubrey's Alpha didn't bristle at the idea and was rather intrigued by the thought of watching Kinsey ride up and down on her cock, fucking herself. And if Kinsey needed help, Aubrey knew how to move her hips.

"B-But we don't have to, if you're not comfortable with—"

"Yes," Aubrey cut off and pushed her fingertips against Kinsey's swollen clit. "I want to watch you fuck yourself on my cock." She loved the bright redness spreading across Kinsey's face. Pulling the fur off them, she picked up Kinsey and turned them parallel to the fireplace. In seconds, she was on her back but lifted her upper body with her left arm.

Kinsey was straddling her lover's hips and leaned in for a kiss. "Are you sure?" she whispered, still uncertain about the reverse of control.

Aubrey grinned and brushed away Kinsey's hair that reflected the firelight. "Yes." She rumbled and nibbled on Kinsey's neck. "Are you afraid now?" Perhaps Kinsey had expected Aubrey to deny the request.

"A little," Kinsey admitted, her voice weak.

"I might be the big Alpha," Aubrey whispered, "but you're the strong Omega." She bumped her hips against the underside of Kinsey and said, "I want to watch you take my cock, use it, and please yourself."

Kinsey was flushed and panting. She pushed Aubrey on her chest and ordered her to lay down.

Aubrey obeyed and situated herself on the fur with her hands flat against the floor. She wanted Kinsey to have full control and waited for her Omega lover to have her way. A smirk played on her lips when Kinsey started to grind her soaked clit into Aubrey's stomach muscles.

Kinsey bent forward, braced herself with Aubrey's shoulders, and rolled her hips in every direction. She gazed down between their bodies, but lifted her head, pushed her hair to one side, and ordered, "Rub your cock for me." Her voice held no room for argument, and she didn't shy away when Aubrey rumbled at her.

Reaching down with her left hand, Aubrey did as she was told and pulled on her cock. She smeared the slick from the head down onto the shaft so it was ready for Kinsey. Her entire length pulsed with jealousy while Kinsey continued to rub her clit. But she restrained her need to fuck Kinsey, who was so beautiful pleasing herself on top of Aubrey.

"Are you hard enough for me?" Kinsey asked, smirking at Aubrey's soft growl.

"Yes." Aubrey hooked Kinsey's wrist and brought her hand back to Aubrey's shaft. When small fingers wrapped around it, she asked, "Is it hard enough for *you*, Princess?"

Kinsey groaned and whispered, "Yes."

Aubrey's Alpha swelled with pride. Her cock hurt with anticipation for Kinsey to impale herself on it, but she clamped down her eagerness. She withdrew her hand and grabbed onto the fur under them, waiting for Kinsey.

Lifting her lower body, Kinsey held onto Aubrey's broad shoulders for support, then started circling her clit around the tip of Aubrey's cock. She seemed to enjoy the friction every time they did it. But then Kinsey tried aligning her entrance with Aubrey's penis, grousing each time it moved away from her.

Aubrey half chuckled until Kinsey fired her a glare. She cleared her throat to rid the amusement that showed on her face. With her hand, she grabbed the base of her cock and held it in place for Kinsey to start taking her in.

Moving one hand under Aubrey's breast, Kinsey gripped Aubrey's side and maneuvered her entrance over the swollen, glistening head that waited for her. Biting her lip, she moaned as the head spread her entrance open and started to stretch her.

Aubrey curled her head back and rumbled at the tight, wet heat that slid over the head of her pulsing cock. She wanted to thrust up and make Kinsey cry out, but instead she clawed the fur. Opening her eyes, she smirked at Kinsey's strained features and hungry eyes. But her smugness fell away as Kinsey slid down her hard length, taking every bit of it without hesitation.

"Oh gods," Kinsey whispered after she finished lowering herself onto the shaft. "That feels so good."

Aubrey growled in agreement and pulled her hand out of the way so Kinsey had better access. She had lost count how many times they had sex, but it was better each time.

Their awkward moments were fewer as they learned what the other liked.

Kinsey remained bent over Aubrey and started lifting her hips then sliding back down the thick shaft. Her groans were long and pleasant. Her face was feverish with desire as her silky muscles slid up and down Aubrey's cock. She increased the pace after a minute and clutched Aubrey harder.

With fingers twisted in the fur, Aubrey did her best to let Kinsey have her way. Her heels dug into the floor when Kinsey increased the pace with shallower strokes on her cock. She gritted her teeth, lifted her upper body, and leaned back on her elbows so she could watch Kinsey. Her new position provided Kinsey with a better angle to hold onto and ride Aubrey's cock. "Fuck," she hissed and growled.

"Touch me," Kinsey ordered, a growl under her command.

Not one to argue such a demand, Aubrey cupped Kinsey's right breast and rolled it, loving its size in her hand. She had sucked and played with Kinsey's breasts multiple times tonight. Every time she bit them, Kinsey's hiss sent a shot of excitement to Aubrey's cock. Even now, her teeth hungered to clamp down on them.

Kinsey peered down at her thighs and watched how Aubrey's full girth spread her open. She whimpered, straightened up, and leaned back some, but tensed from the difficult position. Aubrey propped up her legs and offered support, grinning when Kinsey grabbed onto Aubrey's muscular thighs behind her. With more leverage, Kinsey went faster and moaned or whimpered louder. "Oh gods."

Growling, Aubrey lowered onto her back and used both hands to massage Kinsey's breast or tweak the hard nipples. She wanted to thrust and fuck Kinsey, but she also loved how Kinsey was fucking herself. Kinsey would come up fast, then drop down nearly to the base, encasing most of Aubrey's full length. It was beautiful and sexy, more than Aubrey expected it to be.

But Kinsey's face was red and sweaty with frustration. She snarled and fell forward, her hands on either side of Aubrey's face. "I need more." She panted and nipped at Aubrey's jaw line. She gyrated her hips and caused her entrance to circle the swollen head. "Give me more, please."

Aubrey accepted the challenge and hooked her arms across Kinsey's back. "Hold onto me," she ordered in a growly, hot voice. Kinsey latched onto her shoulders and arms, prepared for a good fucking. She raised her hips and pushed her cock in, testing Kinsey, who moaned in pleasure. With a hungry rumble, Aubrey pulled back her hips, then thrust in again and again. She increased the pace within seconds and made Kinsey cry out.

"Oh fuck!" Kinsey strained against Aubrey's unrelenting hold and spread her legs wider. "Don't stop. Don't stop!" She raised her ass higher, meeting Aubrey's hard drives. Her growls between the screams were deep and pleased with Aubrey's skill.

The pressure in Aubrey's cock was peaking, and she could feel Kinsey clutching her harder. Then a shudder raced down her shaft after the next drive went farther into Kinsey. Aubrey pushed deeper than before, and they both cried out together. Kinsey draped herself over Aubrey, who lifted them up into a seated position.

Kinsey moaned and gasped, but spread her legs out as Aubrey worked the wide knot past her throbbing entrance. With a firm hold on Kinsey's hips, Aubrey sheathed her knot inside her as they both came on each other. Aubrey moaned from the wet heat rushing between their locked bodies. She snarled, then once again bit Kinsey's throat but didn't break the skin.

With her arms around Aubrey, Kinsey clutched her lover and ground her hips a few times, encouraging another wave of cum from Aubrey. She tangled her fingers into golden hair and rested her head against Aubrey's. After deep gulps of air, a purr started low in her chest.

"You've become quite proficient in cussing," Aubrey whispered, needing a distraction from biting Kinsey. She blinked away the faint sting in her eyes after she strangled her Alpha's need to bind Kinsey to her. Her voice sounded rough, but she hoped Kinsey didn't notice it.

Kinsey grumbled and teased, "You bring it out of me."

"I bring many things out of you," Aubrey quipped and earned a smack to her shoulder. She pulled her head back and gazed up at her lover, who was sweaty, red, and satisfied for the moment.

"Yes," Kinsey played with Aubrey's hair, then rocked her hips and made Aubrey groan, "and out of you."

Aubrey continued to use her knees to supported Kinsey's back. She ran her hands down petite arms and whispered, "You've changed me." Peering up, she gave her lover a bittersweet smile.

Kinsey ducked her head and kissed Aubrey, who whimpered from the tenderness. After the kiss, she brushed their lips together and murmured, "I hope for the better." She cupped Aubrey's cheek and held her gaze. "Soon you'll be free. You can start your life."

Aubrey swallowed and traced her fingers up Kinsey's arm to her neck, following the collarbone. "Come with me, Kinsey."

Whimpering, Kinsey dropped her head lower until their foreheads touched together. She gathered Aubrey's hands into hers and squeezed them almost painfully.

"I'll take you wherever you wish or find you a peaceful farm to settle on. We can raise our child together." Aubrey closed her eyes tighter as the happy fantasy played out in her head. "It wouldn't be a grand house, but it would be home, together."

Kinsey whined and hooked her hands behind Aubrey's head. Then her warm tears fell onto Aubrey's cheek. "I'm sorry."

Aubrey slid her arms around Kinsey and tightened them, trying not to be too hard. "Please," she pleaded, low and soft so no one heard an Alpha begging an Omega.

"I wish I could go with you," Kinsey whispered, her voice cracking and her features broken when she lifted her head. "I would be happy with such a life."

Aubrey growled, but not at Kinsey. She cursed their different lives that dictated who they could be and who they could be with. Over the days, she had grown close to Kinsey and could almost touch a life that she thought was only a dream. But Kinsey's sense of duty to her kingdom and family was stronger. She respected it enough to not mark Kinsey, who needed to choose her path.

Kinsey pulled Aubrey's head forward into her chest and murmured soft sounds.

For a moment, Aubrey was stiff against her lover. She was lost in her shame and inability to convince Kinsey of a life together. Aubrey's realization that she had a beautiful future just outside her grasp crushed her in the chest. A guttural howl broke free and Kinsey whimpered against her, clutching her harder. Every tear that fell from the Alpha's eyes was a broken hope for what she could have had with Kinsey.

"Sssh," Kinsey coaxed in a cracked voice. "Everything will be okay." She stroked Aubrey's hair and tried using her sweet pheromones to calm Aubrey, but it was too late.

Aubrey cried out again, growling and rumbling in defeat. She hid her face in Kinsey's chest and held onto her for what felt like the last time. Soon she would have nothing except for her wretched freedom that she earned by impregnating the princess of the Kingdom of Tharnstone. Within months, a baby would be born without its sire.

In reaction to Aubrey's anguish, Kinsey's tears fell onto Aubrey's head, and she echoed Aubrey's sobs. She twisted her fingers into blond hair and whispered, "I swear you'll see your child."

Our child! Aubrey screamed, then rocked their joined bodies. She gasped for air and inhaled Kinsey's soft scent that seeped into her strained muscles. After a moment, Aubrey panted a few times and loosened her grip on her lover.

Kinsey nuzzled Aubrey's head, then continued to run her fingers through Aubrey's strands. She purred low and used her pheromones to ease the last of Aubrey's distress. "Take to me bed?" she asked while wiping the trail of tears from Aubrey's cheeks.

Aubrey took a deep breath and nodded. Soon their time together would end. They expected at first light to be separated, either voluntarily or by force. Their last hours together would be difficult but would mean everything to them.

With gentleness, Aubrey extracted herself from Kinsey, then shifted onto her knees. She scooped Kinsey up, stood, and adjusted her small lover in her arms. Once they were in bed, Aubrey made love to Kinsey for the rest of the night until they exhausted each other. The few hours of sleep didn't prepare Aubrey for the next cold days.

* * *

At dawn, Aubrey and Kinsey were startled from their sleep by Gerald's loud arrival. He ignored their nudity and Aubrey's Alpha posturing, instead snapping at them to get dressed or covered. Aubrey had nothing to wear, not caring about it. But she picked up Kinsey's forgotten nightgown and helped her put it on in a hurry.

Gerald explained that King Wilmont was on his way with a handful of guards, prepared to separate them after a full day of hearing the nonstop screaming. The couple's mixed scents had permeated the outside hallway, spread across the second floor, and even crept down to the ground floor. There wasn't anyone in the castle unaware of Kinsey and Aubrey's mating.

Upon hearing the marching of boots, Gerald bolted out of the room and prepared to delay the entourage a few seconds so Kinsey could finish getting dressed. His voice echoed in the hall but was overpowered by King Wilmont.

Kinsey urged Aubrey to at least use a fur, but when her father burst into the room, she stepped in front of Aubrey. She blocked everyone's view of Aubrey's nude form, almost. Kinsey argued with her father, but failed to get any more privacy with Aubrey.

Instead, Wilmont snapped at the guards to take Aubrey away to the dungeons. He smirked when Aubrey resisted, still driven by her rut and need to protect Kinsey.

Two guards went down after Aubrey tossed them. But she stilled after Kinsey came to her and asked her to go with the guards. Aubrey puffed up and glared at the bruised guards before she focused on Kinsey, who used her pheromones to settle everyone in the room.

Wilmont folded his arms and grunted when Aubrey, an Alpha, heeded Kinsey's wishes.

A guard snatched Aubrey's forearm, but she jerked it free and glanced one last time at Kinsey. She didn't like the heaviness in her chest or the worry in Kinsey's features. But she allowed the guards to pull her arms up and shackle her again, still a fucking slave.

Marching forward, Aubrey paused near Wilmont, who lifted an eyebrow after he visually appraised Aubrey's bigger cock size. She growled and bared her teeth at him but noticed Kinsey had an amused look. After a huff, she was shoved out of the room. Walking through the castle, several people jumped aside and giggled or whispered about Aubrey's Alpha nature. She could tell they no longer doubted her abilities, and it fueled her Alpha.

In the dungeon, she was shoved into the same tiny space as the first day she arrived at the castle. Later she was tossed fresh clothes that fit her better than the earlier set. She found that the cloth rubbed against the sensitive head of her hard cock. Her rut would stay with her for a few more days, just as Kinsey's heat would linger.

Aubrey had no idea how long she paced the dungeon, but it had to be days. She received meals and drinks while other prisoners came and went from the cells. The dungeons reeked worse than last time, but her sense of smell was stronger during a rut.

One day the prison guards set up the hose and started pumping water through it. This time, Aubrey didn't mind the rush of cold water against her raging body. She snarled and snapped at the guard who brushed her down with soapy water. After they left the cell, she flung the wet hair from her face and tossed the wet clothes into the aisle. Within the hour, she was given clean attire that felt less itchy and smelled pleasant.

Three guards returned, opened the cell, and shackled her wrists together. She was taken from the dungeon and escorted to the great hall, which was lined with several soldiers. The base of the dais was several steps in front of her;

prison guards flanked her on all sides. The door to her left opened, and King Wilmont emerged first, followed by Kinsey.

Wilmont and Kinsey climbed the dais and stood in front of two thrones meant for the king and queen. Kinsey stood to her father's left and a step behind him. Her gaze was fixed on Aubrey; her features were drained and eyes puffy.

Aubrey wanted to rush to her lover and comfort her, but the guards would stop her. She rumbled low until Wilmont spoke up.

"Princess Kinsey of the Kingdom of Tharnstone is with child," Wilmont announced. He stared with dark eyes at Aubrey, matching her Alpha with his own. "Your duty is done, *degen*." He signaled a prison guard, who unlocked the shackles and removed them. "You are now free to go."

Aubrey looked from Wilmont to Kinsey, who was biting her lip and cupping her stomach. She was pulled toward Kinsey until a guard blocked her path.

"Escort the *degen* beyond the castle bridge," Wilmont ordered, his voice thin with patience.

Kinsey shook her head at Aubrey and mouthed *go* to her.

Aubrey remained until the guards hooked her arms and forced her back. She snarled several times but didn't lose eye contact with Kinsey until they were too far apart. With a low bark, she jerked free and turned from the nobles, accepting her new future. She followed the guards from the great hall but stole a last glance and discovered Kinsey had walked off the dais, following Aubrey's wake until Wilmont called to her.

Closing her eyes, Aubrey left the great hall and went with the guards into the inner ward. The sun was midway in the eastern sky, giving her plenty of time to figure out a plan. As they crossed the bridge, Aubrey glanced over her shoulder at Tharnstone Castle, which held complex, messy, and beautiful memories.

Once on the other side, the soldiers at the guardhouse allowed her to pass, and then her way back to Kinsey was cut off by iron gates. She held onto the resealed gates and watched the three castle guards walk down the bridge. Lifting her gaze, she studied the emblem of the House of Wymarc on the waving flags on the castle. She banged her hands against the iron gates and considered climbing them, but she would be dead in seconds.

"Keep moving, *degen*," a soldier ordered and halfway unsheathed his sword in warning.

Aubrey growled at him but listened and walked away from the gate. She stepped onto the street and stood there for a moment, unsure which way to go. For once, she had nothing except her freedom, and it settled heavily on her shoulders. After a sigh, she walked in the same direction from which she had arrived in Coldhelm. With only the clothes on her body, she was unsure how to survive without an owner to give her food, clothing, and shelter. Even though the days were warm enough, the nights could hit freezing temperatures. Perhaps freedom didn't out rate bad food, tattered clothes, and leaky roofs.

As she walked the street, she noticed people looking at her differently now. A few came too close and sniffed her, trying to figure out her breed. She growled at them to back off, amazed that they listened to her for once. But then one person in heavy bronze armor emerged from the crowd and cut her off.

Aubrey rumbled low and held Gerald's concerned features for a long moment. She let out a sigh and asked, "Is she okay?"

Gerald dipped his head and replied, "She is okay." He canted his head and shifted closer, able to lower his voice. "But she is concerned for you." Reaching into his cloak, he produced a leather coin purse that was plump. "You are to take this."

Aubrey backed off and said, "I don't wish to be paid."

"It's not a payment. It's a gift." Gerald squeezed the bag, and the coins tapped together. "She said you would refuse but that you would understand her fears for your well-being." He held out the heavy purse and said, "If you don't take it, she will worry over you until she is sick, which is not acceptable for a pregnant Omega."

At the mention of Kinsey's pregnancy, Aubrey whimpered and looked away before she nodded at the truth. She swallowed down her pride and accepted the money that might equal the amount her father had been given when he sold her into slavery. "Tell her thank you."

Gerald nodded, then reached into his cloak again. "And this is from me." He showed a sheathed dagger. "I hope you don't need it, but you may." When Aubrey opened her mouth to argue, he slapped it to her chest, held it there, and grunted at her grumbling. "You're welcome."

Aubrey huffed but wrapped her other hand around the sheathed blade and smiled at him when he let go of it.

"Where will you go?" Gerald asked after he took a step back.

Aubrey pursed her lips and looked to her right, toward the south. "Lower Light," she whispered, then turned her attention back to Gerald.

Gerald gave a soft rumble and said, "You have a long journey, then." He took a deep breath, then prepared to depart from Aubrey but hesitated and whispered, "The princess wanted me to remind you that she gave you her word."

Closing her eyes, Aubrey wondered how long it would be before Kinsey could carry out her promise. Would it be two, four, or seven years before she could meet her child? She doubted it would happen before the death of King Wilmont, who guarded his daughter with an iron fist. King Wilmont would live to be a hundred with Aubrey's luck. By then, the child would be an adult who'd have no desire to meet Aubrey. Grappling with her fears, she refused to break down here in front of Gerald and strangers. Though difficult, she blinked away the tears, held Gerald's stoic features, and said, "I know she will, one day."

Chapter 10

Aubrey wiped the sweat off her brow, then raised the sledgehammer and brought it down on the large metal. She continued working the hot metal over the anvil, needing to thin it. This was her first true attempt to forge a practical piece for one of her mentor's customers. The final item had to be one of three wrought iron hinges for the town's church. If she could forge it to the correct size and length, then her mentor would allow her to produce the other two. If Aubrey failed, she would return to forging horseshoes and nails until her technique improved.

Off to the right, her mentor Rudyard was busy talking to a potential client, who was a noble outside the town. Aubrey heard bits and pieces of the conversation about the noble's desire to have a special, ornate decoration made for his great hall. Rudyard's legacy as a fine blacksmith in Lower Light had grown over the years.

Much to Aubrey's luck, when she arrived in Lower Light six months ago, Rudyard had been in search of an apprentice, especially a striker. At first, Rudyard had brushed off Aubrey's request to apprentice with him, until he tested her with a sledgehammer. He had a bright glow in his eyes after Aubrey demonstrated her strength. A driven, strong Alpha in his forge worked to his advantage.

By midafternoon, Aubrey completed the hinge and waited for Rudyard to check her work. She wiped the sweat from her palms onto her leather apron, grabbed a tankard of water, and gulped it. Near the end, a solid smack came between her shoulders, and she choked on her last mouthful of water.

"Keep it up, striker." Rudyard flashed her a smile and punched her bare shoulder, then was beckoned by a customer on the other side of the forge.

Aubrey wiped her face but grinned to herself after noticing the iron hinge on the workbench hadn't been tossed to the scrap pile. Glancing at the sun, she decided there wasn't enough time to complete another hinge, and it could wait until tomorrow. There were a few orders for horseshoes that she could handle over the next two hours before they closed the forge.

Going behind a different bench, Aubrey grabbed her satchel and pulled out an apple and jerky from inside. She leaned against the bench, ate her snack, and watched the locals mill about in the street. Today was busy and would become busier when the fall festival began. Like every day since her first day as a freewoman, she thought about Kinsey and rubbed the round, heavy metal pendent that rested against her collarbone. It was stamped with a dragon on one side and a woman's face on the reverse side. A tiny hole had been punched through the top for a chain. Aubrey wore it so the dragon faced forward while the woman was forever kissing her skin. The pendent had been tucked inside the coin purse that Gerald gave her many months ago.

With a sigh, Aubrey did a mental count of how much time was left before the baby was born. As of today, Aubrey estimated that Kinsey had three to three and half months left. Throughout the Kingdom of Tharnstone, it was no secret that Princess Kinsey was pregnant and expecting a child at the beginning of the new year. What stirred the rumor mill was who sired the child and whether the royal family would ever give a name. Aubrey often overheard conversations between people in the streets about the royal family and the mysterious pregnancy. The nobles tended to be the ones who discussed it the most, while the common folk were more excited for the birth.

Aubrey struggled to ignore it or not growl at people discussing it. As the final months of pregnancy approached, her mood grew darker and only her apprenticeship with

Rudyard gave her direction. If she wasn't learning at the forge, she was rebuilding the cabin home on Rudyard's property that he allowed her to stay in as part of her pay.

Tossing the apple core, Aubrey picked up her gloves and returned to work. She focused on producing horseshoes for one of their regular customers, who bred and trained fine horses for sale. While heating up more metal, she spotted two sisters about her age. They were both Betas who'd been curious about Aubrey from the first day she started working, and they often stopped by to chat. But Aubrey used work as an excuse to keep them at arm's length.

Today, the one Beta girl Edda left her sister's side and came over to the forge alone. She wore a soft pink top that showed off her generous cleavage. "Hello, striker."

Aubrey rotated the metal inside the forge, then worked the bellows to encourage the fire. When Edda and her sister Gylda first introduced themselves, Aubrey withheld her name from them and told them that she was the blacksmith's striker. Since then, the sisters used it like a pet name.

"You're looking hotter than normal," Edda teased, grinning at Aubrey's sweaty features.

Aubrey rumbled and used the backside of her gloved hand to rid herself of the droplets on her brow. With a whip of her head, she flung the short strands from her sticky face. "It's a busy day."

"Perhaps you should come to the tavern after work today." Edda indicated her sister over her shoulder and said, "Gylda and I will be there." She hooked her arms behind her back and rocked on her feet.

"I have projects to do at home," Aubrey brushed off.

Edda pouted and argued, "Don't you ever take time for fun?"

Aubrey eyed Edda over the top of the forge before she pulled out the metal with the tongs. She held the bright metal over the anvil, picked up a hammer, and prepared to forge it into a horseshoe shape.

Edda sighed loud enough to be heard over the strikes. "We'll still be there if you change your mind." She coed for good measure, then left Aubrey to her work.

Sighing, Aubrey shook her head and returned her focus to her job.

"Those sisters stop here almost every day," Rudyard said from his spot at the other work bench. He was writing or sketching something for a future job. "Why do you torment them so?"

Aubrey rolled her eyes and replied, "I'm not interested."

"They clearly are." Rudyard looked across the forge and stared hard at Aubrey. "You are a strange Alpha." He returned his focus to the journal and muttered, "Most Alphas would have fucked those girls twenty times over by now."

Aubrey grunted and couldn't deny that Edda and Gylda were beautiful. They came from a middle-class family and were fascinated by Aubrey being an Alpha. The fact she was learning blacksmithing added to her mystique and appeal. But neither Edda nor Gylda was who Aubrey wanted in her bed nor crying out in passion under her. As much as Alphas were known for only thinking with their little heads, Aubrey was different, and Kinsey had chosen her for that reason.

By late afternoon, Rudyard started to shut down the forge, like other businesses around them. He encouraged Aubrey to finish the current horseshoe, which she hardened it and tossed into the bin for shoeing another day.

"Can I help you?" Rudyard asked, walking to the right corner of the forging stand.

Aubrey heard Rudyard speaking to another customer behind her, but she was packing her few things in the satchel. She and Rudyard often walked together to the property he owned just outside of town. Sometimes Rudyard would invite her to go with him to one of the taverns, but she always refused the offer.

"I wish to speak to your apprentice," the customer replied, his tone firm.

Aubrey turned and shouldered the satchel on her left side. In the dim sunlight, she couldn't make out the man's face.

Rudyard huffed and stepped aside as Aubrey joined them. "You're popular today, striker."

Aubrey grunted at the remark and slipped between two workbenches. With a scowl, she neared the stranger, whose features started to bring back difficult but special memories. "Gerald."

Gerald was unfamiliar without his bronze armor. Instead, he wore a black leather cuirass that went past his hips. His cloak was a deep red and almost hid his sword, other than the distinct hilt. "Hello, Aubrey."

Aubrey's first instinct was Kinsey, who could be endangered if Gerald was here. Her heart lurched at the idea, and she opened her mouth but was cut off.

"She's safe," Gerald said, holding out a hand to calm her. He rumbled low and whispered, "She sent me."

Aubrey peered over her shoulder when Rudyard came up to her. She didn't want her mentor to overhear her conversation with Gerald, having kept most of her past to herself.

"I can wait for you or—"

"Don't wait for me," Aubrey said, offering him a smile. "I'll find my way home."

Rudyard gave a firm nod, glanced once at Gerald, and left the forge in the setting sunlight.

Alone now, Aubrey turned to Gerald and demanded, "Why did she send you? Is she okay? Is she—"

"Yes." Gerald waited until Aubrey stilled herself, then he asked, "Do you have time to share a table at the Red Bearclaw Inn?"

Aubrey bit down her questions, not liking that Gerald was here rather than with Kinsey. She huffed but nodded and joined him on the walk to the inn. He was probably staying at the inn, which also served food and drink. During the walk, Aubrey did her best to hold back her questions and kept her hands to herself rather than shake answers out of Gerald.

The inn's tavern was busy, especially with strangers. In two days the town would be abuzz with locals and out-of-towners for the autumn festival. Lower Light was known for the excitement that the Apple Harvest Festival brought to the region, especially the cider.

"This way," Gerald said, seeming to already have a table in mind.

Aubrey weaved between people, bumping into a few, who growled at her. She snarled back, showed her teeth, and they submitted to her Alpha dominance in a heartbeat. Since being released from slavery, she had learned what it meant to be an Alpha in the social ladder. Even though she was poor and free, her status as an Alpha gave her some leverage with idiots. They respected her power that she had once bottled as a former slave.

Gerald came to a table in the far corner and stepped aside, hand on his sword hilt.

Aubrey faltered when a petite woman with dark, wavy hair cascading from under a hood and piercing blue eyes peered up at her. The Alpha's breath caught as she stared at a ghost or a trick; she was unsure. But then the woman stood from the chair and revealed her protruding belly. "Kinsey," Aubrey rasped.

Kinsey smiled and cupped her stomach. "Hello, Aubrey." With her other hand, she pulled the cloak's hood off.

Crossing the space in two wide steps, Aubrey dropped the satchel and gathered Kinsey into her arms, needing to feel that her lover was here. She inhaled Kinsey's special, sweet scent and whimpered as it filled her again. Her heart felt less heavy, and she fought the burn in her eyes. "Kinsey," she purred and nuzzled soft, pale skin.

Kinsey echoed Aubrey's sounds, and her cheeks were damp when Aubrey looked at her. She smiled at Aubrey, and her voice was rough. "Can you sit?"

Aubrey stumbled over her words but managed a nod and took the chair next to Kinsey while Gerald sat on the opposite side of the table. "I…." Her heart was wild and loud in her ears, outweighing the tavern's crowd. "Are you okay?"

Kinsey softened at the care, touched Aubrey's hand, and replied, "Yes, but I am worn out."

Gerald huffed and said, "We should have rested in Wind Cliff for the night." He ignored Kinsey's eye roll and looked to Aubrey. "But the princess was much too excited to see you."

This time, Kinsey blushed and fired off a glower at Gerald. "I thought you said you would sit at the bar while I visit with Aubrey?"

Lifting an eyebrow, Aubrey looked between the pair and admired their playful nature that reminded her of siblings.

After a gruff sound, Gerald stood and slipped past Aubrey but not without patting her on the shoulder.

Aubrey centered her full attention on Kinsey and stared at her as if waiting for her to vanish from the chair.

Her mind flew in every direction, and she was unsure what to ask first. She nearly felt dizzy and touched her forehead. But Kinsey's delicate touch anchored Aubrey, and she swallowed as the initial rush washed away, leaving her disjointed. "Why... How...." She shook her head, still fighting for which question to ask first.

Kinsey blinked a few times when her eyes glistened over. She curled her fingers over Aubrey's larger hand and whispered, "I'm sorry I'm here without sending word first, but everything happened very suddenly."

"What happened?" Aubrey asked. Just as Kinsey opened her mouth, a barmaid arrived at their table to offer them food and drinks. Aubrey held back a growl after being interrupted, but her sharp pheromones made the jumpy barmaid stutter.

"I-I'm s-sorry I—"

"It's okay." Kinsey smiled at the barmaid, her own scent calming the tense situation and unraveling Aubrey's annoyance. "Are you hungry?" She looked to Aubrey, then touched her large belly. "I am." She crinkled her nose and whispered, "Hungry for two."

At the reminder of Kinsey's pregnancy, Aubrey's natural need to care for her pregnant lover came to life. "We'll each take a dinner, drinks, and fruit." She charmed the barmaid with a smile, then turned back to Kinsey when they were alone again. "How did you travel here?" She didn't notice guards, knights, or Kinsey's family.

"By foot and rides with merchants," Kinsey replied.

Aubrey read between the lines and whispered, "You ran away."

Kinsey leaned back in the chair, seeming to find relief from the comfortable position. "I left." After a sigh, she whispered, "Under the cover of darkness, I'll admit."

Aubrey huffed and concluded that Kinsey had used the hidden passage in the undercroft. "Does anyone in your family know?"

"Agatha. Although she is unaware that I traveled here to Lower Light," Kinsey replied, her voice soft. She was distant for a moment, then had a weak smile. "Gerald and I left late one night nearly a fortnight ago. We used the hidden passage in the undercroft that leads to the underside of the castle bridge. On the underside of the bridge, there's a walkway that took us across the rift, then into another tunnel that let us out a few streets away from the guardhouse at the bridge gate."

Aubrey tilted her head and said, "You know that passage well."

"Yes." Kinsey grinned and whispered, "As a child, I was very bored and explored every nook and cranny of the castle."

After a grunt, Aubrey leaned against the table and studied Kinsey in the lamp light. Despite Kinsey's having traveled for so long, she was beautiful, glowing, and healthy appearing, other than the darkness under her eyes. Aubrey wanted to pull Kinsey into her lap and touch every part of her body, especially her round stomach. Her Alpha was humming with excitement and even pride.

Kinsey parted her lips, but the barmaid returned with their drinks. She sipped on hers and sighed with contentment, then stared into the tankard. "I wanted to leave with you six months ago," she whispered. "Every day after you left, it became more difficult to stay in Coldhelm." Lifting her head, she gazed into Aubrey, reading her. "I fought harder to stay, for the kingdom's future."

"Then what happened?" Aubrey leaned closer, almost into Kinsey's space. She tried to respect their distance, unsure what Kinsey might be comfortable with. Already Kinsey's sweet scent was affecting her, but she ignored her Alpha's rising hunger.

Kinsey frowned and stared at Aubrey, at a loss for a moment. "I snapped." A growl started in the back of her throat that startled Aubrey. "At first, my father would make comments that he hoped the child wasn't a degenerate."

Aubrey responded with her own snarl. She saw dots of red in her vision when she thought of King Wilmont. *That arrogant bastard*, she seethed.

"The remarks turned into threats as time went on," Kinsey said, heat in her voice. "He swore the child would be banished and not carry the Wymarc name." She bared her teeth between her growly explanation. "Then it turned into threats to kill the child."

Aubrey swallowed a furious howl, knowing it would stir the entire tavern. Already people were looking in their direction due to the strong pheromones pouring off her. She pulled away, bent forward, and curled her hands into fists. Her growl was low but violent, leaving her body trembling and sweating.

Kinsey huffed and gulped for air, then said, "He wanted my agreement that I would allow Luca to impregnate me if our child was a degenerate."

Closing her eyes, Aubrey paced her breathing, but Kinsey leaned in closer to her and released soothing pheromones even though the conversation was ugly. "Did you agree?" she asked, hearing her voice shake with fire.

"No," Kinsey snapped, then puffed. "I left."

After a deep breath, Aubrey straightened up and looked at her former lover. Her rage settled, for now. There was more to the story by the worry on Kinsey's face.

"I struggled for so long," Kinsey whispered. "Every day I asked myself why did I want to leave. I worried that I was giving into my Omega instincts rather than doing what was logical. So I fought with myself. I forced myself to stay, thinking it would get easier."

Aubrey rumbled but let Kinsey continue to vent about their months apart.

"I believed that I needed to stay so I could rule my father's kingdom. If I left, I was being selfish." Kinsey bit her lip and bowed her head closer to Aubrey. "But then one day I realized that I was no different from you when you first came to the castle." She peered up, eyes watery, and whispered, "I was beating down my Omega."

With a sigh, Aubrey agreed with Kinsey's epiphany; she had watched Kinsey battle her Omega self. She suspected that King Wilmont had started retraining Kinsey to suppress her Omega in hopes she could rule the Kingdom of Tharnstone without distraction or weakness. A marked Omega was a useless one in King Wilmont's eyes. But his plan to ensure an heir had backfired on him, because Aubrey triggered Kinsey's Omega to life.

"I don't want to be constantly at war with myself," Kinsey whispered. "Not anymore."

Aubrey rumbled in agreement and nodded. "This is part of who we are."

Kinsey smiled and touched Aubrey's knee, squeezing it. The heat of her hand warmed more than just Aubrey's skin. "You changed me too, Aubrey." She clutched Aubrey harder and whispered, "You helped me see that there are good Alphas, nothing like my father."

Aubrey growled and flashed her teeth, then chuffed before saying, "There are Alphas who wish to lift their Omegas, not tear them down." She wanted to say more, but the barmaid returned with the meals. At Kinsey's big eyes, she grinned and watched Kinsey eat first. Her former lover was famished, and it pleased Aubrey to see her eating well.

"If you truly wish to be queen, then you should be queen," Aubrey said between bites of turkey. "If your heart isn't there, then you will be miserable, and so will your people." She pushed around the peas and whispered, "Your people have had enough misery."

Kinsey grunted but studied Aubrey while she turned the fork in her hand. "If I choose to be queen, would you consider being at my side?"

Aubrey choked her on mouthful of vegetables, but a tiny pea was stuck in her throat. She coughed and patted her chest several times.

Kinsey gave a soft whine, clapped Aubrey's back, and pushed the tankard closer.

After swallowing the weak wine, Aubrey cleared her throat and raised an eyebrow at Kinsey. She rumbled and pursed her lips after a second, longer rumble. "Can you have both?"

Shrugging, Kinsey speared a few sliced potatoes on the fork and replied, "I would be queen. I could have anything."

"But a degenerate Alpha as a mate?"

Kinsey snarled low and corrected, "She-Alpha."

Aubrey grinned and canted her head, then turned back to her meal. "I would consider it." She ate more turkey but was ready for whatever else Kinsey might say. Her answer brought a slight smile to Kinsey's features.

"What if I didn't want to be queen?" Kinsey waited until Aubrey swallowed, then asked, "Would you still consider being at my side? I would have little to my name once my dear father writes me off."

"I said I would care for you," Aubrey whispered, but her tone was firm. "I meant it."

Kinsey shrugged and played with the last few peas on her plate. "You could have a sweet Beta or cute Omega back at home."

"Do I smell like I have one?" Aubrey asked, leaning in closer so Kinsey could scent her.

After a deep inhale, Kinsey replied, "You smell like iron and fire."

Aubrey huffed, finished the last mouthful of potatoes, and pushed the plate away, ignoring the bread. She gazed at Kinsey, and a slow throb started in her cock.

Kinsey leaned in, straining against her belly. "And you smell like an Alpha with a hard cock."

With a snarl, Aubrey said, "You haven't lost your crassness, Princess."

Grabbing Aubrey's thigh, Kinsey dug her nails through the leather pants and whispered, "I never said my mouth was as refined as my curtsy, Alpha."

Aubrey's body hummed from the flirting. She would have picked up Kinsey, set her in her lap, and kissed her senseless if they weren't in public. The longtime pressure in her chest was easing the more they spent time together. *But this won't be permanent*, she reminded herself. Kinsey might be considering a life other than being a ruler, but it was no guarantee. Her thoughts were distracted by the return of the barmaid, who dropped off a plate of fruit and took the dirty plates.

Kinsey snatched a few slices of red and green apples, humming as she enjoyed every bite.

Aubrey took a handful of grapes, popping them into her mouth one by one. For a moment, she admired Kinsey and wished they were alone rather than in public. Perhaps they were better off in public or else Aubrey wouldn't control herself. "What do you wish to do now?" she asked.

Kinsey slumped against the chair and nibbled on a slice of melon. "I refuse to return to Tharnstone Castle as long as my father is alive."

"Even if the child is an Omega or Alpha?"

Kinsey rumbled and folded her arms after putting the melon rind on the plate. "Even then." She vibrated with thunder, which was new for her. Her Omega instincts were on the surface, and her sole focus was the unborn child in her belly. "I will not let him manipulate my child's life."

Aubrey smiled despite the situation. All she could smell was a protective Omega rising within Kinsey. She was driven wild by it but clamped down on her desire before she made a mistake.

"I don't want her or him to go through what I have been through." Kinsey's gaze shifted to the plate of fruit, staring at it for a minute. She sighed and ran a hand through her hair before focusing on Aubrey again. "But Father will search for me."

Aubrey blew out a growly breath, then touched Kinsey's knee. "Stay with me." She leaned closer and squeezed the softness under her hand. "I don't have much, but I have—"

"You have everything," Kinsey cut off, then grabbed Aubrey's hand. "I don't have to stay long if you—"

"Stay," Aubrey repeated, firm and with conviction. "Have the birth here, then decide what to do." She wanted Kinsey to stay indefinitely, at least with her, whether it was in Lower Light or another place, but as long as they were together.

Kinsey nodded and whispered, "I didn't come to Lower Light to impose myself on you. I wished to see you."

"I know." Aubrey's lips tugged with a smile. "Just as you know I will care for you." Her eyes lowered to Kinsey's stomach. "Both of you." Even though she was promising to provide for Kinsey and their future child, she was no fool to the reality that Kinsey was capable on her own. Kinsey was educated in math, reading, writing, healing, and other skills that would give her the ability to find work. However, Kinsey was still an Omega who reveled in hearing an Alpha willing to care for her. Aubrey was grateful that Kinsey was willing to accept it, at least for now.

Gerald returned, interrupting their conversation. He appeared tired but content after a good meal. "It is late, my princess."

Kinsey nodded, then peered up at her personal guard. "I plan to return with Aubrey for the night." She smiled at his downturned expression and said, "You'll have the room all to yourself, and you'll sleep better without my snoring."

Gerald grumbled and shifted on his boots, then opened his mouth only to be silenced with a look. "Very well. I shall bring down your things." He returned a few minutes later with a leather bag and handed it to Aubrey. "Rest well, my princess. I will see you in the morning." He turned to Aubrey and said, "Good luck." He earned a backhanded smack to his arm from Kinsey but said goodnight and left.

Aubrey eyed Gerald's receding figure and reminded herself to thank him later for protecting Kinsey. He was dedicated to her, and Aubrey admired him for his loyalty. He was better than most Alphas. "Are you ready?"

After taking the last bunch of grapes, Kinsey stood up and asked, "Is it a long walk?" She covered her yawn with a hand.

"Not too long," Aubrey replied. She fished out the coin from her satchel that she'd left on the floor earlier and paid for the food. With both bags across her chest, she led the way through the busy tavern and allowed Kinsey to go out the door first. Just as she turned, a familiar Beta approached her.

"Sister!"

Aubrey smiled big and greeted, "Hello, little brother." She held out her arm, which he took and yanked her into a quick hug. "You're out late."

"The night is young, and you're getting old."

Rumbling, Aubrey turned to Kinsey, who had an awed look. "This is Kinsey." She knew better than to announce that Kinsey was the princess, if anyone would even believe it. Holding out her hand to the Beta, she said, "This is my brother, Corin."

Kinsey looked between the two siblings before smiling at Corin. Coming closer, she exchanged a handshake with him, then cupped her stomach. "Younger brother?"

"A couple of years," Corin replied, then he lifted an eyebrow at Kinsey. "I don't believe you're from here." Her brother's smile was charming and his golden hair appealing – his boyish features often gave him what he sought.

"No." Kinsey pursed her lips and said, "I'm from Coldhelm, actually."

Aubrey saw the gears turning in Corin's head. She hadn't told her brother what happened to her in the Tharnstone Castle. The details about her freedom were brief and left untouched because Aubrey didn't wish to discuss it. In her mind, her past as a slave was done. "Kinsey arrived this afternoon and is tired from her travel," she said, curbing Corin's curiosity before he pushed for more details.

Corin held up his hands and said, "Say no more." He smiled at Kinsey. "Hopefully we'll have another time to talk." He smirked at Aubrey and teased, "If my sister's big Alpha self doesn't chase you off."

After a huff, Aubrey pushed her brother toward the tavern and said, "Goodnight, brother."

Corin turned as the pair started down the street. "Goodnight, ladies."

Kinsey glanced over her shoulder while she followed alongside Aubrey. "Your brother?"

"Mmmm."

After a chuckled, Kinsey asked, "Have you seen your other siblings or parents?"

"Only Corin." Aubrey bit her lip and reflected on the first month she had arrived in Lower Light. She had seen one sister and one brother from a distance but hadn't approached them. She had run into Corin in a pub. He had hugged her to the point that her ribs almost cracked in half. To be reconnected with him was a blessing. As a kid, she had been closest to him of everyone in the family. They had spent a lot of time catching up and then always shared a meal once a week since then.

Aubrey's parents lived on the same farm as in her youth, and two of her siblings continued to live with them, caring for them and the farm. Her other sisters and brothers had married and moved to neighboring towns, except for Corin. Her family was aware of her return, but they steered clear of her. Aubrey hadn't approached any of them but was happy to rekindle a relationship with Corin.

"Will you see your parents eventually?" Kinsey walked closer and adjusted the cloak around her body.

Aubrey frowned and glanced at Kinsey before turning down another street that would take them out of town. "If I do, it will only be to see my mother."

Kinsey dipped her head in understanding and touched Aubrey's forearm in comfort. "I'm glad you found Corin again."

Softening, Aubrey nodded and said, "I am too." With him back in her life, she realized how much she missed having family. Corin told her what their brothers and sisters were doing whenever she asked him. It was enough for now.

Tilting her head, Aubrey asked, "What became of Luca and Eldon?" She heard Kinsey's soft rumble.

"After several discussions, Luca agreed to join my father's army." Kinsey had argued heavily with her father about Luca's fate, not wanting him put to death. She cared for him and felt he deserved his freedom. Sighing, she said, "He will earn his freedom in three years, provided he doesn't die in the meantime."

"And Eldon?"

Kinsey groused and shook her head. "I argued for his freedom with Father, but Eldon had little to no value in Father's eyes."

"He was killed?"

"He was returned to Sir Philip, who then sold Eldon to a slave owner." Kinsey gave a pained sound and whispered, "The slave owner has several coal mines."

Aubrey frowned after learning Eldon's fate, which would be a slow death or a sudden but painful death. Her disdain for King Wilmont seemed to have no end, but she refused to carry her hatred through life like she had before meeting Kinsey. One day, she would let go of what happened to her as a child and young adult, but it would take time.

"How do you like being a blacksmith?"

Aubrey chuckled and replied, "I'm a striker." She and Kinsey passed the last home, following the road out of town. The night was cool, signaling the onset of autumn. The moon was close to full and would provide them with light.

"An apprentice, then?" After Aubrey's nod, Kinsey rumbled low and said, "I would like to see the forge."

"Tomorrow." Aubrey was making plans now that Kinsey was here. For a moment, it jarred her how her future had changed direction again. There was no guarantee that Kinsey would stay long term, but Aubrey felt lighter. She wanted it to last, but Kinsey seemed unsure about her plans, and that made Aubrey's stomach sink. Her wandering thoughts were cut off by Kinsey's grabbing her arm.

"Thank you," Kinsey said after hooking her arm through Aubrey's own. "For taking me in after everything that happened between us."

Aubrey rumbled low and long before she sighed. "What happened in Tharnstone Castle was confusing at the time but beautiful." She held Kinsey's gaze for a beat but focused on the remaining stroll to the farm. "I've had much time to reflect on it since I was freed."

"So have I," Kinsey murmured and squeezed Aubrey's bicep, then halted their walk. She turned to Aubrey and said, "I am sorry for what you went through, all of it."

Clutching Kinsey's hips, Aubrey lowered her head closer and whispered, "Do not apologize for your father's doing."

Kinsey cupped Aubrey's warm cheeks and argued, "I am still responsible. I went along with it."

Aubrey huffed and shook her head. "Did he give you a choice? A real choice?"

After a sigh, Kinsey bit her lip and withheld her answer. "I still—" She was silenced by Aubrey's lips in a tender kiss that grew heated in seconds. Moaning, she trailed her hands behind Aubrey's head and twisted her fingers in golden strands.

The kiss was meant to be brief, but Aubrey heard a soft sob between them. She whimpered in return and pulled Kinsey against her, feeling the protruding belly push into her. Their kiss grew harder and desperate to consume each other after being apart for so long. Aubrey gasped afterward and ran a thumb across Kinsey's swollen lip. Her cock pulsed with need, and she could have taken Kinsey against a tree. But it wasn't safe in the dark, on the road, and with Kinsey both pregnant and tired.

With linked hands, Aubrey continued the walk to the farm and directed them down a dirt road after a minute. Their conversation and kiss brought back memories from their last day together in Tharnstone Castle. The sex had left Aubrey wanting for months, but she never gave in to any urges.

It was also the first time Aubrey had been in a rut. Even today, she still felt a measure of disgrace that her rut had been induced by medicine. It cheapened and charred her first experience, even more so because it was with Kinsey. Since then, Aubrey had considered whether or not Kinsey's heat was also forced by medicine and suspected it was, so that Kinsey had the best chance to become pregnant. Even so, Aubrey swelled with excitement when she looked at Kinsey's expanding belly.

"I wish I could see the farm," Kinsey said as they neared the shadowy farmhouse.

Aubrey rumbled and promised, "Tomorrow." She took them to the right, to a smaller building that glowed under the moonlight. Pausing at the base of the steps, she said, "It's not much." Upon her second day of work with Rudyard, she started rebuilding the cabin-like home on his property. Often Rudyard had to help her, especially when she built the A-frame. But she put much of her energy into it alone. So far, the tiny home had a bedroom, small kitchen space, and sitting area.

"We'll make it work," Kinsey said, smiling and squeezing Aubrey's hand.

Climbing the steps, Aubrey guided Kinsey up and opened the door. While Kinsey waited, Aubrey lit a few lamps and allowed everything to come to light in the small home. She hooked the back of her neck while standing in the open space between the kitchen and sitting area where the fireplace had been built by Rudyard's friend.

Kinsey folded her arms and grinned at Aubrey, who cleared her throat.

"I've been building a dining table." Aubrey indicated the open space to Kinsey's right. "It's in the barn."

"And chairs for it?" Kinsey asked, a teasing tone in her voice.

"Rudyard knows a carpenter that will trade with me." Aubrey felt the heat in her face and wished she had more to offer Kinsey. "This is the bedroom." She brought Kinsey into the next room at the back of the home.

Kinsey followed and stood in the center, turning in the small space. She gazed up at the A-frame ceiling and smiled at it, seeming to like the bare timbers. To the left were empty shelves, a crude stand with a washbasin, and more shelves with a few folded clothes.

Aubrey studied the bed that she had built into a nook. She had used long, cedar boards and nailed them into the wall at either end and into each other. It was platform that allowed for storage underneath it and was easy to put bedding on. But it was only large enough for one person, specifically an Alpha like Aubrey. There was still enough wall space that Aubrey could expand it, but it would take time and supplies.

"I'll sleep on the floor," Aubrey said.

Kinsey turned and showed her wide eyes. "No." She glared and argued, "We can share it."

"There's very little room." Aubrey studied Kinsey's stomach, imagining how much larger it would be by the eighth and ninth months. The bed needed to be enlarged if they were going to share it long term. "I'm used to sleeping on the floor." After building the platform, she had slept on it without any mattress but used two furs, one underneath her and one over her. Only a month ago, she had purchased a mattress that was stuffed with bedstraw. Aubrey's first night on the mattress had been a battle, and it had ended up on the floor a few times since then.

"We'll make do," Kinsey insisted, then turned to Aubrey. "Is there an outhouse?"

Aubrey nodded and replied, "When you go out the door, go to your left, and it's next to the house."

Kinsey rumbled in agreement and said, "Then I will start there." She headed to the front door but paused when Aubrey told her to take the burning lamp beside the door.

Alone for a moment, Aubrey considered how to handle the sleeping arrangements. In Tharnstone Castle, all the beds were oversized and too comfortable in Aubrey's opinion. She had slept several times on the stone floor in the castle, using the blankets to stay warm. Staring at the bed, she knew they'd have to sleep on their sides and pressed together. Aubrey growled as her cock hardened again. Sleep would elude her tonight.

Kinsey's return stirred Aubrey, and she decided to use the outhouse next. She placed Kinsey's satchel on the bed, then excused herself. Aubrey had hoped the short time alone and the fresh air would give her a chance to settle down. But the cabin was alive with Kinsey's honey-like scent that made Aubrey's skin itch.

In the bedroom, Kinsey was buried under the blankets and fur. Her few items had been moved to an empty shelf. She brushed her hair back and watched Aubrey prepare to lie down. "Your hair has grown some."

Aubrey played with it, shoving the longer strands from her face. "I have trouble finding someone to cut it." Her excuse was often that winter was coming, and it could wait until spring. Already the evenings had a slight chill to them.

"Do you wish to keep it short?"

Aubrey kicked off her leather boots, tucking them under a shelf next to her one pair of shoes. She shrugged and considered the question. Slaves and serfs were best known for having short hair, a symbol of their status in society. Once being freed, she should have let it grow out, but she was also an Alpha. It was common for Alphas to keep short hair, even shaving and tattooing their scalps.

"I like it short," Kinsey said.

Aubrey pulled off her gray tunic and set it aside for tomorrow's work. She shimmied out of her leather pants that protected her at the forge. Now only in a breast wrap and undergarments, she was able to wash away today's ash from her exposed skin, especially her face. Behind her, she felt Kinsey's eyes burning into her back. Drying her face, she turned her head sidelong and said, "Perhaps you can cut it, then."

Kinsey chuckled and shifted under the blankets. "I would enjoy that."

Aubrey grinned to herself, then hung the towel on the bar next to the basin. She reached for a fresh knee-length tunic.

"You won't need that," Kinsey said. "Remove your breast band and drawers, then lay with me."

Swallowing, Aubrey chewed on her lip, then returned the tunic to the shelf next to a new pair of underpants. At first, she began to remove the last of her clothing but first turned off the lamps in the house, then returned to the bedroom where one lamp burned on the nightstand. After taking off the undergarments, she crawled under the blankets with Kinsey, who rested on her side and faced Aubrey.

"You will be more comfortable if you turn the other way," Aubrey suggested.

"I know." Kinsey reached under the blankets and collected Aubrey's hands, drawing them to her.

Aubrey sucked in her breath when her palms pressed against Kinsey's bare belly. But her next breath hitched in her throat and she went still.

"She's moving around," Kinsey whispered, holding Aubrey's wrist with one hand and resting the other over Aubrey's fingers. "Can you feel her?"

Continuing to hold her breath, Aubrey was lost in the sensation of the surreal movement in Kinsey's stomach. She sucked in some air, then moved her hands to one side when the baby pushed there. Her eyes burned the longer she felt the baby shifting inside Kinsey. A whine broke free from her chest, causing Kinsey to press their foreheads together.

"You're going to be a mother soon," Kinsey whispered.

Aubrey struggled with the lump in her throat and gasped a little, then tasted a hint of salt in her mouth. "Mine?" she asked with a tremor in her voice.

Kinsey cupped Aubrey's cheek and whispered, "Yours." She nudged her face closer, placing a feather kiss against Aubrey's lips. "Ours."

Aubrey whimpered, then crashed their mouths together. She kept one hand against Kinsey's stomach while her other tangled in wavy hair. Hungry moans passed between their lips as their tongues clashed with months of buried need. In seconds, her cock stiffened and throbbed at the tip. She tore away from Kinsey, gasping for air. "I want…." She struggled to voice how much she wanted Kinsey.

"I know." Kinsey stroked Aubrey's face and smiled at her under the warm lamp light. Her eyes were fiery blue and inviting to Aubrey.

"But it's late, you've traveled so far, and I don't want to hurt you with the pregnancy." Aubrey stiffened when Kinsey chuckled at her.

"Always the protective Alpha." Kinsey's smile grew and her expression was tender. She continued stroking Aubrey's features, trying to brush away the worry lines. "I am weary, but I've waited too long to be with you again." She leaned in again and whispered, "I've heard sex is even better during pregnancy."

"Kinsey," Aubrey murmured and massaged the lower portion of Kinsey's scalp. "I—" Her speech was silenced by Kinsey's thumb covering her mouth, but when her mouth was freed, she whispered, "I'm not as…" She felt the heat in her face and wanted to back away, but she made herself say it. "I'm not as big as I was during the rut."

Kinsey grinned, shrugged, and whispered, "I think I'll be happy with your size since I'm not in my heat."

Aubrey was still flushed from admitting her defect, but Kinsey's arousal hadn't faded after the confession. In fact, Kinsey smelled even more excited, which sent a shiver down Aubrey's spine. Then a nimble hand grabbed her cock, which swelled to a fuller length that surprised Aubrey. "Fuck," she cursed.

Growling, Kinsey tugged on it from the base to the tip and said, "It feels perfect to me." Her lips ghosted across Aubrey's own while her right hand went under Aubrey's shaft. With two fingers, she slipped into Aubrey's slick entrance and hit the sensitive bundle of nerves that sent shocks through Aubrey's stomach and penis. "And probably even better in me."

"Kinsey," Aubrey hissed, thrown off by Kinsey's forwardness. Their first time together had been awkward at the start, and Kinsey had been submissive for most of it. She had been an Omega in heat, relying on her dominant Alpha lover to satisfy her needs. Without the heat, Kinsey was persistent and sure of what she wanted from Aubrey. The next demanding pull of her cock made Aubrey snarl. She was still the goddamn Alpha here! But she resisted the primal urge to shove Kinsey on her back, climb on top, and thrust her cock into her. Kinsey was pregnant with their child.

As if reading Aubrey's concerns, Kinsey smirked but continued massaging Aubrey's sensitive spot. "The worst positions for me are ones on my back. I should stay on my sides, upright…" She nuzzled Aubrey's nose, then went lower and sought out Aubrey's neck, which vibrated with soft thunder. "Or on my hands and knees." She nipped at delicate skin, encouraging Aubrey.

Aubrey gasped for air when Kinsey pushed against her vaginal wall. "Then get on your hands and knees," she ordered, growls vibrating in her chest. She groaned when she shifted off the bed and allowed Kinsey the room to get into the right spot at the top of the bed. Aubrey rubbed the tip of her cock, smearing the slick over the head. Kinsey's sweet pheromones were calling to Aubrey, and she did her best to remain in control.

Kinsey shoved her hair to one side after she situated herself on the bed. She looked over her shoulder and studied Aubrey in the soft light. "Don't make me wait any longer, Alpha."

Aubrey lifted an eyebrow at the old pet name that Kinsey used to call her. There was a depth of emotion in it. Getting on the foot of the bed, she reached between Kinsey's thighs and rubbed the swollen, soaked clit.

Rocking her hips, Kinsey moaned and bowed her head. She swayed her body back and forth when Aubrey massaged her thumb over the hard bud.

For a moment, Aubrey watched Kinsey's greedy motions and enjoyed the high from the sweet slick that waited to coat her cock from tip to base. She had never expected to have the beautiful Omega presenting herself again. Every night in bed was filled with loneliness and bittersweet memories about Kinsey. But tonight was different and would change her future, just as her first night with Kinsey.

"Please, Aubrey," Kinsey begged. "I need you inside me." Her aching words speared Aubrey's heart.

With a pained rumbled, Aubrey scooted forward and massaged the head of her cock against Kinsey's entrance.

"Please," Kinsey whispered. "Don't make me wait any longer." The pressing need in her voice undid Aubrey, who hooked Kinsey's hips.

Aubrey pushed through Kinsey's entrance and savored the slow pace of her cock spreading Kinsey open. The tight, slick walls wrapped around her shaft the deeper she pushed into Kinsey. Her long moan was echoed by her Omega.

"Fuck," Kinsey whispered after a soft pant. "I missed this feeling."

Aubrey whimpered in agreement and nudged the last bit into her lover. Her memories and imagination couldn't recreate how good it felt to have Kinsey clenched around her throbbing length. For a few seconds, she remained still and allowed them both to feel close again. But then the raw need to fuck Kinsey overwhelmed Aubrey. When she pulled out most of the way, Kinsey groaned and whimpered in brief dissatisfaction. But Aubrey growled and thrusted into Kinsey, filling her again.

Kinsey cried out and braced herself for Aubrey to start fucking her. She screamed each time Aubrey smacked her hips into Kinsey's ass. Her pants matched Aubrey's grunts, and her rocking her hips showed Aubrey how much she was loving the pace.

Aubrey clung to her petite lover and drove into greedy muscles that tightened more around her cock. Kinsey demanded that Aubrey go faster, split her open, and fill her completely. Pumping harder, Aubrey growled and cried out as her chest grew heavier. Then at the base of her shaft, she felt the slight ring swell and bang against Kinsey's entrance.

"You have a knot!" Kinsey demanded between gasps, slight awe in her voice. She slapped her hand against the wall in front of her head, holding her body back as Aubrey pumped her harder.

"Yes," Aubrey snarled, knowing the knot was smaller than when she was rutting. She hesitated with her next thrust when Kinsey dropped her upper body. It was a silent plea for Aubrey to mount her and knot her, just as she had done the very first time they had sex. Unable to deny her lover, Aubrey got onto her feet and positioned herself over Kinsey, pushing her cock even deeper. She restarted the pumping and used the wall to her left to keep her weight off Kinsey's back.

"Fuck," Kinsey swore into the pillow. Her curse sparked a shock in Aubrey's stomach. "Knot me, please, Aubrey." Her demand was laced with deep need, an urge to be joined again after so long.

Aubrey pumped harder and gritted her teeth between the low growls. Her cock ached the more Kinsey's inner walls clutched her. Kinsey's cries were perfect and made Aubrey go faster until Kinsey's scream turned raw, holding Aubrey's buried cock in place. Aubrey howled as Kinsey shuddered underneath her. But she rocked her hips and worked her knot into Kinsey, who gasped and whimpered below her. The final connection sent a sharp jolt through Aubrey, giving her the orgasm she'd held back.

Kinsey groaned when Aubrey's cum released deep in her. She clawed at the edge of the bed and whispered, "More."

Aubrey snarled and tightened her hands around Kinsey's sides, just under her breasts. She growled low and started rocking her hips against Kinsey's ass. She moaned as the throbbing head of her cock massaged against Kinsey's inner walls. "Fuck. You're so tight." Kinsey's clenching muscles made it easy for Aubrey to come again, giving Kinsey what she wanted. Dropping her head back, Aubrey allowed them to revel in the sensation of being knotted and fucked after too long.

"And you're bigger than you think you are," Kinsey said, smugness lacing her words. "But your cock feels so good in me."

Aubrey rumbled and nudged her cock, but the knot was still too swollen to pull out. She dropped to one knee, then slid her arms around Kinsey and picked her up. She stiffened from Kinsey's soft hiss, sensing her knot straining against Kinsey's locked entrance. Going slower, she sat back on her butt with Kinsey in her lap and scooted backward until she pressed her shoulders against the wall. With her legs spread wide enough, Kinsey was close enough for the knot to remain comfortable.

Kinsey rested back into Aubrey's muscular body, which supported her weight. "Thank you," she whispered and turned her head toward Aubrey.

Aubrey had one hand propped up behind her and placed the other against Kinsey's stomach. "Do you want more?" In truth, she could fuck Kinsey all night, even though they had time now. But she wanted Kinsey to get plenty of sleep after traveling while being pregnant. She felt one of Kinsey's hands drift lower and realized Kinsey was rubbing her own clit.

"Yes," Kinsey replied, nibbling at Aubrey's throat. "I've been using my hand almost every night since you left. It hasn't been enough for me."

Aubrey's rumble was deep as she pictured Kinsey using her fingers to thrust inside herself. Someday soon she would have to ask Kinsey to show her. But right now, she wanted to satisfy Kinsey's sexual needs. "Then stop touching yourself." She hooked Kinsey's wrist, feeling the inner muscles tightening around her cock again. Kinsey had to relax her muscles for Aubrey to separate them.

Kinsey gave a displeased sound but tangled their hands together. "I can't help it. I love the different kind of orgasm from my clit too, especially when you're stuck in me."

Aubrey twisted her head and bit Kinsey's neck, getting her to submit to her. She rumbled, held Kinsey in place by her throat, and nudged her cock out after sensing the knot was gone. Kinsey whimpered but remained still as Aubrey withdrew from her. Once free, Aubrey released Kinsey's neck and said, "I'll fuck your clit with my mouth."

Making a pleased sound, Kinsey nuzzled her lover and whimpered from the promise. "Now?" she murmured.

"Now." Aubrey sat up with Kinsey against her body, then separated and lay down on the bed. "Come here." She grinned at Kinsey's hesitation, but she helped Kinsey straddle her hips. From her position, she admired Kinsey's large tummy and wondered how much bigger it would grow in the coming months. Soon she would find out, and it brought a smile to her face.

Kinsey mirrored the smile and covered Aubrey's larger hand. "What now?" She rubbed her soaked clit across Aubrey's stomach muscles, groaning with each stroke.

Aubrey cupped Kinsey's ass cheeks and urged her forward. "Closer." She smirked at Kinsey's timid manners, but pulled her to her face. "I want you in my mouth." After a few more tries, she finally had what she wanted against her lips. She had missed the smell and taste that was Kinsey, and she breathed in the sweet slick that waited for her. Kissing and nipping, she teased Kinsey, who whined above her. Unable to resist any longer, Aubrey dragged her tongue between the slit and hit Kinsey's pulsing clit.

Kinsey gasped, then gave a long moan when Aubrey did it again. Demanding more, she nudged her hips forward and pushed into Aubrey's mouth. She yelped when Aubrey clawed her ass and jerked her closer, suddenly sucking hard. Kinsey cried out but rocked her hips.

Growling, Aubrey played with the swollen bud in her mouth and urged wonderful whimpers from her lover. She licked and tasted every bit of Kinsey's arousal, unable to get her fill. Kinsey's moans and screams caused her cock to harden again. But first she would have Kinsey come in her mouth.

Kinsey leaned forward, slapped her hand against the wall, and rode Aubrey's face. "More," she demanded in a growly voice. She started to shudder but didn't stop thrusting into Aubrey's mouth. She cursed several times between her grunts or yells.

Aubrey growled deeper than before and latched onto the straining clit, working it with her tongue and lips. Kinsey stiffened above her, trembled, and clawed into Aubrey's shoulder.

"Fuck!" Kinsey quaked and called out her lover's name, toppling until strong hands held onto her.

With an eager tongue, Aubrey caught every drop given to her before she kissed Kinsey's burning skin. She rumbled with pleasure and listened to Kinsey's panting, loving the continued shudders. After a minute, Aubrey helped Kinsey lie down on the bed, facing the wall. She curled up behind Kinsey after snaking an arm underneath her lover's protruding belly.

Kinsey whimpered and reached for Aubrey's cock that rubbed against her clit. She massaged the pulsing head and smeared the slick down the shaft. Peering over her shoulder, she said, "I've thought about you every night."

Aubrey rumbled and nuzzled her lover's neck, which was flushed and damp. "I thought about you every day." The necklace pressing against her collarbone was a constant reminder of Kinsey and their time together.

Whimpering, Kinsey lifted her leg over Aubrey's hip, then gripped halfway down Aubrey's penis. "I would think about our last day together." She circled the aching head around her entrance. "About how you took care of me during my heat, even though you were in a rut."

Closing her eyes, Aubrey failed to stop a whimper at the messy memories from her first and last moments with Kinsey. They were beautiful and difficult for her she'd always wished it had happened differently for them. Aubrey was left with a hint of doubt about the depth of their attraction to each other since their heat and rut had been induced by herbs. She was still certain that Kinsey was the most gorgeous Omega ever and would always call to her Alpha. But she wanted it to be natural, along with their child's conception.

"I will always care for you," Aubrey whispered, but heard the tremble in her voice. She covered it with a kiss to Kinsey's temple while she waited for Kinsey to push in her cock. But Kinsey remained still, other than a soft rumble.

Kinsey withdrew her hand, then turned to face Aubrey. "What is wrong?" She caressed Aubrey's cheek and said, "I can smell your distress."

"It's nothing." Aubrey leaned in and brushed their lips together until Kinsey pulled back.

Ducking her head, Kinsey narrowed her eyes that pierced Aubrey's thick skin. "Tell me, please." Her pheromones were shifting the longer Aubrey resisted her. Kinsey smelled inviting and soothed the tension in Aubrey's shoulders, making it easy to confess what was buried in Aubrey.

"I wish that my rut and your heat weren't forced on us." Aubrey swallowed, then her frown deepened when Kinsey smiled at her.

"They weren't," Kinsey whispered, her smile widening to reveal her canines. "When I realized you'd triggered my heat, I sent word to the healer, Lind, to give you a sleeping agent so that my father wouldn't know."

Aubrey jerked back and opened her mouth but words failed her.

"Unlike my father, I sensed your rut the day Orman examined you." Kinsey started to trace Aubrey's jaw line then her temple, cheek, and lips. "That was why I was horrified that you didn't wish to bed me, even though you were starting to rut for me."

Aubrey recalled the terrible fever at the time. She had thought it was a fever from her shoulder wound, but a rut made more sense. "I wanted you, but I—"

"I know." Kinsey pressed their lips together and whispered, "I know, and I'm sorry." She kissed Aubrey again but it was brief. "After our time together, I silently swore to you that I would find a way for us to be together." She pulled Aubrey's hand to her stomach and murmured, "All of us."

"I hope this is the way," Aubrey said, hooking her hand against Kinsey's neck. "I can't and I won't let you go."

"I don't want to go, not without you." Kinsey smiled but her eyes gleamed with tears about to fall. "I want to be the Omega to your Alpha."

They smashed their lips together, growling and whimpering at each other. Their tongues warred, and salty tears mixed into the kiss. Aubrey poured her heart and dreams into the frantic kiss that ended with whines. She then helped Kinsey turn around again, and their bodies molded together. Once Kinsey's leg was back over her hip, Aubrey thrust into Kinsey without any restraint.

Kinsey released a deep moan and curled her head back, closer to Aubrey. "Give me everything, Aubrey." She cried out from the next hard thrust. "Fuck me!"

Starting with a punishing pace, Aubrey pumped her hips and drove her hard length through Kinsey's silky walls that clenched around her. Her right hand squeezed and rolled Kinsey's breast, then she hooked Kinsey's thigh with her left hand. She forced Kinsey to open wider for her, to take her cock even deeper. Together, she and Kinsey cried out as they chased the pleasure racing between their bodies. The fullness throbbed in every inch of Aubrey's cock, but she would only come with Kinsey.

"Don't stop! Please don't stop." Kinsey trembled and shook against her lover. She reached behind and wrenched her fingers in golden strands, forcing a furious snarl from Aubrey. "More!" Her demand was met with frantic pounding, and Kinsey screamed as she was tipped over the edge.

Aubrey felt the first contraction that locked around her cock, causing cum to burst free. She and Kinsey were hit with aftershocks, but Aubrey urged her swollen knot to push into Kinsey. With a grunt, she drove it in and locked them together. She was left panting and rocking her hips against Kinsey's ass.

Again and again, Kinsey trembled and bucked against the hard length completely buried inside her. She gasped for air, then twisted her head to better expose her neck to Aubrey. Her whines were needy and submissive.

Aubrey was drawn in and scraped her teeth over the soft flesh. "Kinsey," she whispered and rumbled, wanting to sink her canines in. Kinsey could be hers and only hers for the rest of their lives. Her eyes stung from pained memories, and the ache rose in her chest again.

"Bite me," Kinsey whispered, digging her persistent nails deeper into Aubrey's scalp.

Whimpering, Aubrey withdrew her mouth and nuzzled Kinsey's ear. "But your fath—"

"Don't mention him," Kinsey cut off. She closed her eyes, then she started to shake from more than pleasurable aftershocks. "Please bite me. Take me, Aubrey."

After another whine, Aubrey wanted to sink her canines into the sensitive flesh below Kinsey's ear and mark Kinsey as hers. Nothing else made more sense to her. When they first met, Aubrey was awakened by Kinsey, her scent, and her Omega. Her attraction and draw to Kinsey were new but certain, like the sunrise every day. But if she bound Kinsey to her, then Kinsey's future as a queen could crumble. By default, Kinsey's mate would assume power, but the Kingdom of Tharnstone would forbid a degenerate Alpha to rule. The crown would go to the next in line – Agatha.

Aubrey released Kinsey's thigh and snaked her arm across Kinsey's protruding tummy. "You will never be queen."

"I don't wish to be queen," Kinsey whispered, shaking harder. "I have never truly wished to be queen. To be cold and brutal or sentence people to death and slavery." She clutched Aubrey's hand on her stomach and fought a quiet sob. "I wish to be your Omega. To be bound only to you."

Aubrey groaned and brushed her hot lips across Kinsey's throat. She felt Kinsey arch her neck into the delicate touch. Her heart thundered against her chest, then a predatory growl rattled deep in her chest. She licked the pulsing, salty skin that waited for her. "Mine," she snarled and dragged her canines across the soft flesh.

Kinsey gasped and clawed Aubrey's hand. "Please," she rasped.

With a growl, Aubrey applied more pressure with her sharp teeth and started puncturing the skin. Her Alpha howled in her chest as the first droplet of blood touched her tongue. Kinsey's very essence merged with Aubrey's, binding them as lifetime mates. As her claim solidified itself, Aubrey nudged her hips and shifted her cock, causing Kinsey's silky walls to clench again.

"Mine," Kinsey echoed, then panted as she remained locked in Aubrey's hold. Her moans continued until Aubrey withdrew her canines.

Aubrey licked the bite mark a few times, then released a shaky breath. Already she felt the gentle shifts in her mind and body. She was taught from an early age what it meant to be bound to one person, to care for them and sense everything between an unbreakable link. Now as Kinsey's Alpha, she had both social and legal rights as family, just as Kinsey did as her Omega. Where she had once been broken by her old family's rejection, she found it mended by Kinsey's love and acceptance.

Kinsey wiped her face and whispered, "I needed you to bite me months ago." Her voice cracked, and she started to cry.

Struck by the tide of distress and troubled pheromones, Aubrey became frantic to soothe her new mate. She hastened to withdraw her buried length, but gently, then rolled Kinsey onto her back and crawled on top. "It's okay, Kinsey." She caught some of the tears with her lips.

"I should have asked you then." Kinsey seethed and clutched Aubrey's shoulders. "I should have left with you. I was so stupid to stay."

"No, no." Aubrey worked her forearms underneath Kinsey and hugged her against her body. Her rumbles grew louder as she released comforting pheromones to ease Kinsey's pain. "We're together and mated to each other now. No one can force you again." She chuffed, nudged Kinsey's cheek, and whispered, "*No one.*"

Kinsey nodded into her mate's neck. She stroked Aubrey's hair and nuzzled the closest ear. "I'm sorry. I believe I'm exhausted."

"And pregnant," Aubrey quipped and smiled after Kinsey's huff. "It is late." She lifted off Kinsey, then helped her get under the blankets and fur. Once they were both settled into place, she drew Kinsey's back into her body. After a happy rumble, Aubrey breathed in her mate's unique scent and couldn't have enough of it.

Between yawns, Kinsey muttered, "You're getting hard again."

Flushed, Aubrey cursed her body's natural reaction to Kinsey's nearness. She felt like a whelp of an Alpha rather than a mature one. Maybe one day she'd learned how to control herself around Kinsey, especially when they had a little one running around.

Twisting her head, Kinsey whispered, "I could be convinced to fuck more."

Aubrey groaned from the effects of the curse word, but nudged Kinsey's head away from her. "I'll be fine. Please rest."

"Wake me if you can't sleep," Kinsey insisted, her voice already drowsy. Within minutes, her breathing deepened, but her hand stayed laced within Aubrey's own.

Burying her face into Kinsey's hair, Aubrey closed her eyes and focused on their breathing patterns rather than the soft ass pressed against her penis. For a moment, her mind drifted back to the biting mark and how it filled her to finally have Kinsey as her Omega. Tears burned in the corner of her eyes, and she whined until Kinsey squeezed her hand in her sleep. With their hands pressed against Kinsey's stomach, Aubrey pictured their future in a few months when they had a newborn. It felt like a dream, but soon it would be real and all theirs, together. *I'm so blessed.*

Aubrey started to purr, and she murmured, "Home."

Epilogue

K insey finished heating the hammered pot of cider over the stove, then brought it to the kitchen table where three ceramic mugs waited. While she filled the mugs, the booms and bangs overhead grew louder but softened again. The noise came from the bedroom area and were signs of progress.

With the three mugs in hand, Kinsey left the cabin, wrapped around the right side, and neared the back of the home. She found a seat on a chopping block and waited for someone to near the roof's edge. Running her hand through her hair, she thought she would be accustomed to the shorter length, but it was still strange to her. Two days ago, she had shortened her waist-long hair to her shoulders.

She was happy since starting her new life. She was happier than she could ever recall, and so was Aubrey. They settled into the cabin together without any trouble. Kinsey confided that she had brought gold coins with her, which they agreed to hide under a floorboard in their bedroom. Her other items consisted of a few pieces of clothing and the

Kingdom of Animals book. Nothing else was necessary from Kinsey's old life as a princess.

But as Kinsey sat there, she considered their long-term future in five or ten years. Before she left her family, she had snuck to Agatha's room. For over an hour, she and Agatha conspired over the future of the Kingdom of Tharnstone, especially once their parents were old. It was plausible that their father would die early in battle or by an assassin's hand. The kingdom would now go to Agatha, who was troubled by the idea and begged Kinsey to stay. Unlike Kinsey, Agatha wasn't educated in politics, finances, trade, and civil issues, whereas Kinsey had been studying for them.

Kinsey was positive that the kingdom would refuse to follow her as queen if she was mated to a She-Alpha. But they would follow Agatha without question and whomever she chose as king, if she did choose. Kinsey doubted that their father would allow Agatha near any Alpha after his plans to have Kinsey impregnated backfired on him.

After a heated argument, Agatha agreed to Kinsey's leaving Tharnstone Castle, as long as she promised to return to Coldhelm if Agatha needed her help. Kinsey couldn't be queen, but she could be an advisor to Agatha and shoulder some of the responsibilities. By then, Kinsey might be ready to return to Coldhelm and take on the duties if Aubrey agreed to it. She kept the arrangement a secret from Aubrey right now, unsure if it would even happen. Nor did she want them to lose focus on the upcoming birth.

Aubrey knew Gerald was traveling between Lower Light and Coldhelm once a month. He would meet with Huxley in a tavern and exchange letters between the sisters. Kinsey was relieved to learn that her mother was stable after essentially losing two children, both to her husband's heavy hand. Kinsey suspected her mother understood Kinsey's choice to leave. In her most recent letter, she promised her sister that they would visit so Agatha could meet her godchild, or godchildren. Rubbing her enlarged stomach, Kinsey smiled at the thought of having more than one baby.

Lifting her gaze, Kinsey spotted Corbin, who was the first to emerge near the ladder. He laughed at something either Aubrey or Gerald said, then he spotted Kinsey, who signaled the hot cider. Smiling big, he hurried down the ladder and took the offered drink. He hummed and sipped on it. "You make the best cider, Kins."

Kinsey rolled her eyes at her brother-in-law's nickname. "How's the project?"

"We're getting close." Corbin pursed his lips and said, "We should finish it in the next few days."

"I hope so, since we're having company soon." Kinsey had encouraged her mate to host a small gathering for the end of the year.

"How are you feeling?" Corbin asked between swallows of cider.

"Excited and nervous," Kinsey replied, resting a hand on her protruding belly. She expected to give birth the first or second week of January. The child's birth was one of the reasons she had pushed Aubrey to have a gathering, because their time with friends and family would be cut back by the newborn. "And rather weary."

Corbin touched Kinsey's shoulder and squeezed it. "I hope my sister has been caring for you."

Kinsey shook her head at him, picked up another mug, and said, "Take this to Gerald. Tell Aubrey she has to come get hers." Corbin took it from her after he drank the last mouthful. While she waited for her mate, she studied her belly. She had reached her final month of pregnancy, and soon life would change again for her.

Aubrey hurried down the ladder and traded a smile with Kinsey. "You should be resting, not spoiling us."

"I wanted fresh air." Kinsey gave her mate the hot cider but received a soft kiss first. "Is there much left to do on the roof?" She and Aubrey had decided to add a second bedroom for their child. The additional roofing was close to completion, while the interior needed to be finished last.

Aubrey peered over her shoulder and cupped the steaming mug between her hands. "We have about another day's work, but I need to work at the forge tomorrow." She took a seat on the frozen ground at Kinsey's feet. "Then I'll finish the interior in a few days."

With a frown, Kinsey shook her head and said, "You're working too hard."

"I wish to have it completed before our child is born." Aubrey sipped on the cider, then rumbled and gave a content sigh. "I think it's wiser to complete it rather than have banging when the baby is trying to sleep."

Kinsey agreed, but she still worried about Aubrey exhausting herself with the project to expand on the cabin, which had developed more character over the months since Kinsey moved into it. "I hate to see you tire yourself." Since Kinsey's arrival, Aubrey had dedicated much of her time to improving and filling the cabin for them. The kitchen had been completed, a dinner table and chairs added, and the bed widened. One day Aubrey had brought home two pots and a skillet that she forged herself. Last week, the town's resident carpenter gifted Aubrey and Kinsey with a bassinet for the baby. To add to the generosity, Rudyard paid for the wood to expand the cabin and gave them the nails from the forge.

"I'd rather tire myself now so I can focus on our child later. You will need time to heal," Aubrey said. Ever since Kinsey arrived, Aubrey's spirits had lifted, and her smiles were frequent. Aubrey was often quiet by nature, but she had opened up with Kinsey over time.

Kinsey softened at her mate's concern and care. As she studied Aubrey, she realized how thankful she was to have Aubrey as her mate and friend. Many Alphas would hold their newborn for a few minutes, return the baby to their mate with final approval, and then leave the child rearing to the Omega. However, Aubrey was a different kind of Alpha, who would share the parenting with Kinsey. Some part of her wondered if it was because Aubrey was a She-Alpha and harbored a maternal side in her. Regardless, she was excited to raise the child together.

"Have you decided on a name?" Kinsey asked, crossing her arms over her belly and leaning forward. "I prefer Devon after my brother."

Aubrey grinned over the rim of the mug. "I still think Binsey is a fine name."

Kinsey snorted low and narrowed her eyes at the ongoing joke. "We are not naming her that."

Chuckling into the mug, Aubrey finished the contents, then placed it on her knee. "How certain you are that the baby is a she?"

"Pregnant mother's intuition," Kinsey said grinning and rumbling. "But we should have two names ready."

"In case it is a boy."

Kinsey lifted an eyebrow and argued, "In case it's twins."

"Twins?" Aubrey's eyes widened, and the mug teetered on her knee from her body's jarring movement. She blew out a breath, then dragged her fingers through her hair. "Twins," she whispered in awe and stared at Kinsey's belly. "Are we having twins?"

"I am quite large." Kinsey straightened up and held either side of her stomach. After studying her belly, she smirked and whispered, "I do recall us making certain I was pregnant." She shivered from Aubrey's soft growl. "Many times over."

Aubrey was flushed and opened two buttons of her jacket's collar. "Yes, I remember."

Kinsey chuckled and admired the color on Aubrey's face, already smelling an excited Alpha. *It's good to see I can still make her hard even when I'm as big as this cabin.* She bent forward, at least as much as her stomach allowed her. "What will you do if it's triplets?"

Aubrey whined, dropped her head in her hands, and whispered, "Grow plenty of injor herb for morning-after tea."

Not expecting the response, Kinsey barked with laughter and pictured copious amounts of injor covering their garden this coming spring. The herb was a powerful contraceptive that female Omegas, Betas, and even Alphas took in tea form the morning after sex.

"Are there triplets?" Aubrey asked, her voice weak and eyes watery.

Taking pity, Kinsey shook her head, then rested a hand on the front of her stomach. "But twins are possible." She watched the seriousness grow on Aubrey's features, and she waited in silence.

"I love the names Devon and Shaw."

Kinsey was thoughtful and considered the handwritten list that she kept in the cabin. "I still like Teon and Ranald too." She agreed with Aubrey's first two choices, finding the names universal for a boy or girl.

"What of your grandfather's name?"

"Randall," Kinsey whispered, more to herself. As a child, she had been close to her mother's father and loved all his tales about animals. Her time with him had been brief, a few years, before he died early. Randall had been an Alpha but kinder in his older years compared to his early days as a warrior. As a child, Kinsey ignored the bloody stories about her grandfather and held onto her childhood memories of him, needing to believe at least one Alpha in her family was gentle.

"It's a good, strong name."

Kinsey smiled and said, "The name means shield wolf."

Aubrey rumbled low, then nodded once. "It is a very good name, then."

"For an Omega," Kinsey teased, then shifted her attention to Gerald coming down the ladder. Since settling in Lower Light, she attempted to persuade Gerald to live his life rather than guard a fallen princess. After being marked by Aubrey, Kinsey couldn't return to Coldhelm and become the future queen. Aubrey's bite had freed Kinsey from her life as a royal. Now she wished that Gerald would accept her new life as a commoner and end his vow as a guard.

"Corbin needs your help," Gerald said to Aubrey, hands on his hips.

Aubrey smirked, grabbed the mug, and stood up. "You mean he needs my muscles."

"Yes, but he wouldn't admit that."

Aubrey set the mug near the other empty one, then kissed Kinsey on the cheek and nuzzled her.

Kinsey watched her mate climb the ladder and imagined the muscles flexing under the clothing. She sighed, then peered up at Gerald, who set his mug beside the other two.

"Thank you for the cider." Gerald squatted next to Kinsey and gazed up toward the cabin's roof. "How are you feeling?"

Kinsey lost count how many times people asked her about her health, but she was grateful for the concern. "I'm ready to give birth," she admitted and grinned at Gerald's smirk. "The first seven or so months were wonderful, but I'm ready."

Gerald chuckled and bowed his head for a moment. "It won't be long now." He pursed his lips and said, "Aubrey told me that there's talk of Tharnstone soldiers searching the region for you. Is that why you cut your hair?"

"Yes, I thought perhaps it would change my appearance. It'll grow back." Frowning, Kinsey stretched her legs and considered how well the soldiers would search for her. "Have they been seen in Lower Light?"

"Not yet." Gerald sighed and whispered, "There's also a reward if anyone finds you."

"Then it's good that I've spent most of my time on the farm."

Gerald bobbed his head, then stood up and stretched his legs. "You still carry the dagger?"

Kinsey patted the hidden weapon under her cloak.

Gerald nodded, then went back up the ladder to help the others. His movements were a bit strained, perhaps from being an assistant cartwright for two of the cartwrights in Lower Light.

For a while longer, Kinsey remained on the chopping block, but she returned to the warmth of the cabin after a chill settled over her. She re-stoked the fireplace and sat by it while reading a book that Aubrey had bought her two weeks ago. On the small table beside her was another book, but it was for children. However, Kinsey was using it to teach Aubrey how to read. Later they would pass it on to their child, whom Kinsey would school.

Tomorrow would be a full day for Kinsey. Like Aubrey, she had work to do for the forge; Rudyard took her on as a bookkeeper. It had happened by accident when Kinsey had gone to the forge the day after she first arrived in Lower Light. Aubrey had been working on a job, while Rudyard was away to work with a client. A potential customer had arrived at the forge to discuss pricing for twenty locks.

Aubrey did her best to handle his inquiry, but Kinsey sensed that the prospect was about to walk away due to Aubrey's inability to barter and handle numbers. Kinsey had stepped into the conversation and charmed him with both her intelligence and smile. Rudyard had returned a few minutes toward the end of the conversation and witnessed the handshakes between Aubrey, Kinsey, and the new client.

Rudyard had asked Kinsey to help him with his sales and finances. She readily agreed, needing some amount of work. With Kinsey's skills, Rudyard better understood how much his materials cost and what profit margins he needed to make so that his forge could grow. After the incident, Aubrey built up the courage to ask Kinsey to teach her how to read, write, and calculate numbers. For the most part, Aubrey was an easy student, but her frustrations with adding measurements showed at times.

As nightfall approached, Kinsey prepared a meal while Aubrey was on her heels the entire time. She both cooed and grumbled when Aubrey stood over her shoulder, especially in the past month. Her Omega loved the attentive Alpha, but Kinsey was still capable of many things and understood her limits. After dinner, Kinsey retired to bed while Aubrey practiced writing.

The next day Kinsey kissed her mate farewell for the day. She focused on the finances for Rudyard all morning, then needed a break. Closing the leather book, she decided to make the soup for dinner tonight. Aubrey would bring home bread and a few other items from the market.

Leaving the cabin, Kinsey started toward the root cellar that was shared between the cabin and farmhouse where Rudyard lived with his mate and four kids. In the cellar, she collected several items for tonight's meal, set them outside the cellar, and closed the doors. Kneeling, she prepared to pick up the leather bag of items but faltered when she spotted two strangers walking down the dirt lane. Even from a distance, Kinsey recognized their glinting armor.

The Tharnstone soldiers would be near her any minute. She tried holding down her heart-racing panic, knowing Aubrey would sense it and arrive too late. After taking a deep breath, she grabbed a bit of dirt and rubbed it on her face. She checked that the dagger was hooked to her hip under the crimson cloak, then picked up the bag.

Kinsey shouldered the bag and continued toward the cabin as if a normal day. She paused when the two soldiers called out to her. She went toward them and waited, praying that she could handle the situation. But as the soldiers approached her, one soldier's familiar features made her heart fall into her stomach. For a moment, she and Luca stared at each other until the other soldier's growly voice cut through her awe.

"We are looking for Princess Kinsey Wymarc of the House of Wymarc," the soldier said and frowned as his attention lowered to her pregnant stomach. He reached to a pouch on his side, opened it, and asked, "What is your name?

Kinsey moved her hand closer to the jars in her bag and looked from Luca to the other soldier. "It's Devon." She waited to see if Luca would contest it and gained an inch of hope when he remained silent.

The soldier narrowed his eyes and retrieved a folded-up piece of cloth had an image of Kinsey. "The princess is pregnant, like you." He opened the cloth, held it up, and looked between it and Kinsey.

"Yes, I'm aware that Princess Kinsey is pregnant." Kinsey shook her head and argued, "As are hundreds of other women in the kingdom." She glanced at Luca and willed him to defend her rather than side with her father, who would reward Luca well if he found Kinsey.

The soldier reached for his sheathed blade after lowering the cloth. "You look very similar to the princess. It is our duty to take you to Coldhelm."

Kinsey wrapped her hand around the jar, preparing to smash it against the soldier's head. Her breath caught when Luca grabbed the other soldier's elbow, halting him.

"Let me see the image again," Luca insisted, retrieving the cloth from him. He opened it, held it up, and looked between Kinsey and it. "I see a few similarities, but Princess Kinsey is much more beautiful. Her hair is longer." He folded up the cloth and pointed at Kinsey. "This girl's neck is marked."

The soldier frowned and pushed the sword back into the sheath but still held onto it. "Who is your Alpha?"

"Her name is Aubrey," Kinsey replied, knowing that no one from her family was aware of Aubrey's birth name. Her body continued to shake, but she kept her voice even. "She's a striker at a forge in town."

With raised eyebrows, the soldier asked, "A degenerate Alpha?"

Kinsey did her best to contain her growl from the insult about her mate. "Yes, she's an Alpha."

Luca snorted and turned to his companion. "There's your proof. Princess Kinsey wouldn't be bonded to an Alpha." He then held out his hand at Kinsey. "Nor would the princess be caught dead in such a hovel. She's probably hiding in some aunt or uncle's manor, not a farm." With a rumble, he asked, "Have you seen or heard anything about Princess Kinsey's whereabouts? Perhaps conversation at the market?"

Kinsey shook her head. "I rarely go to the market. My Alpha likes me home, pregnant, and bare

footed."

The other soldier snorted and huffed. "A wise Alpha."

Fighting to roll her eyes, Kinsey stayed silent and waited for their final conclusion. She exchanged a glance with Luca, who kept a hand on his dagger's handle.

"We're wasting our time," Luca said, then jerked on his companion's shoulder. "Let's go."

After a huff, the other soldier nodded and turned with Luca, who headed down the lane.

Kinsey felt the strength drain from her knees while she watched the soldiers leave the farm. She crumbled to the ground and wiped a few tears from her cheeks as she watched Luca vanish around the bend. *Thank you, my friend*, she silently called to him.

After a minute, she made it over to the cabin's steps and sat there, trembling and panting as she pictured being dragged back to her father. King Wilmont would ensure that Kinsey stayed in Tharnstone Castle, using Kinsey's newborn as leverage. He might even threaten to have Aubrey arrested and murdered if she didn't follow his wishes.

Kinsey was unsure how long she sat on the steps, but running boots caught her ears. Without looking up, she already sensed her mate's frantic need to find Kinsey.

"Are you all right?" Aubrey asked with a sheathed blade in hand.

"I'm okay," Kinsey replied, hugging herself and peering up at Aubrey. "Tharnstone soldiers were here looking for me."

Aubrey growled and asked, "Where are they now?"

"Gone." Kinsey stood up and sought out comfort from her mate, who drew her into a hug. "Luca was one of them."

Aubrey stiffened and rumbled low. "What happened?" She tipped Kinsey's face back, studied her features, and wiped away some of the dirt.

Kinsey relayed the story and shook her head toward the end, leaning heavier against Aubrey. "I'm sorry I scared you."

"I wish I had been here sooner." Aubrey kissed her lover's head and said, "Come on. It's cold out here." She picked up the satchel and guided Kinsey into their home.

After the incident, Aubrey spoke to Gerald about the Tharnstone soldiers, who were circling Lower Light like vultures. Gerald, Aubrey, and Corbin rotated days to spend with Kinsey rather than leaving her alone, in case the soldiers decided to visit again. On the second-to-last day of the year, the Tharnstone soldiers left the area and continued their hunt in another part of the region.

On the last day of the year, Aubrey finished the second bedroom that branched off from their own. Kinsey stayed near, helping some. She found herself checking and rechecking that they had everything they needed for the child. The clothes, blankets, and bassinet were clean and ready. Corbin had given them a rocking chair, which Aubrey set up in the new room. Kinsey sat in it several times, rocked, and watched her mate finish the window trim in the new room. One day it would be full of memories; but until then, it was empty and waiting for new life.

Hours later, their cabin's sitting room and kitchen were bursting with company and merriment. Hot ciders were traded, both spiked and traditional. Soup, bread, fruit, and cheeses were shared among friends, along with old and new stories. Several times Aubrey was clapped on the back for approaching motherhood. Kinsey received hugs, praises, and loving whispers as people left one by one.

Aubrey groaned after settling into the bed next to her mate.

"It was a long day," Kinsey agreed and adjusted the blankets, grateful for her Alpha's body heat. But it was hard to find a comfortable position at first. Mild pain had started inside her abdomen yesterday afternoon when she was preparing dinner. She knew the signs of early labor, but she had kept the news to herself, not wanting Aubrey to cancel the gathering.

"Very long." Aubrey had started her day before sunrise, finishing the new room and then helping Kinsey prepare for this evening's celebration for the new year. "But I enjoyed seeing everyone."

Kinsey smiled and curled up to Aubrey's side. "So did I." She snuggled closer when Aubrey hooked her shoulders. "Now we wait."

"Any day now," Aubrey whispered and started to purr, coaxing Kinsey closer to slumber.

Any hour, Kinsey argued in her head. She rumbled in happiness and whispered, "Sweet dreams." She drifted off within minutes when Aubrey's purrs grew deeper.

At first, Kinsey slept well, until sharp, distinct pain started in her stomach and down her spine. She was jolted to life, discovering the mattress was soaked from her waist down. Her wrenching cry stirred Aubrey, who sat up alarmed but ready to handle the situation.

"Contraction," Kinsey rasped and clutched her lover's bicep.

Aubrey scrambled out of bed, lit the lamp by their bed, and grabbed her jacket to cover her nude body. "I'll send Rudyard to get the wisewoman."

Gritting her teeth, Kinsey snapped, "Hurry, Aubrey!" She cried out while Aubrey raced out of the cabin. After the second contraction, she heard Aubrey slam the front door. "Aubrey?" she called, needing her mate's help and support.

"I'm lighting more lamps," Aubrey replied, voice tight and shaky. She rushed into the room with two burning lamps, which she set up around the room. Shedding the long coat, she yanked on leather pants and a tunic from the shelves. She scrambled into them, then grabbed several worn towels and placed them on the foot of the bed.

Kinsey was breathing hard and sweating, and she tossed the blankets off her burning body. She felt secure as her mate continued to prepare for the childbirth. They had practiced everything several times, but Aubrey had been paranoid that she would freeze and forget what needed to be done. But in the heat of the moment, Aubrey seemed to revert to her controlled nature from slavery and used it to focus on the situation.

Another contraction hit Kinsey, pain sparking in her abdomen and shooting up her spine, demanding that her body prepare for the birth. She cried out and dragged her heels through the blankets. "Aubrey," she whined toward the end of it.

Aubrey finished cleaning her hands and arms with water and soap. She hastened over to the bedside, then piled the pillows together and used a balled-up blanket to lift Kinsey better. Before she could move, Kinsey grabbed her and held their foreheads together. They rumbled at each other for a heartbeat, needing the moment before chaos engulfed them.

"You and the baby will be okay," Aubrey whispered, sharing a quick kiss. They had discussed the dangers of Kinsey's going into labor and how childbirth could kill her and even the baby. But being an Alpha, Aubrey was controlled and determined to not allow that to happen. It had spurred her to take it upon herself to learn from Kinsey and the local wisewoman Alma how to deliver a baby.

Kinsey whimpered, nodded, and shared a final kiss before they both became mothers. Her entire body jerked from another contraction that was stronger than the last two. Screwing her eyes shut, she felt Aubrey rush off to finish preparing for the birth. The pain and shifts in her body were increasing incrementally. She knew it would only be minutes before she would need to push.

Aubrey reemerged and placed a bite stick in Kinsey's hand. But before she could leave the bedside, Kinsey snared her again and bared her teeth. "They're coming!"

Aubrey jerked back and asked, "They?" She grew pale under the lamp light. "How many?" she squeaked and trembled in Kinsey's hold.

Before Kinsey could respond, a contraction wracked her petite frame and forced another scream. She grabbed the bite stick and clutched it with ferocity. Again, Aubrey left her side and her movements were still frantic. Kinsey suspected Aubrey was doubting everything now that Kinsey was certain there was more than one baby. Being an Omega, her awareness of her body was much keener than a Beta. For most of the pregnancy, she had been certain that two babies were developing inside her. By the last three months, Kinsey wasn't quite sure how to tell Aubrey, who was already wired by expecting one child.

Aubrey took her position at the foot and shifted the blankets until only one covered Kinsey's upper body. "Let me see," she ordered, her voice commanding like an Alpha.

Kinsey groaned as the latest contraction eased for a second. She opened her legs for her mate, allowing Aubrey to examine her. The front door opened and closed, signaling Alma's arrival.

"How are we doing?" Alma asked, hurrying into the room.

Kinsey responded with a sharp cry and arching back.

Alma took Aubrey's side and said, "That sounds promising." Kinsey shot her a dirty glare, but Alma smiled back and bent over Aubrey's shoulder. She started to coach Aubrey on what to do and reminded Kinsey of the labor process.

"I fucking know, Alma!" Kinsey pointed the bite stick at her.

Alma moved closer to Kinsey and pushed the bite stick toward her face. "You might need that soon, dear."

Kinsey could have swatted Alma with it, but she respected Alma far too much. Alma was called a wisewoman in Lower Light, but Alma was closer to a healer or physician with all her knowledge, especially about females. Alma had handled nearly a hundred births in and around Lower Light, making her a revered midwife. Much of Alma's work as a midwife was done without charge, but middle class and nobles often gave her money after a child's birth.

A new contraction washed over Kinsey. Her cry filled the cabin, but Alma spoke loud enough for Kinsey to hear what was happening next.

"Kinsey is opening up to allow the baby to pass through," Alma reminded.

"Babies!" Aubrey was growly and tense, but Alma didn't seem put off by it.

Alma smiled big and looked at Kinsey. "You spoil your Alpha."

Kinsey was prepared to chuck the biting stick at Alma, but the next contraction already started. "Aubrey!" A cramp started in her right leg and caused her to whimper. She tried to reach for it, but Aubrey was already massaging the calf muscle for her.

"Things are going to happen quickly here," Alma said. "Omegas are extremely fast compared to Betas."

Aubrey's rumble was loud and agreeing while she continued to massage Kinsey's calf.

"Remember that we want the babies to come out head first, face positioned down toward the bed." Alma waited for Kinsey's cries to settle, then she said, "We'll be able to turn them some once the head is visible enough."

Aubrey agreed, then a minute later announced, "I see the first head."

Kinsey whimpered and already sensed the first baby close to being born.

"Start pushing, Kinsey," Alma ordered.

Already feeling the urge, Kinsey bit down on the stick and pushed. Aubrey was determined and communicated the baby's position even though Kinsey sensed it. Alma coached Kinsey on her breathing and when to push versus resting. But the first baby cry brought a brief instant of happiness to Kinsey. Her need to comfort the newborn overwhelmed her, but Aubrey refocused her on the second birth.

Alma had the first baby wrapped in a blanket after cutting the umbilical cord. She cradled the baby while she coached both mothers on the second birth. Her voice was gentle but encouraging, keeping away any chaos. She cooed at the baby and said, "Such a handsome Omega. What's your name, sweetie?"

"Randall!" Kinsey looked at her baby nestled in Alma's arms. "His name is Randall." She sensed her mate's pride filling the room, making Kinsey smile for a beat. As the second baby pushed through, she didn't need the bite stick and found the next birth a little easier. But Aubrey had to turn the baby, who was facing slightly to the side but mostly downward. The last birth was faster, and the baby's cry was joyous to Kinsey and her mate.

"Take Randall to your mate, Aubrey." Alma traded newborns and took care of the rest of the delivery.

Aubrey rumbled in annoyance but heeded Alma's command. She cradled the swaddled baby and took a seat beside Kinsey, allowing them both to enjoy their first one.

"And a beautiful Alpha," Alma announced, handing the twin to Aubrey, who adjusted both babies for them to see.

"Hello, Devon," Kinsey greeted, kissing both.

"We need to finish up," Alma said after a minute.

Aubrey understood and moved off the bed. She held the babies, beaming at them but looking from them to Kinsey.

Kinsey continued having milder contractions and followed Alma's instructions until she completed the labor cycle. Alma started cleaning up and wiped Kinsey down while Aubrey placed each child in Kinsey's arms. "They're gorgeous," she whispered, then looked at Aubrey, who squatted down beside the bed. "Do you like their names?"

Aubrey hadn't lost her smile and leaned over, pressing a kiss to Kinsey's temple. "Of course. They're fitting." She continued to purr and stared at the twins.

Alma emerged from the second bedroom and said, "I'm going to make us some tea." When Aubrey tried to get up, Alma pushed her back down. "I know my way around a kitchen."

Kinsey nuzzled the twins, inhaling their scents, which were delicate and distinct to each. Her rumbles grew deeper as she took in their early features, such as Randall's light hair and Devon's darker hair. Already they appeared quite different from each other, rather than just being an Omega and an Alpha. They were both rare breeds and would face the similar hardships that Aubrey had as a child. But the children had Aubrey's experience to help them and an unbreakable family.

"Two?" Aubrey whispered, awe returning to her features.

Kinsey chuckled and nodded. "Two, my Alpha."

Aubrey leaned in and nudged Kinsey with her nose, then hooked an arm across Kinsey's chest. "Thank you for everything you've given me." She smelled spicy, a bit dominant, and all passionate. Her scent was perfect to Kinsey; it called to her heart.

Kinsey sought Aubrey's lips for a tender kiss, then whispered, "I love you." She felt a few of Aubrey's tears against her skin. Her heart was full and her young family was all that she needed after struggling to find her way in life. Once upon a time she was trapped in a golden future that held little value until she met Aubrey, who fought and waited for her. Kinsey had more than she could have ever dreamt.

"And I love you, Kinsey."

The End

Enjoy More Lexa Luthor

The Alpha God
An F/F Sci-Fi Romance Series

Join Charlie, a mercenary for hire, who returns home to Kander for a job that's offered to her by the planet's sole ruler, Kal. As a female Alpha, Kal is rare among her kind but driven to protect her planet even if it means hiring someone that dislikes her people. Quickly Charlie learns there's more to the mission than just money especially after she unravels more secrets while also having a secret affair with Kal.

Learn more at www.LexaLuthor.com

About the Author

Lexa Luthor is an avid writer and reader of the Omegaverse trope especially F/F pairings. In her books, each main character(s) is a strong-willed female, who navigates difficult situations but always ends up finding love with their mate. Every tale has a twist and is gripping, sexy, and even a bit adventurous.

When not writing, Lexa enjoys binge watching television shows like Game of Thrones, Gentleman Jack, or The L Word. Her other favorite hobbies are playing cornhole, rooting for the Kansas City Chiefs, and laying around the pool in the summer. At times, Lexa finds time to read romances (both dark and fluffy) and great sci-fi books but nothing else can beat a steamy, downright erotic F/F romance with biting, knotting, and slightly possessive love.

Visit her website at LexaLuthor.com for more information and be sure to sign up for her newsletter for the latest release information, bonus material, and freebies.